Ho Zanzibar

Colin South

Copyright © Colin South 2020

The moral right of the author has been asserted

This is a work of fiction. Names, characters, places and incidents are either a product of the author's imagination or are used fictitiously, and any resemblance actual persons, living or dead, business establishments, companies, events or places is entirely coincidental
ISBN: 9798458623285

To James

Preface

It took just forty-five minutes for the Silver Airways' Saab SF-340 twin turboprop to carry Dr Mark Hill from San Juan's Luis Munoz Marin Airport in Puerto Rico to Terrence B. Lettsome International Airport in the British Virgin Islands. Dr Hill stepped into the midmorning sunshine to find a surprisingly modern, though small airport. The heat brought him out in a sweat just walking from the aircraft to the terminal building. By the time he got there he was already carrying his jacket over his arm, and had loosened his tie. It didn't take him long to collect his suitcase and make his way outside. He knew the jetty where he was to catch his boat, was only a short distance from the airport, but he didn't fancy lugging his suitcase all the way, especially in this heat. Stepping outside he found the usual line of taxis found outside any airport, anywhere in the world. He stepped up to the first in line, and leaned in through the open window. "I need to catch the ferry to Hotel Zanzibar." he said.

A big grin lit up the driver's face. "You must be Dr Hill."

"Yes, I am," he replied, somewhat taken aback.

The driver jumped out, came round the car and took Dr Hill's case and put it in the boot. "We were told to look out for you, Sir. We're all told when a guest is due in so we get them to the right boat" he explained. Turning to face the other taxis he shouted, "It's Dr Hill, I got him." The other drivers acknowledged him with a smile and a wave.

The drive to the jetty was no more than five minutes. Alongside the airport runway, then round to the dock at the end of the beach. A blue and white boat, about sixty feet long, two decks and an upper promenade deck, sat beside the quay. On the quayside, a van and a pickup truck were unloading boxes and crates onto the boat. They were being carried up the gangplank and checked off against a list carried by a man in pristine navy blue trousers, dazzling white shirt with navy blue epaulettes and an officer's blue and white cap. Dr Hill's driver carried the suitcase up the gangplank and plonked it down on the deck. "Thomas, this is Dr Hill" he said with a grin that never seemed to leave his face.

"Thank you Benjamin," said Thomas. He turned to Dr Hill and extended his hand. "Welcome aboard Dr Hill." They shook hands, "I'm

Thomas Philips, Captain of the good ship Island Sun. Please go on inside and make yourself comfortable. The steward will get you something to drink and something to eat if you're hungry."

"Thank you, that's very kind," said Dr Hill, feeling suddenly weary from his journey. It had already been over twenty four hours since he left Heathrow, London. "How long is the crossing?"

"It takes about two and a half to three hours, depending on wind and currents. They tend to be a little unpredictable once we get out past Guana Island. We should be away in about half an hour."

Dr Hill stepped into the welcoming coolness of a well air-conditioned saloon, dumped his case beside a bench seat and went over to the bar. A smartly dressed steward was diligently polishing glasses. He put glass and cloth down as Dr Hill walked towards the bar and asked what he would like. Dr Hill opted for a beer. The steward popped a can of Red Stripe and carefully poured it into a glass. He placed it on the bar top, condensation already forming on its side. Dr Hill picked it up and took a swallow. Glorious cooling nectar slid down his throat. He took another big swallow. "You may care to open another one of those," he said, between mouthfuls. He took his second beer over to the bench, where he'd dumped his case. He sat down, then slumped back in his seat and placed his glass on the table. He wasn't just weary, he was bloody knackered. Finally, he took off his tie, rolled it up and put it in the pocket of his jacket, that lay beside him on the bench. He took out his iPhone. There was a signal, but no messages.

Soon the sound of the auxiliary engine was replaced by the deeper rumble and vibration of the main engines. There was a movement and sway as the boat cast off and moved away from the quay. The throb of the engines and the gently, barely noticeable, sway of the boat soon had Dr Hill nodding off.

He was roused by the boat's increased movement. He sat up, blinked and looked around. His half finished glass of beer sat on the table, its contents swaying from side to side with the motion of the boat. "We're just passing Guana Island," said the steward to Dr Hill's unasked question. "The sea's more open once we get out here." Dr Hill nodded his thanks. The steward got on with doing whatever it was he was doing behind the bar. Dr Hill looked around. He appeared to be the only passenger. He got up and went over to the stairs in the centre of the saloon, then up onto the promenade deck. He squinted in the brilliant sunlight, its reflections glittering back from the sea. He took his sunglasses out of his shirt pocket and put them on. Walking over to the port side, he lent on the rail and watched a green forested island pass to the port stern.

"Guana Island" said a voice. Dr Hill turned to see Captain Thomas Philips standing by the open bridge door. Dr Hill went over to join him. Captain Philips led them round to the promenade deck in front of the bridge. He stood at the front rail, hands resting loosely on it, "About another hour and three quarters, I should think."

Dr Hill lent against the rail beside him. "The swell will be getting bigger as we move out of the shelter of the islands. We're almost into the Atlantic, out here. How's your sea legs?"

"They're fine," smiled Dr Hill, "I could do with a good blow after being cooped up on aeroplanes for over twenty-four hours."

"Well, enjoy the trip." Replied Captain Philips. He turned to return to the bridge.

"Excuse me, but am I the only passenger on here today, Captain?"

Captain Philips turned back to him, "You are indeed, Dr Hill, but we also have some supplies to deliver, and two passengers to pick up and take back to Beef Island, tomorrow." He turned and disappeared into the bridge. He reappeared beside the helmsman, checking their heading. Dr Hill turned back to the rail. The wind in his face and the odd spray from the bows refreshing him after his long travels. Looking at the horizon he peered to try and see their destination. Nothing yet, not even a smudge on the line where the sea met the sky.

He thought back to the reason for this journey. The bizarre circumstances and stories that led up to this. How it all started nearly ninety years ago. How it had occupied his life, on and off, for the past thirty odd.

Part 1

Chapter 1

1984, George Orwell's dystopian future. Mark Hill, junior analyst at MI5's Curzon Street House, often thought he wasn't far out. He'd been with MI5 close to two years, coming straight from Oxford on a graduate entry scheme. Today was his turn in room B2/7 - basement 2nd level, room seven, a musty and dank room in the very bowels of the building. B2/7 went by the nickname Looney Tunes. This rather large room contained the files of some of the more outrageous and plain barmy escapades of MI5 and its predecessor, the Secret Service Bureau. It was a dusty, unused room, the age of its contents given away by the fact that many of the filing cabinets were wooden. The room was in the process of being cleared, as it had been earmarked for use by the ever expanding computerised archive. The process of clearance was to go through the files, and chuck out all the old, irrelevant stuff and put anything useful to one side, ready for putting on to the computers. To this end, Mark was being kept company by two carts. One had sections to take the files, the other had two large burn bags. The procedure was to start by the door and work your way down the left hand side, and back up the right. Take a drawer full of files over to the desk, speed read though them and toss anything unwanted into the burn bag, the others would then be trundled away to be digitised. This mostly boring, but sometimes intriguing task had been given to all the junior analysts. They each spent a day here, in turn. The clearance, so far, had taken three weeks and they were only halfway down the left hand side, and it was Mark's fourth stint in Looney Tunes.

Just after lunch he was nearing the bottom of his current pile, when he pulled a folder towards him with the words Làngfèi shíjiān, hand written in red fountain pen, on the cover. Across the top left hand corner the words Watching Brief had a line through them. Inside, the cover sheet gave a brief summary of the contents, and a note about curious incidents that had occurred between the end of World War Two and 1967. It was signed *Andrew Henly, Senior Analyst/Market Interventions*. A quick speed read through its contents had Mark sitting back in his chair wondering what on earth he'd just come across. He put it to one side and quickly went through the rest of his pile. Three went to be digitised, two into the burn bag. He pulled the Làngfèi shíjiān file towards him, again, and read it through, more slowly, this time. The service had discovered this mysterious artefact's properties from decrypting a piece of paper written in code, and in Chinese. The slip of paper was enclosed in the file. Mark held it in his hands. Quite a small single sheet of paper crammed with Chinese characters, just two words in English, Swifts Bank. It would seem the author of the file was one of those that decrypted it. Then, there was a brief mention of a team involved, referred to purely by their initials, E.B., C.C., N.T, and E.T. The last one made him smile, thinking of the hit movie from two years previous. There was one name given though, Paul Rivers. The man that had disappeared with the subject of the file. Other papers detailed market incidents that gave the impression of someone who knew what was going to happen weeks, sometimes months, in advance. A mining company, with significant funds tied up in an exploratory gold mine in South Africa, was on the verge of collapse. What was thought to be significant deposits turned out to be just a small seam. The shares plummeted. Just when it was thought it would go under, a significant amount of shares were purchased, at a rock bottom price. It enabled the company to continue exploring for a further month and half when it hit a rich seam. The shares rocketed. Shortly after, a major South African gold mining concern bought them out. The purchaser of the shares more than quadrupled its investment. The purchaser, and beneficiary of the sale was simply noted as Billingforth. The name underlined in red.

A rumour about the bonafides of the directors of a property company caused its value to fall. When it was on the verge of going into liquidation it was bought up at a heavily reduced price. It's properties were then sold off separately, making it's purchaser significant profits. The purchaser's name? Billingforth. Mark read several more similar incidents, each one brought up the name Billingforth. All attempts to trace Billingforth came up against a brick wall of offshore shell companies. Then, in 1967, it had been archived. No explanation, just the usual slip of paper clipped to the inside of the cover marked "Archived 12/01/67".

Mark looked at his watch, it was getting late. He wanted to take this to his boss, Tom King, and he would be going home soon. Mark picked up the folder, went out into the labyrinth of corridors and wound his way to the Head Archivist's office. Sally Brunswick had been at Curzon Street House forever. No one can remember a time when Sally wasn't in charge of the archives. A jovial, dumpy little woman, with a preponderance for luridly floral dresses, and a wild mop of curly grey hair. She called everyone 'Dear' regardless of rank or gender. It was felt that should there ever be a royal visit to the archives, instead of curtsying to the Queen, Sally would just say "Hello, Dear" which is exactly what she said to Mark when he knocked and entered her office.

"Hi, Sally," said Mark. "This file, from Looney Tunes, can I sign it out for reference?"

"Let's have a look, Dear." She took the folder from him and had a look inside the cover "Good Lord, one of Andrew's little projects."

"Did you know him then Sally."

"Oh yes, Dear. Lovely man. What he didn't know about dodgy banking wasn't worth knowing. Split his time between here and GCHQ. Most of his time over there. I'm surprised to see one of his files still here."

"Any idea why it was archived then?"

"Yes, he retired. We all had a little party at a pub down the road. A double celebration as it was his sixtieth birthday as well. His friend came, too."

"His friend?"

"His man friend, called Johnny. Everybody knew he was gay, but nothing was said despite the regulations. He was such a brilliant analyst, and no one doubted his loyalty. They made a point of deep vetting Johnny once a year."

"Right," said Mark, somewhat surprised, given the Service's attitude to homosexuality at the time. "Anyway, the file, can I sign it out?"

"Of course you can, Dear." Sally pulled a ledger towards her, and entered the reference number, off the file cover, into it, then turned it round for Mark to sign.

"There's mention of obtaining the subject of the file from the bank" said Mark, as he signed the ledger. "Do you know anything about it?"

"No, I'm afraid I don't Dear." Sally became quite serious. "Make sure it stays in your sight, and is locked in your department's safe when it's not." She tapped the file with the end of her pen. "Off you go, now."

"Thanks, Sally, will do." Mark picked up the folder and took the lift up to the second floor.

Chapter 2

He crossed the outer office and knocked on the door of the officer in charge of his department. The glass fronted office looked out over three groups of desks, arranged in twos, facing each other. Tom King bid him enter. A dumpy, untidy little man, looking about ten years older than his thirty-six years. The room stank of cigarette smoke, and there was one burning in the ashtray on the desk.

"What is it, Hill?" His manner abrupt as he sat back in his chair, took the cigarette from the ashtray and took a long drag. Then exhaling a long plume of smoke.

"It's this file from the archives, Sir."

"What about it?"

"Well, it refers to several unexplained financial, I suppose you could say coups, Sir. Starting just after the war, up till '67. All linked to one shady, untraceable company, in turn linked to a series of incidents back in the '30's."

"If it's been archived, it's of little relevance to us now, obviously."

"Well, Sir, it seems the reason it was archived is because the officer analysing it retired."

"Who was it?"

"Bloke called Andrew Henly."

At the mention of Andrew Henly, Tom King visibly pricked his ears up. "Andrew Henly, eh? One of the best analysts we ever had. If you wanted to know about dodgy banking, he was your man. Here, let me see." He stretched an arm out to Mark, who stepped forward and handed him the file. He plonked it down and looked at the cover, and the title Làngfèi shíjiān. "Shit," said Tom King, quietly. He looked up at Mark, "Have you read this through?"

"Yes, Sir, well mostly. I skimmed through some of it and spent a bit more on others."

"Like, erm...."

"The bloke that took off with whatever this was?" offered Mark.

"Yes, quite. Christ, I thought this had been burned ages ago. What the fuck made you bring this up here? Why didn't you sling it in the burn bag along with all our other embarrassments?"

"I think it may be quite relevant to some recent market moves, and the name Billingforth rings a bell."

"Shit," said King, only louder this time. He looked at his watch, "Right, come with me. He heaved himself out of his chair and lead Mark across the outer office, much to the surprise of the staff who watched their little procession to the lifts. As the lift doors closed behind Mark Hill and Tom King, speculation started to bubble up. Even more so when they saw the lift indicator show it going up to the fourth floor.

Tom King marched them over the soft, sound deadening maroon carpet of the fourth floor to a door marked "Sir Michael Saris". This was the office of Corporate Desk. The head of the department that oversaw all things corporate and financial within the United Kingdom. Its prime function was to prevent money laundering and the financing of terrorist groups, particularly the IRA.

Tom King rapped hard on the door, and walked straight in, dragging Mark Hill along in his wake. Sir Michael was busy with some papers, pen in hand. He sat up, somewhat startled by King's sudden eruption into his office. "Tom?" was all he could immediately say.

"Sir Michael, sorry, but this has surfaced."

"Ok, ok, slow down. What's surfaced, and why have you brought, erm.." He pointed at Mark with his pen.

"Oh, this is Hill, a junior analyst. He found this." He handed the file to Sir Michael, who took it off him with a bewildered look. He stood back to wait for Sir Michael's reaction.

As he looked down from King to the cover of the file his eyes widened. He looked back up at King with his mouth half open, a look of mild horror on his face. "What the holy fuck? I thought this was dead and buried." He looked over at Mark. "Hill, why the fuck didn't you burn this? Stick it in a burn bag at once." He grabbed the file and thrust it towards Mark.

Mark was opening his mouth to speak, but King beat him to it. "It's author was Andrew Henly, he tied several untoward market events to one name, Billingforth."

"According to Sally it was Henly's pet project. It was archived the day he retired," added Mark.

"Well if it's been archived, why bring it up here now?"

This time Mark got in first. "Billingforth rings a bell. I'm sure I've seen it in conjunction with some recent market activities."

"Surely, if Andrew had felt it worthwhile at the time, he'd have passed it on for someone to carry on?" queried Sir Michael.

"Looks like it slipped through the net. He had some fairly big stuff on the go, at the time, if I remember. Quite a big handover on then, a lot of it down at GCHQ"

"Does he know about… you know?" asked Sir Michael, indicating Hill with a wave of the file he was still clutching."

"Rivers disappearing with Làngfèi shíjiān? Yes, Sir Michael. He has a rough idea." King glanced at Mark. "Haven't you?"

"Yes, Sir."

Sir Michael dropped the file down on his desk and sat back in his chair. He dragged his hand down his face, then pressed the intercom on his desk. "Doris, I'm not to be disturbed for the next hour."

"Yes, Sir Michael" came the tinny reply.

"Well then, gentleman," said Sir Michael, "I think you'd both better take a seat so that we can discuss this." King and Mark drew chairs over to the desk and sat facing across from Sir Michael, "What do either of you know about this?"

"Only what I've seen in there," answered Mark.

"Just the usual rumours and departmental chat," said King, "An op that went tits up and a field officer that buggered off with this bizarre artefact. He then went dark, and was never seen, or heard of again."

"In that case, let me fill you in," said Sir Michael. "Andrew took a specific interest in this as he was part of the team that deciphered the original note about the artefact, this Làngfèi shíjiān. They worked out what it was and what it was supposed to be able to do." He then went on to take them through the story of Làngfèi shíjiān, from it's appearance on UK shores, to Paul Rivers' disappearance. "Then Andrew Henly picked up on it following the war. 'K' and Bant thought they'd buried it, but Henly dug it out. 'K' died in 1942, Bant a year later. Henly had risen quite considerably in the ranks. Spent much of the war at Bletchley Park. Further promotion saw him in a senior position that had him spending sometime in London, but mostly at Bletchley, then GCHQ, as it became. Word got around Curzon Street House, towards the end of his career, that he had a pet side project, that had been going on for years, involving a mysterious disappeared artefact, and a rogue agent. Upon his retirement, Curzon Street House must have assumed it was archived for destruction at GCHQ. GCHQ thought the same, but at Curzon Street House."

"Whatever happened to Swifts Bank?" asked Mark.

"It was bought by Martin's Bank in 1939. They had their Safe deposit vault raided. Emptied the whole show. The claims against them were colossal. Its general manager, Sir Bernard MacIntyre, resigned over it, and died a broken man in 1938.

"However, Hill, you seem to think there's some connection between this Billingforth, that Andrew Henley had been keeping an eye on, and some present day activity?"

"I do, Sir. I'd really like to go through the file with a fine tooth comb. Particularly the deals involving Billingforth."

"Very well. You keep this very much to yourself, d'you hear."

"Yes, Sir."

"Report only to Tom, here. In his absence, me. You do not discus it with anyone else excepting the later financial aspect. Is that clear? Especially not Làngfèi shíjiān. You're to look purely into this Billingforth outfit, and any connections between it and our current investigations." He held the file out towards Mark, who stood up and took it.

"Yes, Sir," said Mark.

King got up. "Thank you, Sir Michael"

"Thank you for bringing it straight to me, Tom."

Mark and King left Sir Michaels office, taking the lift back down in silence. Back on their floor most of the staff had left for the day. Those still there were the late shifters. They came in at two p.m. and worked till ten, then the graveyarders took over. Their task, to monitor the foreign markets around the globe. They paid the returning pair scant regard. At his office door King held out his hand. "I'll take that now, Hill," he said, somewhat brusquely. "It stays in my safe over night. We'll discuss it further in the morning. Right now it's time to go home. I'm late already."

The following morning Mark Hill retrieved the Làngfèi shíjiān file from Tom King. King was his usual morose self, keeping hold of the file when Mark took it. "You can concentrate on this until the end of next week, when I shall expect a full report. If there's no more movement involving Billingforth, and you are no nearer finding out who, or what is behind it, it goes on the back burner, OK? You'll maintain a watching brief, but you'll concentrate on more current things."

Mark took the file back to his work station and fired up his computer. Once logged on he looked at the cursor blinking next to the glowing green 'C:' He typed in Billingforth, and the command line for a deep search, hit enter, and sat back, waiting for it to work it's magic. In the mean time he went back to the file, and started to read through it again. He found it difficult to believe this Chinese artefact had some weird and wonderful power. However, the fact that this man, Rivers, had seen fit to run off with it did lend it some credence. Was there some connection with Làngfèi shíjiān, and the raid on the safe deposit vault? He was pondering all this when King came over and handed him an old and battered manila file. "You may find this interesting." He said, "Managed to get this from Personnel Archives" and walked back to his office. Mark opened it. Inside we some old, faded typewritten forms detailing Field Agent Paul Rivers. Designated Superior, Reginald Cockscombe. Mark took Designated Superior to mean Handler, in todays parlance. Held to the top of the front page, by a rusty paper clip, was a faded photograph of a very nondescript, dark haired young man. In the margin, at the bottom left of the front page, was written "If found, L.S. to be returned to this office. P.R. to be dispatched forthwith." And signed 'K', all in red fountain pen.

Mark half stood, and peered over at Tom King's office. King was in his usual position, sat at his desk. He looked up, saw Mark looking over at him, gave him a knowing nod, and went back to whatever was on his desk. Mark sat back. If this Làngfèi shíjiān thing, this magic machine, and this Paul Rivers are still out there, worth a massive fortune, he had a sentence of death on his head. Not that anybody, apart from Mark, Tom King, and probably Sir Michael Saris, knew that.

The blinking cursor changed, and a whole slew if data started filling the screen. The screen told the story of Billingforth. After a brief look at the post war years, he concentrated on post 1967. He figured Andrew Henly would have gone as far as he could at the time. With all MI5's computers, Mark felt he still wouldn't get much further, he'd just hit the brick wall that much sooner. Through the late '60's, early to mid '70's there was nothing of note. Billingforth cropped up now and then. Just ordinary trades, nothing especially noteworthy about them. Then in 1979 Billingforth was heavily involved in the acquisition of Merlin Finance. They specialised in commercial finance and had invested heavily in some quite big ventures. Unwisely, it would appear. Although the businesses were functioning and going concerns, their growth was minimal, just enough to keep going. Merlin had virtually all its capital tied up in these companies. With such small returns, it now had a cash flow problem. To overcome this, it had borrowed a little too much at an uncompetitive rate, from the banks. Merlin Finance was about to go tits up. Suddenly in steps Billingforth. It buys Merlin, lock stock and overstretched barrel. Over the next few months it restructures its loans and pays off the bank. It forecloses on the slow businesses, and seizes their assets. In mid 1980 Billingforth sells everything. All Merlin's business, and all the assets its seized. It walks away making a hefty 51% clear profit on its investment. Then it all goes dark again.

Mark's investigations lead him to Billingforth's owners. They turn out to be a company called Drake Holdings, registered in the British Virgin Islands.

Chapter 3

Three days before his deadline, Mark Hill knocked on Tom King's office door. In his hand was an interim report he'd put together the night before. King looked up and beckoned Mark in adding his customary "Come".

He held out the report in its green 'live' folder. A diagonal red stripe denoting its secrecy - like all the folders in MI5 with the exception of those Above Top Secret, which had an additional purple stripe. You didn't carry those around in your hand, you carried them around in a locked briefcase, chained to your wrist if leaving the building. Which still didn't stop the odd one being left on the tube. "Sir," said Mark, as he handed it over, "You may find this rather interesting. There's a definite link to the British Virgin Islands. I'd like to see if someone out there could have a ferret around and see if they can find out any more about the parent company, Drake Holdings."

"You angling for an expenses paid trip to the Caribbean, Hill?" said King, with a sour look on his face.

"No, Sir," said Mark, with a look of complete innocence. "I thought maybe somebody already out there could sniff around."

"You know, of course, that there isn't anybody anywhere near the British Virgin Islands. Just who do you think would do it?"

"Isn't there somebody in Jamaica, Sir? Mind you, if there really isn't anybody, it might well be worth my while going out there to have a look-see for myself."

King took his time looking through the file, leaving Mark standing in front of his desk. Eventually he looked up. "No, I'm afraid you won't be heading off to sunnier climes at Her Majesty's expense any time soon, Hill. Leave this with me and I'll see how we can proceed." He all but waved Mark away back to his desk. "But keep digging," he added as an afterthought.

On deadline day King ventured out of his office, and made his way over to Mark Hill's work station. Mark was pawing over a printout when King broke in on his concentration. "Hill, I have some good news for you."

Mark looked up, somewhat startled,"Oh?"

"Yes, the Station Chief from Barbados happened to be in the British Virgin Islands, on unrelated business. Asked him to have a nosey round, see what he could see. You know?"

"Oh yes." King now had Mark's full attention.

"Yes, he managed to unearth a bit more info for you. Not much, I'm afraid, but something, none the less." He held two sheets of A4, closely typed on both sides.

"Thank you, Sir."

"And I'm extending your time on this. Give it another two weeks." With that, he turned and wandered back to his office. A few heads appeared above their computer monitors. A chap called Gavin, at the desk opposite Mark peered round his monitor.

"And what are you up to to winkle His Lordship out of his kennel?"

"We have a little off-shore naughtiness going on, Gav. Just the usual."

"So why the royal visit? He doesn't even leave his glass tower when the fire alarm goes off."

"I think he wanted to show off. He managed to get the Station Chief in Barbados to ferret around on B.V.I.

The fact he was already over there doesn't enter into it. King got a Station Chief to do him a favour."

Gavin gave a short laugh and went back to work. Mark read through the papers King had given him. King had been right, despite the four sides of closely typed data all it boiled down to was that Drake Holdings owned one company, and that company was Billingforth. It also said that although Drake holdings had an office in the British Virgin Islands, it was part of another company, Mallard Holdings, which happened to be registered in the Cayman Islands. Mark sat back with a sigh. Wheels within wheels. It was like a Russian doll that just went on and on. He also had a little inward smile at the names; Drake Holdings, Mallard Holdings. Who would he find behind them? Goose and Partners? Swan and Associates?

To say Drake Holdings had an office in the British Virgin Islands would be something of an exaggeration. It had a room in a small office building just off Main Street in Road Town, the capital of the British Virgin Islands on the island of Tortola. This room was just big enough to swing a cat without giving it serious concussion. It contained a steel desk, on which there was an antique looking telephone, a tatty office chair, and a steel filing cabinet that had seen better days. This office was manned by a Mrs Winifred Styles, a rotund and matronly native Tortolian, of indeterminate age, who once a week cycled to the main post office and got all the post from the Post Office box that was Drake Holdings correspondence address. She then pedalled over to the office, where she spent about ten to fifteen minutes putting all the post into one big pre labeled envelope that she got from the filing cabinet, and sealed it up securely with Sellotape, also obtained from the filing cabinet. Then taking said envelope back to the post office and sending it off. Occasionally, if something out of the ordinary arrived in the PO Box, and by out of the ordinary that meant anything not in a heavy white envelope with a crest and the name Billingforth on the back, then she used the telephone to inform the person at the other end. Sometimes she would be asked to open it and tell them what was inside. More often than not, she would then be told to chuck it in the bin. This entailed going round the back of the building with a battered metal waste paper bucket, putting the unwanted correspondence in there, squirting some lighter fluid over it and lobbing in a lit match.

Chapter 4

A week went by. Mark was getting nowhere. No other signs of activity from Billingforth, Drake Holdings or Mallard Holdings. Historic trawls and recent digging came up blank. It appeared that Billingforth was the only company owned by Drake Holdings and, although more difficult to verify completely, it would seem Drake Holdings was the only company owned by Mallard Holdings.

Ten days later Mark received a further report from the agent on The Cayman Islands. On two occasions they had seen someone open Mallard Holding's P.O. Box. On each occasion a different person. They had been followed. All the way to the harbour, where they got into waiting tender that took them out to a larger vessel, moored off shore. And each time it had been a different vessel. Enquiries at the harbour resulted in the knowledge that the vessels were both bound for the British Virgin Islands. That was all, no specific island listed.

This all resulted in a further meeting with Sir Michael, upstairs. "So what's happening, Hill, owt or nowt, as they say?"

"I can find nothing since they sold off the Merlin acquisition, in 1980, Sir. It's just been small regular stuff. It's as if they just want to keep a hand in, keep the name there."

"Do you think they're getting ready to pounce again?"

"I really don't know, Sir. I rather think that's why that Andrew Henly was keeping an eye on them. You've no idea it's going to happen until it happens."

"Quite, point taken. So nothing significant for four years, just bits and bobs. It's as if they're waiting for something."

"Given the details in the file, I think they already know what's going to happen. We just have to wait and when it does happen, follow the money while the trail's still warm."

Tom King, who had been sitting quietly during this exchange, now broke in, "Shall we just keep a watching brief then, Sir Michael? Get things in place to move at a moment's notice."

"Yes. Tom, that's how I think we should proceed. Put some triggers in place so any sudden, or aggressive moves by Billingforth are flagged for immediate follow up and possible action. Have a chat with our colleagues across the river. See if they can set up a small swift action protocol in the relevant neck of the Caribbean. Ready to activate at a moment's notice."

"I'll see to it right away, Sir Michael." King and and Mark stood.

"Thank you, gentlemen." Sir Michael dismissed them with a nod to each. He was already pulling a folder towards him as they left the room.

Seven months later. Christmas and new year had come and gone. A cold, wet and windy January morning saw Mark Hill trudge along the street, then through the side entrance into Curzon Street House. The man on the security desk told him not to drip all over the place as he signed in. In the office, he hung has coat on the rack by the door and joined Gavin in the kitchenette, just off the main office.

"It's only just boiled." Gavin informed him. Mark spooned Nescafe into a mug, poured the water in and fished the milk out of the fridge. "His Lordship's off" added Gavin as he watched Mark put the milk back in the fridge. "Flu. May his suffering be long, and he leaves us all in peace."

"You do know his wife's got leukaemia, don't you, Gav?"

"I know, poor cow. No need for us to suffer, though, is there?"

"That's what I like about you, Gav, you're all heart." Mark took his coffee over to his desk and logged on to his computer. The first thing he did, once logged on was what he did every morning, checked for any unusual market movement pertaining to Billingforth. As usual nothing untoward. He was about to switch to his current investigation. The KGB seemed to be moving money through the city through a number of obscure companies. The usual follow the money routine. He was suddenly struck by something, and scrolled back several pages, then back some more. To say Billingforth wasn't doing much was an understatement. It was doing nothing. No sign since mid December. Usually there was something happening with Billingforth every week or ten days. Suddenly nothing for just over a month. He conducted some more searches, using different parameters. Still nothing. He used links to go back in to Billingforth's registration. Again nothing. Still registered, but not trading, or doing anything. Back into the history to have as look at what it had been doing prior to mid December. "Shit," he said quietly. Printed out the results and phoned Sir Michael Saris.

"Show me what you've got, Hill," said Sir Michael, as soon as Mark walked into his office.

Mark handed Sir Michael the printout. "Billingforth have gone dark, Sir. Not a peep out of them since the middle of December. However, for the six weeks running up to that all it did was sell. Bits here, bits there. No pattern, nothing big all at once. Just a gradual selling of all its holdings. It now owns nothing. I've currently got a backdoor program running to see what's in the current account. Its liquid assets must be phenomenal."

"So you think it may be preparing something big?"

"Impossible to say, Sir. Nothing's happened for weeks. Nothing big in the markets. No big institutions struggling. Nothing to suggest it's about to pounce. And there's the gap between sell off and now. In the past it's quick. Too quick to let anybody know what's happening until it's too late."

Sir Michael looked over the printout on his desk. All he said was "Hmm." He seemed lost in thought for a moment or two. Then he spoke. "How come the system didn't pick up on this before?"

"The algorithm was set to flag up sudden moves. This wasn't sudden, or significant. Just a gradual sell off and a cessation of trading. It wasn't programmed to look for nothing happening."

"Any thoughts? I know Tom King's your boss, and the next move would normally be his decision. However, he's off with the flu. So, I'm asking for your input. You found this, and brought it to our attention. Have been with it ever since."

"I'd like to dig deeper, see if this current account search reveals anything. Money syphoned off to another company, that sort of thing. See where it takes us."

"Very good. What are you doing at the moment?"

"The KGB money laundering scheme. It's me and Gavin Taylor."

"Right, give it all over to Taylor. Does he know about Billingforth?"

"No, Sir. You asked me to keep it under wraps. Just yourself and Mr King."

"Good man. You'd better tell him you're working on a special assignment from me. Possible infiltration of the market by offshore assets of a foreign power. Keep it suitably vague. Mind you, it's not that far from the truth."

"Yes Sir." Mark picked the printout up from the desk.

"Good work, young man," said Sir Michael as Mark headed for the door.

Chapter 5

Over the next week, or so, Mark set to work. Using all the algorithms at his disposal, plus the back doors into various financial institutions' systems, he followed the money and Billingforth.

Then, one mid afternoon he hit pay dirt. He hissed a quiet "Yes!" And tapped his fists against the edge of his desk. Drake Holdings now had a new company, in its portfolio, Harlequin. No Holdings, no Associates, no And Partners; just plain Harlequin. And Harlequin was the sole owner, now, of Billingforth. Money had been syphoned off from Billingforth every which way. Some as capital assets for Harlequin, other payments into various Swiss bank accounts, and some as commission payments to Drake Holdings. Billingforth was now nothing more than a name in Harlequin's ledger.

So what did this shiny, new Harlequin do? That was the next challenge for Mark, because it didn't seem to do anything, it didn't trade on any markets. It just sat there, comfortably well off, with a shade under US$1billion on current account. Waiting. Waiting for what, though? This was the frustrating thing for Mark. How do you second guess someone that already knows the future? Not some future guessed by some sophisticated algorithm, someone who actually knows their future because they've been there.

A couple of days later Gavin leaned around his monitor. "You keeping an eye on any of the big boys, Mark?"

"Which big boys do you mean?"

"High end wealth managers with dubious and unknown clients. I'm seeing some strange market moves by them."

"Strange in what way?"

"Sudden purchases of rock bottom shares, stuff that looks as though it's about to go into administration, stock worth next to bugger all. One or two of these boys buys into it. I've got one here, bought up nearly forty percent of the stock of Seascape Ferries hours before the Government put in place a rescue package and the shares bounced right up. They were on the verge of ceasing trading, no-one with an ounce of market savvy would have gone near them with a ten foot pole. Yet here's matey risking a fair old wedge of client's funds on the Trade Minister's coin toss coming down right side up."

Mark was interested to say the least. "Well, I'm not looking at them, per se, but it might well be connected with my operation. Send me the details across, plus any others, and I'll have a look."

"Sure thing," said Gavin. "By the way, what is it you're looking at?"

"Something along similar lines, Gav, but going way back, and all offshore."

"Well, good luck with that. Sending that stuff across now."

And there it was, dates, names and figures. Mark printed it off and compared it to his own sheets. This was recent stuff, so no need to look back too far. All post Billingforth. Then the pattern emerged. Harlequin didn't appear to be doing anything, but a substantial sum of money was transferred in to its accounts always two days after the share price jump that these shady big boys had bought into. He chose the saving of Seascape Ferries as a starting point. Looked at the wealth fund managers, in this case Booth and Partners, a very exclusive, very discrete wealth fund manager. Unless your personal wealth was in excess of £50 million, they wouldn't give you the time of day. That limited their client base to high end media moguls, oil sheiks, and organised crime bosses. It used funds from all clients to buy the Seascape shares, and gave them 65% of the profit, keeping 35% as commission. That commission came to just over £12 million. 50% went straight back out to a Swiss Bank account. A Swiss bank account that seemed familiar to Mark. When you're dealing with bank account numbers, and number sequences day in day out, you get to recognise them when they pop up again. He went through the Harlequin file and bingo, there it was. 50% of Booth and Partner's commission went straight to Harlequin. He checked back through Booth and Partners accounts and found something surprising. They made a regular payment of a straight £1m to the Harlequin account every month. The commission split was a bonus on top of that. It was a lightbulb moment, flash, and it was all so obvious. Harlequin wasn't trading, because it didn't have to anymore. In this modern electronic age, the financial motherlode was intelligence. If you could provide infallible market intelligence to the right people, they would pay a fortune for it. They would even pay a retainer to ensure they received said intelligence as soon as it became available.

Chapter 6

For over two years Mark Hill kept an eye on Harlequin, and its clients. Whenever one of them made a quick killing on the markets, soon after, there was the payment to Harlequin. No amount of investigating could determine how they came by their information. Even an approach to the newly formed Crown Prosecution Service proved fruitless in going for Insider Trading. Mark was getting nowhere, and spent less and less time looking into it. Then one afternoon, after one of his occasional checks into Harlequin and its clients had brought the usual result, he decided to take another look at the actual file. Tom King had moved on, promoted to a higher desk in the directorate. Mark's immediate boss was now George Fellows, a much older man, whiling away his time at a desk job before he retired. Mark tapped on George's door, and stuck his head round. "Afternoon, George, mind if I get something from the safe?"

"Be my guest," replied George, leaning back in his chair, "Anything interesting?" George had a habit of opening the safe, once he was in his office, and leaving it open till he left.

Mark rummaged around until he found the file with Làngfèi shíjiān written on the cover. "Just want to have another look at this." He held up the folder so that George Fellows could see the front. He got an unexpected reaction.

"Bloody hell! When did I get that in my safe?"

"It's been there since Tom had the office. I found it in the archives a couple of years ago."

"Don't tell me, you've kept a watching brief ever since, and found fuck all."

"Well, in a manner of speaking, yes."

"Take a pew, Mark. Let me tell you a little something about that Làngfèi shíjiān file." Mark sat in the chair opposite George Fellows and put the folder down on the desk. George reached over, picked up the folder and flipped through it. "The man that initiated this file, Andrew Henly, the man who, along with a colleague, managed to decipher this." He held up the slip of paper covered in Chinese characters. "Nearly went potty trying to find out what was going on. He spent the war at Bletchley Park, then later worked between here and GCHQ. Brilliant analyst and cryptographer. I worked with him, briefly, not long before he retired. I saw him with this once. He told me that what was in here could change the world if only he could find out the source. He also told me that most of the information, the story he called it, had been omitted. Either not placed on record, or deleted. Removed from the file and destroyed, just before the war." George closed the folder and sat back. "You should go and see him, have a chat. He's still alive and quite compos mentis last I heard. Living on the South Coast somewhere. Personnel will give you his address, if you ask nicely." He held the folder out to Mark, signalling the end to their little chat. "Now, if you'll excuse me, I've got some really boring crap I have to finish before the end of day for those of higher station." His popular euphemism for anybody senior.

Mark took the file and went back to his desk. He sat there for a short while just looking at the folder, then came to a decision He reached for his phone and dialled personnel. He was told that if he wanted the address of a retired officer, he'd have to come down, in person, and fill out a form. Half an hour later Mark was back at his desk with Andrew Henly's current address and his ex-directory telephone number. He took a deep breath and picked up his phone. It was answered after the third ring, "Yes?" A curt bark.

"Andrew Henly? This is Mark Hill, at Curzon Street House." It was the only thing he could think to say without blurting out Làngfèi shíjiān.

"What do you want? I've retired. I've other things to do."

"I wondered if I might pick your brains over something."

"Really? I can't think what."

"Does the file titled Làngfèi shíjiān ring any bells?"

There was a long pause, then "I'll call you back."

Before he could hang up Mark said "It's Mark Hill, extension…"

"I'll find you." He cut Mark off and hung up.

Mark put the phone down, sat back and looked at it. Well, that went well, not. He was reading through the file again when his desk phone rang. He picked it up, "Mark Hill."

"Andrew Henly, here." Mark sat up in surprise. He didn't really think Andrew Henly would actually call back, let alone this quickly. "If you really want to know about Làngfèi shíjiān then you'll have to come down to me, here, in Brighton. I'll not discus it over the phone. I suggest tomorrow, at 11 o'clock. You have my address, I take it?" Mark confirmed he did. "Good, tomorrow, then. Oh, and by the way, I suggest you book yourself into a hotel for the night. This could take some time." He rang off. Mark looked at the phone for some time before he moved. Then he checked his diary for the next couple of days. Nothing that couldn't be put off or given to someone else.

He stuck his head round George Fellows door for the second time that afternoon. "I'll be out of the office for the next couple of days, George. Going to see Andrew Henly."

George smiled up at Mark."Good man. Just don't become obsessed, like him. Let us know what he has to say. I'd be fascinated to know more about this."

Chapter 7

It transpired that Andrew Henly actually lived in Hove. At just after 11am, the following morning, a taxi deposited Mark Hill outside a row of four storey Georgian townhouses, on Brunswick Terrace, with a fine view across the road and promenade to the English Channel beyond. He went up the steps, found the bell for Andrew Henly's flat, the top one, and pressed. After a brief pause there was a buzz and the door unlatched. Mark opened the door and went inside. Across the road a figure watched him go in, looked up at the flats, turned and looked out to sea. A grey day over an even greyer English Channel. He walked off along the front. Inside Mark found a well kept vestibule, with potted plants and Regency wallpaper greeting him. In front, carpeted stairs with a highly polished balustrade. Mark started up the stairs, looking up the stairwell. A face appeared over the balustrade at the very top. "We're up here." Called Andrew Henly, and ducked back out of view.

Andrew Henly's apartment was big. It was the entire top floor of the house. A huge lounge, with large windows looking out over the front. He bade Mark sit on one of the two small leather, two seater chesterfields by the fire place. A welcoming fire crackled in the grate, its warmth driving away the late autumn chill. Between the sofas a low dark wood chest, that acted as a coffee table. Andrew Henly sat down opposite. He seemed surprisingly spry for his age. He held himself upright, almost regimentally so. His movements were sure, not at all doddery. The real clue to his age was that he was very thin. His clothes, brown corduroy trousers, open neck check shirt and yellow V neck sweater, seemed to hang on him. Also the liver spots on his obviously old hands, and on his bald head. The white hair round the sides neatly trimmed. His brown eyes had a gleam of excitement to them, behind his gold rimmed glasses. "So," he said, "You want to know all about Làngfèi shíjiān, do you?"

"Yes, please, Sir." replied Mark, a little in awe, not just of his surroundings, but of the man himself.

"Good," said Andrew Henly. "And it's Andrew, not Sir. I'm not your boss, and I've retired from the service. But first of all tea." He got up and disappeared into the kitchen, "Any preference? Earl Grey, Assam?" He called out

"No, I'm easy," replied Mark.

"Excellent, PG Tips it is then."

While he was in the kitchen making the tea, Mark delved into his briefcase. He brought out a legal pad, a cassette tape recorder and a couple of C90 cassettes. He took a pen from inside his jacket, and placed it beside the pad. Andrew returned with the tea tray, placed it on the chest and sat down. "Do you mind if I record this?" asked Mark.

"Not at all," was Andrew's response. "But you're going to need a damn sight more cassettes than those." He grinned and nodded at the two tapes Mark had got out.

"Not to worry, I've got more in my briefcase."

"Very good. Right, Làngfèi shíjiān. Where to begin?" He poured the tea and passed a cup to Mark. Poured his own, took a sip, then placed his cup back in the saucer. "Where to begin indeed." I have some files of my own in my study, which you're welcome to look at later. May clarify some of what I'm about to tell you. I was going to ask how far you've got, but I'd hazard a guess at not much more than me."

"No. We've identified some companies, all registered offshore. British Virgin Islands, Cayman Islands etc. The latest an outfit calling itself Harlequin, just seems to deal in market information."

"Yes, of course." Andrew nodded to himself, "In the Information Age information is the ultimate commodity, and Làngfèi shíjiān gives them access to the most accurate information possible. What's already happened in the future."

Mark looked a little surprised. "We thought that they may have access to information through sources we couldn't possibly find, but the future?"

"That," said Andrew, "is what Làngfèi shíjiān is all about. That is why it is so powerful, and that is why it must be found. Couldn't, in my time, but with the more modern resources at your disposal I'm hoping you can.

"Switch on your recorder, take notes. I'll start right at the beginning. This is before I came on the scene, you understand. Also, the events later on I wasn't party to at the time, I only found out the details later."

Part 2

Chapter 8

London, on a cold, foggy November morning in 1931. A small, stocky Chinaman with a long white beard and dressed in a formal morning suit, walked into the City branch of Swifts Bank. He was accompanied by his taxi driver who was struggling with a large, sturdy wooden crate. He presented himself at the counter and announced, in highly accented, but precise English, that his name was Lau Huang, and he wished to see the manager. He then presented the young man, behind the counter, with a thick white envelope to give to the manager.

While he waited he took in his surroundings. Everything about the place spoke money. Old, established money. Mahogany panelled walls, marble floor and columns, all the brass-work polished to a pale, dazzling yellow. All the staff immaculately turned out in morning suits, much like himself. Pinstripe trousers, tails and grey waistcoat. What little clientele there was were equally well turned out. A distinguished elderly, grey haired gentleman in a very expensive bespoke suit. A middle aged woman with perfectly coiffured hair and a fur coat. In other circumstances a Chinaman in morning suit would command curiosity and stares, muttered comments and glances. This, however, was Swifts Bank, second only to Coutts, and regarded itself as a cut above the rest. Barons, dukes and some minor royals, both British and foreign were among its clientele. As such, no one paid any attention to him whatsoever.

A door, at the back of the banking hall opened, and a large man of about sixty came through. He too wore a morning suit, in the buttonhole was a single red rose.

Where he got his buttonhole from at this time of year, fresh each morning, was a mystery. He was balding and clean shaven and wore a warm, friendly smile of greeting. As he strode into the room he extended his hand in greeting to Lau Huang. "Mr Lau, it is indeed a pleasure," he said. "I am Sir Bernard MacIntyre. How may I help you?"

They shook hands. Then Lau Huang indicated the wooden crate on the floor. "Thank you, Sir Bernard," he said. "I wish to place this in your safekeeping"

"Certainly, Mr Lau," said Sir Bernard. "Please come through." He beckoned two of his staff over and instructed them to bring the crate through with them.

The other side of the door was a large vestibule with a rather grand staircase leading to a gallery with doors off either end. One end the under manager's office, according to the plate on the door his name was Geoffrey Vicarage. At the other end two doors. One marked Board Room, the other carrying the name plate "Sir Bernard MacIntyre. General Manager".

"Would you care to come up to my office?" Invited Sir Bernard, "I'm sure we can provide you with some refreshment." He beamed down at the Chinaman.

"Thank you, no," said Lau Huang, "If all is in order I should prefer to place my charge into your safekeeping as soon as possible."

"Of course," said Sir Bernard, "Your letter of authority, plus funds, arrived last week. Your letter of today confirms everything. All is, indeed, in order, Mr Lau. We shall proceed to the vault." With that he led them to a set of double doors to the left of the staircase, opened them wide to allow Lau Huang, and the two junior staff carrying the crate, to go through. Then they went down the stairs to the vestibule that accessed the vault.

In the safe deposit vault Lau Huang used a crowbar he'd asked for, to open the wooden crate. He carefully lifted out the ornate bronze chest, it was obviously very heavy, yet Lau Huang handled it without difficulty. He placed it in the largest deposit box in the vault. It was more of a safe than a deposit box, there was no inner box to slide out, inside were a series of hinged metal straps. Lau Huang positioned the chest in the middle, placed the hinged straps over the chest and secured them with a series of padlocks that he retrieved from the wooden crate. He then closed the door on the deposit box and called in Sir Bernard. All the while Lau Huang had been opening the crate and securing the chest Sir Bernard had been outside the vault ensuring he had complete privacy. He entered the vault, inserted his second key into the safe deposit box's second lock, alongside Lau Huang's, and the pair of them turned their respective keys and locked the box. Sir Bernard then called in a member of staff to take out, and dispose of the remains of the wooden crate.

"Is there anything else we can do for you, Mr Lau?" enquired Sir Bernard as they left the vault and ascended the stairs to ground level.

"Thank you, no, Sir Bernard." said Lau Huang, "You have been most accommodating. I have some other business to attend to, in London, before I return to China at the end of the week."

"You return so soon?" enquired Sir Bernard. "Forgive my curiosity, but to come all this way for such a short time."

"Not at all, Sir Bernard," said Lau Huang, "but there is much to be done in China, now that we are at war with Japan. The sole purpose of my visit was to place a certain item in your safekeeping, and trust in your complete discretion."

"Of course." said Sir Bernard. He escorted Lau Huang to the front door of the bank, shook his hand, bade him farewell and watched him walk off into the slowly thinning fog. He turned back into the bank with a wry smile on his face. Funny little man, he thought to himself. He comes all this way from China just to place whatever was in that crate in our vault. He must have money, the funds he sent will pay for whatever it is safekeeping for a hundred years. Extraordinary. Typical of the inscrutable Chinese. Now back to China. No sooner here than back again. He made his way back to his office feeling quite content with himself. That one long term, lump sum payment had almost doubled Swift Bank's not inconsiderable liquid assets.

Chapter 9

Lau Huang awoke as soon as he heard them enter the room. To anybody else they would have been soundless, but Lau Huang was on his guard. He had been expecting something like this since he stepped off the ship at Tilbury. His only surprise was they had taken so long. He'd expected some sort of attack before he placed his charge in the care of Swifts Bank. He was just glad he'd managed to stay just that one small step ahead of them. In a flash he was out of his bed, a knife in his hand. The fighting was fast and brutal, one of his assailants receiving a deep and vicious cut to his arm before they overcame, and killed Lau Huang. They knew they wouldn't be able to subdue him, they would have to kill him. Quickly they set about ransacking the room. It was clear they were searching for something. Everything was gone through. Closet opened and clothes taken out, linings slashed. Drawers taken out, contents strewn around, bedding tossed, mattress and pillows slashed so a covering of feathers eventually settled over everything. It was clear from their demeanour they didn't find what they were looking for. Quickly they left the room. From entering the room, to them finally leaving, and locking the door behind them with Lau Huang's key, had taken twelve minutes. Nobody heard a thing.

It was the chambermaid the following morning, who discovered Lau Huang. Or rather the manager. Finding the door locked, and no response to her somewhat vigorous knocking, she remembered her instructions not to enter and called the manager. He stood outside the room, unsure himself what to do. Then the chambermaid gave a gasp and pointed to the carpet just outside Lau Huang's door. There were four large spots of, what was obviously blood.

"Bloody hell," muttered the manager. Without further ado he unlocked the door. He turned to the chambermaid and told her to wait outside, then let himself in. His shout of "Great God Almighty." brought the chambermaid into the room. At one look at the state of the room, and Lau Huang's bloody, slashed corpse she let out a loud scream and dropped in a dead faint. The manager managed to catch the chambermaid, as she fell, and dragged her out into the corridor. He shouted at the bellboy, who was running up the corridor keen to be in on the action, to run and telephone the police.

Chapter 10

So it was that Detective Inspector Horace Simms, of Scotland Yard, found himself standing in the middle of Lau Huang's room, surveying the carnage. Detective Sergeant Arnold "Tom" Brown came into the room. "I've asked all along the corridor, Guv', both sides, the floor below, and the floor above. No one saw, or heard anything," he said, "Though Christ knows how they kept this lot quiet." His look took in the room.

"It is indeed a mystery, Tom," said Simms. He produced a tobacco pouch and proceeded to fill his pipe, a small briar with a curved stem. Putting the pouch away he produced a windproof Tommy lighter from another pocket and lit his pipe. Clouds of smoke billowed forth around his head as he stood in thought. Tom debated with himself whether to open the window. "Look at all this," said Simms, indicating the room with the stem of his pipe. "Get into the room, kill," He turned a questioning look at the manager hovering in the corridor, just outside.

"Lau Huang" said the manager.

"Indeed, Lau Huang. Kill Lau Huang ransack his room then leave. Lock the door behind themselves and disappear without anyone, anyone," repeating himself to emphasise the point, "hearing, or noticing a damn thing. I suspect they were fellow countrymen of our friend here," poking the stem of his pipe towards the body of Lau Huang before taking another puff and sending out more plumes of acrid smoke. A uniformed constable came up to the room.

"Sir," he called out.

"I wouldn't come in here Davey, boy." said Brown.

"Is it that bad?" asked the constable.

"You could say that," said Brown, "His lordship just lit his pipe."

" I heard that, Sergeant," said Simms. "What is it constable?"

" I've been asking around, Sir, and spoke to the night porter of the small hotel next door. The erm.." he consulted his notebook. "The Consterdine Hotel. He was out the back having a crafty fag about twelve thirty and saw two, what he called 'shifty looking Chinks' walking quickly down the alley past him. They didn't see him 'cos he'd just put his fag out and was standing behind the bins. He only saw them as they drew level. Said he didn't hear them as they were moving so quietly." "Good work constable." said Simms. "See?" he said turning to his sergeant "Told you it would be the Chinese." He heaved a sigh and inspected the bowl of his pipe. Then gave it a couple of good sucks to see if was still alight. It was. More smoke filled the room. DS Brown crossed the room and opened the window. "Making a statement, Tom?" enquired Simms.

"Just felt it a good idea not to smoke the deceased like a kipper, before the coroner's had a look," he replied.

Another constable came up to the room, coughed, said "Bloody hell, is the place on fire?"

"No," said DS Brown, " It's his-"

"Yes, thank you sergeant," interrupted Simms. "What is it, constable?"

"I've just been looking round the back alley, where next door's night porter said he saw them Chinese," he said.

"Yes?" said Simms. "What did you find"

"Blood, Sir, lots of it, and some blood soaked towels. Just by the back door of this hotel."

"Well, he obviously didn't give up without a fight," said Brown.

"No," said Simms, "he certainly didn't. I think he also knew his attackers or, at least, was expecting them. He's been slashed and cut. Stab wounds to several places, not just the chest, but I doubt this is all his blood. Aha." He stooped down beside the bed and, using his handkerchief, picked something up from beside the jumbled and screwed up bedding. He held up an ornate, but blood covered dagger. "And this, if I'm not mistaken is Lau...thing's."

"Huang," prompted Brown, "Lau Huang."

"Indeed, Lau Huang." said Simms. "I think he managed to hurt one, maybe both his assailants. They grabbed the towels from the bathroom to staunch their wounds as they escaped the hotel. Once outside they discarded the towels." He looked wistfully about him, through the slowly dissipating clouds of smoke, "Then buggered off into the night." A constable produced a paper evidence bag and Simms dropped the dagger in. "You've got a contact in Chinatown, haven't you Tom?" he asked.

"Yes, Sir," said Brown, "Huang Xian. He's got his finger in a few pies, most of them a bit dodgy. I'll have a word, see what I can find out."

"Excellent," said Simms, "Pop along and see him. We've done all we can here, I think". While he was saying this Brown had picked up an upended attache case, its contents strew across the floor. He was looking round the inside and noticed something.

"Hang on, Guv'," he said, taking the attache case over to the table by the window, miraculously still upright and in one piece. Placing the open case on the table he started feeling along the inside of one side.

"What is it, Tom?" said Simms, coming over to look over his shoulder.

"There's something in here." Brown took out a pocket knife, and inserted the blade under the lining where it joined the top edge, and peeled it back. Carefully he teased out a piece of very thin rice paper approximately six inches by four. "There you go," said Brown. He handed it to Simms, "Thought I could see something. Surprising his killers didn't find it." One side of it was covered in very closely packed very small Chinese characters. There was one small entry in English, however, just two words, 'Swifts Bank'.

"Probably ran out of time," surmised Simms, "or they just didn't see it. They were in a hurry, and doing all this ransacking, probably by torchlight. Right, I'll get back to the yard with this, the dagger and anything else the lads have found. You take the car and go to Chinatown. I'll go back with the constable, once the Police Doctor's finished up. Whenever he gets here." He took out his pocket watch to check the time.

"Right, will do," said Brown. "Shall I take the note, ask Xian what it says?"

"No," said Simms. "Best we hang on to that for now, get our own people to have a look at it. Besides there could be something vital on there. They could find it useful, tell us any old poppycock and we'd be none the wiser."

"Right oh," said Brown. He left, meeting the Police Doctor on the stairs. "Morning , Sir," he said.

"Morning, Sergeant," said the doctor, and bustled on up to the room. There's a man of few words, thought Brown. Unless he's actual playing with a body, and telling you all the gory details, he hardly says a word.

Chapter 11

Yesterday's fog had virtually gone and a persistent drizzle gave everything a dull shine. The day had a grey, miserableness about it, and when DS Brown drove into Limehouse the drizzle was starting to turn to rain. He turned into Canton Street, pulled up next to an alley. Dirty shop fronts with Chinese characters barely visible through the filth either side of the alley's entrance. The fronts of many properties boarded up. In the street, people were scurrying around heads down against the weather. Nearly all of them were wearing black baggy trousers and high buttoned tunics, the workaday clothes of the Chinese in this part of London. Some wearing Chinese skull caps, some wearing coolie hats against the rain. DS Brown climbed out of the Wolseley, putting his trilby on as he got out. Slamming the door he hurried down the alley to a tiny shop, barely more than a doorway with a small window beside it. Shoving the creaking door open brought a little old lady scuttling into the shop through a worn and tatty beaded curtain, along with the aroma of spices and incense. She wore the traditional black pants, but her tunic was a deep blue with a design of golden dragons. She had a very wrinkled face making it difficult to judge her age, her grey hair in a platted braid that went down her back to her waist. DS Brown put her age between 80 and 100, she was so wizened. She gave the briefest of starts, when she saw Brown. A sight twitch, then a forced smile.
"Meestar Blown," she said, " always a preasure."
DS Brown removed his hat, shook the rain off. "Madam Huang," he said, "Is Xian about?"

Madam Huang shuffled closer to him and looked up. "This abou' dead man in hotel in Horrand Park?" she enquired. Curiosity overcoming her reticence.

"Word gets around fast," said Brown.

"This Chinatown," said Madam Huang, " ob course we know. What he name, man killed?"

"Lau Huang, according to his passport," said Brown, "any relative?"

A shock of recognition flashed across her face and was gone, but not before Brown had noticed it. "Huang not unusual name in China," she said, turning away. "I not know. I get Xian." With that she scuttled back out through the beaded curtain shouting in Chinese. She couldn't get out of the shop fast enough. Other voices joined hers, out the back. Suddenly the voices got louder and more excited. She'd obviously told them why DS Brown was here, and the name of the dead man. Brown smiled inwardly. He didn't have to know Chinese to pick up that they knew who Lau Huang was. The shouting reached a crescendo, then there was a bark from a male voice and everything quietened down to almost a whisper. A minute later a man in his mid fifties, about 5'4" tall, the traditional Chinese platted pigtail down his back and a long drooping moustache, came through the curtain. He had a big welcoming smile on his face. DS Brown always noted the smile never extended to his eyes, they remained cold, dark and hard. No sign of the haze in him that the opium gives, as so many of his fellow inhabitants of Chinatown had.

"Sergeant Brown," said the man, the usual confusion between 'r' and 'l', so common among the Chinese, conspicuous in its absence. In fact he sounded quite well spoken.

" Hello Xian," replied Brown.

"Madam Huang tells me you are here about the murder of the man in Holland Park."

"Yes, his name's Lau Huang. Mean anything to you?"

"Should it?" asked Xian.

"I thought perhaps Madam Huang, and your name, Huang Xian, you know?"

"The name Huang is not uncommon in China."

"Yes, Madam Huang said. Do you know him, or of him? He was killed by two of your fellow countrymen. They sustained some nasty injuries judging by the blood they left behind."

"Let me ask around. See what I can find out. I will let you know if I find anything.

"We normally like to take care of things ourselves, but when one is murdered in one of your hotels it brings us all into disrepute."

"One of our hotels?" said Brown. "You make it sound like another country."

"You think it is not?" replied Xian, with a thin smile. "I will call you tomorrow." He passed a slim packet to Brown, who slipped it into an inside pocket. It was just some herbal tea that his wife said she liked. A little gift for her, now and then, smoothed things a bit if he was late from the pub. However, to an observer it looked as if DS Brown was on the take. A little charade that both of them kept up as a cover for Huang Xian's work as a police informer. Were it known to the Triads, Sui Fong Triad in particular, DS Brown didn't give much for Huang Xian's chances. Payments, to him, made at other times, away from Chinatown. Also a blind eye turned to some of Huang Xian's less than legal activities. DS Brown would only know Xian had been found out if he suddenly disappeared. If that happened Madam Huang would most probably push him out of her tiny shop with a broom, and lock the door behind him. In which case DS Brown would beat a hasty retreat and keep well clear of Chinatown, and Limehouse, for quite a while. He put his hat back on and went back out into the rain to his Wolseley. Huang Xian watched through the shop window as DS Brown disappeared up the alley in the rain. He went through into the back of the shop and had a quick conversation with Madam Huang. She went into the shop, leaving him alone. He picked the receiver up off the ancient telephone fixed to the wall, hesitated for a second or two, then dialled a number.

Chapter 12

The Police Surgeon, Dr Smith, knocked on the open door. DI Simms looked up. "Ah, Dr Smith, good of you to come." He stood back and indicated the body.

"Good morning Inspector," said Dr Smith. He walked over, placed his doctor's bag on the floor by the body and retrieved a pair of pince-nez from the waistcoat pocket of his dark greeny-brown Harris Tweed suit and clipped them onto his nose. Without any further comment he inspected the body. He took his time, at one point pushing the body up on its side to inspect the back. He stood up and removed his pince-nez.

"Well?" enquired Simms, "apart from being stabbed what can you tell me?"

Dr Smith glanced over at Simms, then back at the body, "As you say, he's been stabbed. A ferocious attack from which he defended himself equally ferociously, judging by the wounds to his arms. There are three very deep stab wounds to the chest, two of which could have been the fatal one. We'll know more after the autopsy. It was a double edged blade, something like a dagger, very sharp. The way it's cut through both clothing and flesh I'd say razor sharp, almost as sharp as a scalpel."

"Could this be the murder weapon?" asked Simms, taking the evidence bag from the constable, removing the dagger and showing Dr Smith.

Dr Smith replaced his pince-nez and looked closely at the weapon, "Similar, but not this one. Judging by the stab wounds I'd say the murder weapon was slightly larger, a broader blade. This was probably the dagger the deceased used to defend himself." It confirmed what Simms had thought. Removing his pince-nez, once again, he faced Simms. "I would say this attack was vicious and fast. There are no wounds to the back, whatsoever, so he faced his attackers the whole time. I doubt they got off scot free, The dagger you have could inflict a nasty wound."

"There were two of them and we know he injured at least one." said Simms. "We have an eye witness who saw them leave via the back door. When we checked there was quite a lot of blood, and a blood soaked towel, just outside."

"Quite," said Dr Smith. "Well, as soon as the autopsy's complete you'll have my report. Although I doubt it will tell you anything we don't already know. Good day, Inspector." With that Dr Smith picked up his bag and left.

DI Simms looked around the room. The body on the floor, the shredded bedding and upturned furniture. And nobody heard anything, he thought to himself. The clientele didn't seem the sort to turn a blind eye to a rumpus in the middle of the night. Indeed they seemed more the type to ring down to reception and complain to the night porter about it. Fast and vicious, yet they missed the note hidden in the lining of the attache case. So, he thought, ruthless, but not terribly efficient after the fight. What sort of people carry out this sort of attack and search without disturbing the neighbours. These hotel room walls aren't that thick. Plus this Lau Huang never made a sound. Strange he didn't call out, or make a sound, even while being attacked. I just hope Tom has more luck in Chinatown.

He returned the dagger, in its evidence bag to the constable by the door. "Okay, constable," he said. "I've finished here. Get the body to the morgue and finish up here, thank you."

Chapter 13

DI Simms sat behind his desk, puffing away at his pipe, filling the room with a pungent haze and gazing into space as he thought about Lau Huang's murder. The door opened and DS Brown entered the room waving the smoke away from in front of his face. He coughed a couple of times. "Blimey, Guv", is your waste paper basket on fire?"

"Very funny, Tom," said Simms. "Did you get anywhere with your Chinatown informant?"

"Well, they knew of the murder," said Brown, "but claimed not to know the deceased, though I'm not so sure about that."

"How so?" asked Simms.

"Two of the people I spoke to are called Huang, just like matey. There's a Madam Huang, and then there's my contact, Xian Huang. But, they claim it's quite a common name in China."

"So what makes you think they're lying about knowing him?"

"Don't know, Guv", just something about the way they reacted. Madam Huang almost gasped, but just stopped herself. Xian remained expressionless, almost deliberately so. You know? Like trying to keep a dead pan face when playing poker."

"I'll bow to your superior knowledge of poker, Tom, but I know what you mean. Also I've got an interpreter coming in to look at that note." He leaned forward and picked up a piece of paper off his desk. "A Mr Cheng Zao. Sounds more like a pantomime character. He's coming in tomorrow morning." He stood up and retrieved his hat and coat from the stand by the door.

"Where are we off to now, Guv'?" asked Brown.

"We're going to Swifts Bank, see if they can shed any light on what this Lau Huang was doing here."

"Which branch? There must be a fair few of them in London." They were now going down the stairs towards the side entrance, where their car was.

"I thought we'd try the City branch, first, then work our way out. It's on The Strand."

"I know it, about fifty yards down from Coutts."

Outside it was still raining. If anything it was getting heavier. As DI Simms climbed in, DS Brown ran round to the driver's side and got behind the wheel. "Bloody weather. Yesterday you couldn't see 'cos of the fog, now you can't see 'cos of the blessed rain."

"Such are the vagaries of English weather," said Simms, and took out his pipe and tobacco pouch.

"I'll open the window," threatened Brown. "even in this rain."

"Don't worry yourself, Tom, I'm only going to fill it. I wouldn't dream of lighting up in here. You just don't appreciate the aroma of fine tobacco."

"That's just the trouble, Guv', I do," said Brown with a grin, "but there's no way, on Gods earth, you can call that stuff you burn in there 'fine tobacco'"

"Just drive, sergeant," said Simms, with a smile, and looked out the window at the passers by hurrying through the rain. Umbrellas aloft, hats pulled down. He put the unlit pipe in his mouth and felt the comfort of its weight as he gripped the stem between his teeth. A couple of dry sucks and he savoured the light taste of the unlit tobacco.

"What do you think's going on here, Guv'?" enquired Brown. "I mean that hotel room was a bloody mess, in every sense of the word. Chinese staying in a top class hotel, knife fights in the middle of the night. You don't think the Chinese are expanding their criminal gangs over here, do you?"

"I don't know, Tom," replied Simms. "I get a feeling not. I would have thought your contact would have mentioned it to you if that were the case. Has he said anything?"

"No, Gov, but that doesn't rule it out. He keeps things pretty close to his chest, and these gangs can be pretty ruthless. They may have told him to keep quiet. This kind of attack is the sort of thing they do."

"In a hotel like the Goulbourne? Top class and very discrete. I can't imagine a Chinese gang boss staying there."

In the bank Sergeant Brown went up to a cashier. "Detective Sergeant Brown and Detective Inspector Simms." He showed the young man behind the counter his warrant card. "We'd like a word with the manager, please"

The young man looked somewhat startled, and a few heads turned towards them. "Err..yes, Sir, erm.. if you could just wait here a second, I'll see if he's available." He got up and hurried out the back. In less than two minutes he was back, this time in front of the counter. "Sir Bernard says to come straight through." He ushered them through to the rear of the bank, took them up the stairs and knocked on Sir Sir Bernard's door. Then opened it and announced them, standing back to let them enter. As soon as they were inside he quietly left and closed the door. The office was typical of a prominent bank manager, in charge of a flagship branch. Oak panelling, darkened with age, heavy furniture, the chairs green buttoned leather and mahogany. Sir Bernard sat behind a huge mahogany desk, a brass lamp with oblong green shade on one end, a letter tray at the other and his back to a large sash window. To one side a pair of green leather chesterfields faced each other across a low table in front of a nicely burning fire.

Brown identified himself and DI Simms to Sir Bernard, showing him his warrant card.

"Good afternoon, gentlemen," said Sir Bernard, coming around his desk and shaking DI Simms' hand, first, then DS Brown's. "What can I do for you?"

"I wonder, Sir Bernard," said Simms. "Does the name Lau Huang mean anything to you?"

"Ah," said Sir Bernard, walking back round his desk and sitting down. "This wouldn't, by any chance, be anything to do with this horrible business at the Goulbourne Hotel, this morning, would it?"

Simms and Brown glanced at each other. "Yes," said Simms, "as a matter of fact it does. Do you know this Lau Huang?"

"He is a customer of this bank," said Sir Bernard. "But that is all I can tell you at the moment. The confidentiality of all your customers is paramount."

"It was Lau Huang's body that was discovered at the Goulbourne this morning," said Simms. "He'd been savagely attacked and his room ransacked."

"My God." Sir Bernard slumped back in his chair, slightly. "Do you know why?"

"That's what we're trying to find out, Sir." said Brown. "By the way, how did you come to hear about it? It only happened this morning. Too late for the late edition morning papers, and too early for this evening's first editions."

"I heard from a friend in the City, sergeant. Nothing sinister, or untoward. When this sort of thing happens at somewhere like the Goulbourne it doesn't stay secret for long"

"I see," cut in Simms. "But you can't tell us any more about the nature of his business at the bank?"

"Well, in view of the fact he's been murdered all I can tell you is that he used our safe deposit facilities. Other than that I really can't say. I have no idea what it was, all such matters are handled in secrecy. No member of staff was present while he conducted his business. That is to say while he placed whatever it was into his safe deposit box. It was a big one though, our largest box."

"I didn't realise you had different sizes," said Brown, writing in his notebook.

"Oh yes," said Sir Bernard. "Some people wish to entrust us with larger items that wouldn't fit into a regular size deposit box. Fortunately this one was available after the death of one of our titled customers last year."

"Well, thank you, Sir Bernard," said Simms. "You've been very helpful. I think we've got all we came for."

"There is one thing, though." said Sir Bernard. "How did you know he was a customer here?"

"We didn't." said Simms. "We found a note with the name Swifts Bank on it and we thought we'd start here."

The rain had stopped. Simms and Brown stood on the wet pavement outside the bank. Simms glanced up at the sky then busied himself with the ritual of filling and lighting his pipe. "We touched lucky, there, Sir." said Brown. "First branch we try."

Simms got a good head of smoke swirling, before putting his 'Tommy' lighter away. "More an educated guess." he said. "A foreign national, staying in a top class London hotel. They're not likely to pop off to the Lewisham branch, are they? It was lucky, though. The fact is the bank's name on that piece of paper may have meant something totally different. We'd have been a bit stuck, then." They stood and watched the traffic, a coal lorry grinding past, a bus going the other way. "Come on, Tom, let's go."

"Where to, Guv'?" asked Brown, going around to the driver's side.

"Back to the office." replied Simms. "See what we've got so far and see if they found anything else at the hotel."

Chapter 14

The following morning the rain was back in earnest. DS Brown shook the water from his hat, then coat, before consigning them to the coat stand by the door. DI Simms was already in and seated behind his desk. DS Brown smoothed his hair down and straightened his jacket with a tug at the front.

"'Morning, Guv'," he said. "Absolutely chucking it down out there."

"Yes," agreed Simms. "Let's hope we don't have to go out in it too soon. Any word from your Chinese contact?"

"No, Guv"," he replied, "not a peep, still early days yet. He'll need to ask around, and do it carefully so as not to arouse any suspicions." He pulled a chair over from by the wall and sat down at the side of Simms' desk. "When's this interpreter coming in?"

"He's due any time…" Simms' answer was interrupted by a knock at the door.

The desk sergeant opened the door and said, "A Mr Cheng Zau for you, Sir." He held the door open while a slim Chinaman, about 5'8" tall, wearing a double breasted suit entered the office.

"Ah, Mr Cheng, good of you to come," said Simms, standing and extending his hand across the desk.

"The pleasure is all mine," responded Cheng Zau, shaking the proffered hand and making a small bow by nodding his head.

"This is my sergeant, DS Brown," said Simms.

"Detective Sergeant," said Cheng Zau, shaking Brown's hand and also nodding to him. "How may I help you?"

"A document has come into our possession," said Simms. As he was saying this he extracted the note found in the lining of Lau Huang's attache case, from a manila folder on his desk. "We were hoping you could translate it for us." While he was saying this, Brown had got up and pulled another chair over to the desk. Simms handed the note to Cheng Zau, who took it and sat down. The three of them sat around the desk, Simms and Brown expectantly, Cheng Zau taking a pair of gold rimmed spectacles from the breast pocket of his jacket and putting them on. He studied the note carefully, reading it through, then turning it over to look at the back. He held it up to the light and turned it over several times, in his hands, before returning to again scrutinise the writing.

"I would say, at first glance, that this is possibly in a code," said Cheng Zau, in a precise well spoken voice with just a hint of his Chinese background in his accent. He took a note book and propelling pencil from inside his jacket and arranged the note book alongside the note on the desk. "The characters are quite ordinary for this type of Chinese," he continued. "For instance, this character, here," he indicated the character second down from the top left, "is the character for running water, or a stream. However, it has no context." As he was saying this he was copying the characters into his note book with added notes alongside each character. These notes were also in Chinese. "The characters do not relate to each other. It is just a jumble of words and phrases. I can translate for you, but it will just be a list of words."

Simms sat back looking thoughtful. "That would be a start." He said. "We might be able to make something of it."

"Very well."said Cheng Zau. "I would like, if I may, to take this away and work on it. Whilst the characters are simple, in nature, their lack of context can make them somewhat ambiguous."

"I'm afraid I can't let you take the document out of the office, Mr Cheng." said Simms. "However, you can take your copy," he indicated Cheng Zau;'s note book, "and work from that."

"Very good." said Cheng Zau. He turned to a fresh page in his notebook and proceeded to make an exact copy of the note, even to the extent of including the English words 'Swifts Bank' at their correct place. As he did so DS Brown gave his superior a questioning look and frowned. Simms gave him the merest of expressions that told Brown it was curious, but to let it ride. It was the sort of body language exchange they might make when questioning a suspect.

"So, Mr Cheng," broke in DS Brown. "When do you think you could let us have your translation?"

"Tomorrow morning." said Cheng Zau, "I will need to include all the variances for you." He finished writing and was putting his note book and propelling pencil away. He quickly stood up. "Good day, gentlemen. Until tomorrow morning."

"Sergeant Brown will see you out," said Simms, "and thank you again." He extended his hand and Cheng Zau shook it almost as an afterthought.

When Brown returned to the office DI Simms was studying the piece of paper. "What was all that about?" he said, nodding his head toward the door he'd just returned through.

"What indeed." said Simms.

"Once he'd copied everything down he couldn't get out of here fast enough." said Brown.

"Quite so, Tom," said Simms. "He saw something in this." He waved the note, "something he didn't want us to see. I think we'd better keep an eye on friend Cheng Zau." He leaned across his desk and picked up the phone. "Ah, Sergeant Robbins, the oriental chap that just left, could someone keep an eye out, let us know where he goes. Don't let him know he's being followed." He paused while Sergeant Robbins issued some orders in the background, then confirmed the task was in hand. "Thank you Sergeant." said Simms and replaced the receiver. He looked over at the window. "Still chucking it down. Did Cheng have a coat?"

"Yes," said Brown, "he left it at the front desk, picked it up on the way out." He walked over to the window. "If anything it's raining harder."

That afternoon saw a wet and bedraggled constable standing in front of DI Simms' desk, dripping rainwater on to the lino. DS Brown stood by the window. "So what you're saying," said Brown, "is you lost him."

"That's OK, sergeant," said Simms, addressing Brown by his rank in front of junior officers while at the 'Yard, "Let's just go over it one more time. You say he went to a phone box in Whitehall. Then, after the call, waited near the phone box till a car came along. He then got in the car and had a conversation with whoever was in it?"

"Yes, Sir," said the constable. "I was expecting them to drive off and was getting ready use the box to phone back to the 'Yard, when he got back out again."

"Did you see who was in the car?" asked Simms.

"No, Sir, I was behind the car. All I can say is the bloke he was speaking to was in the back. Our man got in the back and I could see their two heads together, but just the backs. Then he got out again and the car drove off. I took its number and phoned it back as soon as I got the chance."

"Just after you lost him," cut in Brown with a hint of irony in his voice.

"Yes, Sarge'," he replied. "That was my first opportunity. We bussed and walked back to Limehouse. Once we got into Chinatown proper I had to hang back as I stood out like a sore thumb. He ducked into one of those alleys off Canton Street and was gone."

"OK, Constable," said Simms, "I think you did well all things considered. Now go and get yourself dried off, and a cup of tea."

"Thank you Sir," he said, and left.

"Well, Tom, what do you make of that?" asked Simms, after the DC had left.

"I think whatever was in that note certainly spooked him. He bloody understood it, despite what he said."

"I'm inclined to agree," said Simms. "I don't think we'll be seeing chummy tomorrow morning. In fact I doubt we'll be seeing him again at all. You'll have to ask your friend Xian about him"

DI Simms, and DS Brown, buckled down to the onerous task of paperwork, prepared for an afternoon at the desk. They both had reports to write up, evidence to be gone over and cross checked. About three thirty the phone on DI Simms' desk rang. He picked up the receiver. "DI Simms," he announced, listened, then held the receiver out to DS Brown . "It's for you, Tom." he said.

"DS Brown," he said, "Xian." He glanced over at Simms, who stopped what he was doing and paid strict attention to his Sergeant, "Yes…..where…..OK in about half an hour." And he put the phone down. "That was Xian," he said.

"So I gathered," said Simms. "What did he have to say for himself."

"He's got the information we want. He sounded quite excited. Said I'd be surprised at what he's got. Wants to meet up at a cafe in Gerrard Street."

"Bit off his own turf?" queried Simms.

"Yes. Doesn't like to be seen with me too often around Limehouse. Apparently there's some interest in the Gerrard Street area by some of the more wealthy Chinese, looking to expand their businesses. Particularly in the restaurant side."

"Really?" Said Simms, incredulously,."Can't see that taking off."

"You'd be surprised, Guv"," said Brown, taking his hat and coat from the stand. "Hope this bloody rain packs in, soon." And left.

Chapter 15

Cindy's Café, in Gerrard Street, was a fairly small affair with eight, or so, tables. Each one adorned with a red gingham check oilcloth table cloth. Apart from DS Brown, two other tables were occupied. One by a very elderly, but quite smartly dressed gentleman with a cup of tea, the other by a middle aged couple tucking into their pie and mash. The cream painted walls had cheap prints of London landmarks hung on them, and below a dado rail brown painted cheap lincrusta. The large front window streamed with condensation. DS Brown sat at a table one back from the window nursing a cup of tea, when Xian arrived. He was wearing a double breasted raincoat and a trilby hat. He briefly glanced around, saw Brown and came over. As he sat down, Brown caught the eye of the plump woman behind the counter. He asked for another tea, indicating his companion. She must be Cindy, he thought.

He noticed Xian was almost smiling. "Well, you look pleased with yourself." he said.

"You'd be surprised," said Xian, placing his hat on the corner of the table and reaching inside his coat. He pulled out a sheet of paper, folded neatly into four, and slid it across to Brown who placed his hand over it.

"What's this?" he enquired.

"That, Detective Sergeant Brown, are the names of the two men you want, plus where you can find them." Xian sat back in his chair with a smile. Cindy came over with his tea and gave him a bit of an old fashioned look.

"Thank you." said Xian with a smile. Cindy half returned the smile, blushed and hustled back behind the counter. DS Brown gave him a quizzical look, unfolded the paper and glanced down. It was just as Xian had said. The two names, and an address in Limehouse virtually on the bank of the River Thames. He refolded the paper and put it in his pocket.

"Go on," said Brown, "How come all this info, and so quickly?"

"Because, Detective Sergeant, the man who was killed, Lau Huang has special reverence among the more spiritual among us."

"How do you mean?"

"He was from a Taoist monastery, in Manchuria. Many here are part of a sect attached to this monastery. Particularly the triads."

"The triads?" DS Brown sounded incredulous. "I didn't think they held anything in high regard apart from themselves."

"They do with these Taoists." said Xian. "There's something special about this monastery, that is the centre of this sect. Its influence has spread throughout China, even as far as Kowloon, where the triad is from. It is the oldest monastery in China and has been in constant use for over two thousand years. It is rumoured that the senior monk is as old as the monastery."

"What, Two thousand years old?"

"Yes. Well. You know how superstitious we Chinese are. We love this sort of thing."

"So how come Lau Huang was killed by these two, and why are the triad so keen for us to have them?"

"Patience, Detective Sergeant, patience." He lifted an admonishing finger from the table. "He had come to England on a special mission. He'd brought something with him. No one seems to know what it was, but the Chinese Government want to get their hands on it and sent their two agents to get it. They bungled spectacularly, you'll agree. Killing Lau Huang and coming away empty handed. The triad want this dealt with, but their hands are tied. They don't want to draw attention to themselves, particularly another murder of Chinese nationals, and these possibly connected to the Chinese Legation."

"Wow," DS Brown sat back in his chair and puffed his cheeks out. "This certainly opens a whole new can of worms. Thanks for the info, Xian. He took his hand out of his coat pocket. In it was a brown envelope which he passed discreetly around the side of the table to Xian.

"No." said Xian, "This is with courtesy and respect from the triad."

"Sorry, Xian," said Brown, "But neither I, nor Scotland Yard, will be beholden to the triads. Take it. Say it was for expenses or something."

Xian pocketed the envelope. Drained his tea, got up and left. DS Brown gave him five more minutes before he went over to the counter and paid for the teas. At the first phone box he came to he telephoned Simms back at the 'Yard and passed on the information, along with a potted version of the story Xian told him. He left the phone box and went to his car parked a little way down the street. He drove off to meet up with DI Simms and some more officers in Limehouse.

Three unmarked police Wolseleys and a Commer van pulled into Narrow Street from different directions at two minute intervals. The torrential rain hissed on the street, the smell of the Thames rank in the air. They parked up, and the detectives in the Wolseleys got out and made their way towards the alley and the address Xian had given DS Brown. Everybody was moving quickly, if only to get this over with, and out of the rain. The van was parked just beyond the alley and as the detectives approached the back doors opened and four uniformed officers got out, along with a sergeant from the passenger seat. While the detectives were in their raincoats and hats, some wearing trilbies, others fedoras, the uniforms had to forgo their capes to allow freedom of movement. Everybody getting thoroughly soaked in the downpour that hadn't let up all afternoon.

DS Brown looked about. "It seems bloody quiet." He muttered to DI Simms as they approached the address. A filthy dirty door about fifteen yards down the alley.

"I was thinking the same thing." replied Simms. "With this police presence there'd normally be a right hullabaloo, despite the rain."

The uniformed officers now moved quickly passed them and stood ready around the door. "Open up, police!" shouted a sergeant, and without further ado kicked the door open. Whether it was locked or not didn't matter. The door was rotten and just splintered from the frame at the application of the sergeant's boot. The officers rushed inside with shouts of "Police, stay where you are." and, "Police, do not move!"

It was all over very quickly. DI Simms, DS Brown and two others didn't even get to enter the property before the uniforms were hauling out two very surprised and angry Chinamen, shouting away in Chinese. They were handcuffed and put in the back of the van.

"Building's clear, Sir" said the sergeant as he came up beside them.

DI Simms walked round to the driver's side of the van and spoke to the constable at the wheel. "Take then to Canon Row," he said.

"Yes, Sir," said the driver and pulled away with prisoners and officers all on board.

Once they'd seen them off to Canon Row Police Station, DI Simms and DS Brown went back to the building and the culprits' rooms. Inside the dirty and shabby building bare stairs led to two rooms on the upper floor. Each room was bare, plaster coming off the walls in places, leaving the laths exposed. A bashed and battered cot in each room, with a straw palliasse and dirty blankets. Bare floorboards that looked rotten in places. Indeed Simms and Brown were careful where they walked, fearful they may crash though to the ground floor. A worn brown canvas bag in each room held their possessions, which were few. A change of clothes a small amount of money, that was it. In the corner of one of the rooms Simms found some bloodied rags. They'd tried to clean the wounds. He pointed them out to Brown, "Did you notice any bandages, or dressings on either of them, Tom?" He asked.

"No, Guv'," said Brown, "but with those baggy sleeves it's hard to tell."

"Hm, quite," murmured Simms as he continued looking around. After a while he called out to his Sergeant, who was now in the other room, "Anything,Tom?"

"No, Guv', nothing, "Just the bag and change of clothes."

"Right," said Simms, "get uniform to finish off and bring the bags with them. We'll head over to Canon Row.

DI Simms and DS Brown walked back to their car, Brown looking around, even turning and walking backwards a couple of paces. "Unbelievable" he said as he got into the car.

"Looks like your oriental friend was right about wanting shot of them. The triad making sure everyones out of the way so as not to get involved"

"Wish all our cases were like this." Said Brown, "Make life a lot easier."

"You and me, both, Tom." Said Simms, "I was only thinking, this morning, how on earth were we going to proceed with this case."

"How do you want to play this, Guv'?" Asked Brown.

"Let them stew in the cells for a while before we speak to them. I don't know about you, but I could do with a nice cup of tea after all that."

Chapter 16

The stone and redbrick of Shaw's Flemish/Gothic edifice that is Canon Row Police Station glistened wetly in the yellow street light as DI Simms and DS Brown bustled inside out of the rain, the swing doors clattering shut behind them. They were shown straight through and made their way down to the cells. The Custody Sergeant stood up to greet them. A florid barrel of a man with white hair cut in a short back and sides and a fine handlebar moustache, equally as white. "You're not going to like this, Sir." he said with a beaming smile. An old hand who had seen everything in his day. All types of offender, with all types of excuses and some you hadn't even thought of. He'd seen it all, and took it all in his stride.

"What's that, then?" asked DI Simms, applying the flame of his 'Tommy' lighter to the contents of his pipe, and almost disappearing behind a cloud of smoke.

"They're claiming Diplomatic Immunity." The sergeant chuckled, "They're getting quite worked up about it. Well, the one that speaks English does. The other one just sits in his cell, then comes up to the bars and glares at you if you go up to his cell. Makes a change, I suppose. First D.I. claim we've had for about five years. Won't tell us their names, though." He came around his desk with a bunch of large keys in his hand, "Which one do you want first?"

"Really?" said Simms, "Diplomatic Immunity, eh? What else is he saying? Has he said anything about the murder?"

"Nope," replied the sergeant. "Just keeps banging on about Diplomatic Immunity, and we've no right to keep him here. Keeps telling me to telephone their embassy, but I thought you'd want to have a word first. Besides, no point in phoning the embassy without knowing their names."

"Thank you, sergeant," said Simms, "Quite so. Now, who's in which cell?"

"The silent one's at the far end," said the sergeant. "Our noisy friend just two doors down from this end."

"Good," said Simms, "We'll take the quiet one first. He may not speak English, but it might exercise his friend when we march him past his cell. By the way, has anybody looked at their wounds?"

"Wounds?" said a somewhat surprised sergeant. "What wounds? No one said anything about wounds. They haven't complained about any wounds. I haven't even seen any wounds."

Simms and Brown looked at each other. Both thinking the same thing, both getting a sinking feeling. What if these aren't the right men, what if they've slipped the net. Even worse, what if Huang Xian had sold them a pup and it was all a set-up. Get Scotland Yard chasing its tail while the real murderers slip quietly away.

The three of them walked down the corridor to the cell at the far end. As they passed the other man's cell, he immediately jumped to his feet. "I have Diplomatic Immunity." he shouted at the top of his voice, "I demand you contact the Chinese Ambassador!"

"Yeah, me too," came a broad cockney voice from the cell next door, "Hy want diplowmatic himmunity, Ah've done nuffin wrong." Followed by a laugh.

"That'll do, Georgie boy." said the sergeant. "When they make you ambassador of Poplar I might consider it. Until then you just keep it shtum. Here we are, gents," he said as he put the key in the lock of the end cell. The man inside was clearly Chinese. Slight build, about 5'6" and with a look of utter disdain on his face. He was dressed, as were they both, in the black baggy pants and tunic favoured by the inhabitants of Chinatown. His age was about late twenties. As the key turned he stood up and came and stood right by the bars, glaring at them.

"Step back, sonny." said the Custody Sergeant. The prisoner still maintained his surly glare, but after a few seconds duly stepped back a pace. "Further than that," snapped the sergeant. "Stand by the bunk." Another two second pause then he stepped back until the backs of his legs touched the low wooden board and straw filled mattress that made up his bunk.

Simms and Brown glanced at each other. Well, they both thought, we know he understands English, even if he pretends not to. They all went into the cell. "Excuse me, sergeant." said Simms, pushing past. He grabbed the prisoner's left arm and before he could say or do anything, shoved the sleeve up exposing the arm. Nothing . A smooth, muscular unblemished arm. He let it go, all the while the prisoner glowered age him. He grabbed the right arm and the prisoner then started to fight him off, shouting in Chinese. The Custody Sergeant and DS Brown grabbed him and held him while DS Simms held him by the wrist and shoved this sleeve up his arm. The bandage round his upper forearm was clean and tight. Whoever applied it knew exactly what they were doing. A faint line of blood was showing through on the outside, but judging by the colour it had stopped bleeding some time ago. Both Simms and Brown let out audible sighs of relief.

"Do you want me to call the duty surgeon to have a look at that, Sir?" asked the Custody Sergeant.

"Later, Sergeant," said Simms. "For now it looks ok. Let's take him upstairs and have a word."

The Custody Sergeant ushered them out, and together they all marched up the corridor. As soon as they drew level with the other suspect he started shouting. First in Chinese, then continued demanding their release due to Diplomatic Immunity. "That's quite enough from you, matey." shouted the Custody Sergeant, cutting him short. Their prisoner stiffened. For an instant something like fear crossed his face, then immediately replaced by his former glare. They carried on to the desk, where the Custody Sergeant made an entry in the log, and DI Simms signed the prisoner out and into his custody.

The interview room was a bare square room, harshly lit by a naked overhead bulb. The small square of glass bricks, high in the wall, that served for a window showed black against the night outside. The bare brick walls had been painted cream at one time, now showing scuffs and scrapes. Darkening to a light brown towards a similarly dark and stained ceiling, thanks to the countless cigarettes smoked by nervous prisoners and frustrated policemen over the years. In the centre of the room was plain wooden table. On one side a simple wooden chair, on which sat the prisoner. He was faced by DI Simms, busy filling his pipe, and DS Brown, opening his notebook and placing a pencil next to it. He then took out a packet of cigarettes and offered one to their prisoner. The man just glared at them. Brown shrugged, took out a cigarette for himself and tapped the ends on the packet. While Simms got his pipe going, Brown took out a match, lit his cigarette and waved the match out before tossing it into the battered metal ashtray in the centre of the table. Brown smiled to himself as the prisoner tried to stifle a cough as the acrid smoke from Simms' pipe wafted across the table. DS Brown introduced DI Simms and himself. He and Simms then remained quiet for a whole minute.

"Why did you and your friend kill Lau Huang?" Simms said suddenly, not going through any preliminaries. Brown kept his eyes firmly on the prisoner, who glanced from Simms to Brown, then back again. Brown noticed the glare was becoming hard to keep up and was slowly becoming just a stoney, sullen stare. Simms took another draw on his pipe, and sent a stream of blue smoke in the prisoner's general direction with no attempt to direct it anywhere, or wave it away. It hung between them like the start of a London fog. They'd decided, before going into the interview room, to ignore the fact they didn't have their names for now, and go straight in to the attack.

"Well," snapped Brown, continuing his superior's line.

The prisoner spoke. His expression didn't change. He just glanced between the two and in a quiet, but firm voice said, "I have Diplomatic Immunity. I demand you contact the Chinese Embassy and released us immediately."

"No," said Simms, "you have nothing on you to say you have any kind of diplomatic status whatsoever."

"And we found nothing in the place you were staying, either." added Brown, "You and your friend are murderers, plain and simple. Even the Chinese community want rid of you. How do you think we found you so soon? They couldn't get shot of you quick enough." He sat back with a smile on his face.

"Those running dogs of the West will pay for their treachery." said the prisoner, then clammed up. He spoke nothing more for the rest of the interview. They pushed him, badgered him, tried to provoke a response, but he remained stolid and expressionless. Eventually they called a halt, and returned him to the cells.

"Do you think there's anything in this Diplomatic Immunity malarky, Guv'?" asked Brown as they waited for the other suspect to be brought up.

"I don't know, Tom." said Simms. "Let's see what chummy has to say for himself and take it from there. We'll have to let upstairs know about it as a matter of form, but I can't see them bothering too much." The other suspect duly arrived and was brought into the room, now thick with tobacco smoke adding another layer to the stained ceiling. Once he was seated and the introductions made by Brown, Simms decided to change tack slightly. "What brought you and your friend to England?" He asked in quite a reasonable voice, almost as if making small talk.

"I have nothing to say to you, Detective Inspector." said the prisoner, in an equally conversational tone. He was slightly bigger than his compatriot, about 5'8", and stocky, quite broad across the shoulders. He had an almost pleasant face, and smiled amicably at his interrogators.

"Yes," said Brown, "Diplomatic Immunity. You said. We heard you downstairs." Brown leaned forward, resting his arms on the table. "Trouble is, we only have your word for it. No diplomatic passport, no documentation of any kind. Nothing. So there goes your Diplomatic Immunity, straight out the window. So I suggest you start to answer our questions."

"And I suggest you contact the Chinese Embassy." said the suspect with a smile, and sat back in his chair. Brown continued to look at him for a while before he too sat back in his chair. He got out his cigarettes and lit up. "Could I possibly have one of your cigarettes, please?" asked the suspect. Brown glanced at Simms, who gave a slight nod. Brown offered the pack across so the suspect could take one. He then held the match to light it. Waving it out, he threw the dead match into the now rather full ashtray. "All I will say to you is this." Simms and Brown both sat up slightly in their chairs. Brown readying his pencil over his note book. "The person you say we killed."

"Lau Huang," said Simms. "The murdered man's name was Lau Huang."

"Huang is such a common name in China." said the prisoner.

"So I've been told." said Brown, to no-one in particular.

"This Lau Huang," continued the prisoner, "has in his possession something of great importance, that is the property of the Republic of China."

"What's that, then?" asked Brown.

"I'm afraid I cannot tell you, but if it is in your possession, you must hand it over immediately."

"How can we know what you want us to hand over, if you don't tell us what it is?" asked Brown sardonically.

"I demand you hand it over now, and contact the Chinese embassy."

"Now hang on there, chummy." started Brown, but he was interrupted.

"I think you're getting a bit ahead of yourself." said Simms, almost snarling, "You've been arrested for murder. You're not in a position to demand anything."

"I insist you contact the Chinese Embassy," said the prisoner, raising his voice. "I claim Diplomatic Immunity and will say nothing more."

Simms and Brown looked at each other. Simms inclined his head toward the door and the pair stood up. "Perhaps a night in the cells may make you, and your friend more cooperative." said Simms. He opened the door and instructed the Constable standing outside to take the prisoner back to the cells.

In the corridor, Simms inspected the contents of the bowl of his pipe, while Brown lit another cigarette. "I think we'll let them stew for the night." said Simms. "In the morning I'll go and see the Super. He wants an update anyway. I'll show him that note and tell him about our friends claiming Diplomatic Immunity. He'll probably laugh that off, but to be honest, Tom, I don't really know where to go from here. We need some concrete evidence to link these two with the scene of the crime. So far all we've got is your mate Xian's say so, and what appears, on the surface, some unusual cooperation from the inhabitants of Chinatown and Limehouse. Not much to go on, and nothing to stand up in court."

"So what are you saying? We may have to let them go?"

"Without any concrete evidence, we may have to." said Simms, with a grim look on his face.

"What about the wound on matey's arm?" implored Brown.

"Could have been caused by anything. Besides the other chap was uninjured. Anyway," he straightened, easing his back. "Let's see what tomorrow brings, eh?

Chapter 17

The rain had stopped by the following morning, but the day was grey and overcast. The streets still wet and a mist in the air that hinted at the return of the fog. It was bitterly cold and the damp made it creep into your bones. It was almost painful to breath. The cold damp air like ice in the lungs. Anyone with any sense wore a scarf wound about their nose and mouth. As did Detective Inspector Simms, as he made his way into Scotland Yard. The collar of his overcoat turned up, and his Homburg pulled low, trying to have as little of his head exposed as possible. As he barged through the swing doors the Desk Sergeant came over to the desk, away from the warmth of the roaring coal fire at the back of the office. A look of recognition spread across his face as DI Simms pulled his scarf down.

"'Morning, Sir," said the sergeant. "Brass monkeys out there"

"'Morning, sergeant," replied Simms. "Yes, it is a tad nippy." He went on through to the back and up the stairs to his office. He turned at the sound of footsteps clumping up the stairs behind him. DS Brown was unwinding his scarf from round his neck.

"'Morning, Guv'," called out Brown. "Thought you'd already be here."

"Decided to give myself half an hour, after last night. Our friends at Canon Row aren't going anywhere for a while. Oh, and the police surgeon attended our injured friend last night. Said whoever did it certainly knew their stuff. A nasty slash, but neatly stitched. He just put a fresh bandage on it."

As they approached their landing the ample figure of Simms superior, Detective Chief Superintendent Herbert Whitstable loomed over the balustrade of the next landing up, his paunch rubbing against the railing like a boat's fender rubbing against the quayside. "Detective Inspector Simms." He boomed down the stairs at them. "Nice of you to come in this morning." Horace Whitstable never one to miss an opportunity to exercise his sarcasm. "My office in five minutes. You too, Sergeant Brown," he added. He turned and disappeared down the corridor to his office.

"Do you think he was waiting for us?" asked Brown.

"I wouldn't be at all surprised," said Simms, leading the way into their office. There they put their hats and coats on the stand by the door. Simms picked the manila Lau Huang case file off the desk and then he and Brown traipsed upstairs to see Whitstable.

DCS Whitstable's office was possibly twice the size of Simms'. A fire roared in the grate and Whitstable stood with his back to it, erect with his hands clasped behind him. He bellowed "Enter," to DI Simms knock. Simms entered, with the manila envelope under his arm, followed by Brown. "Well, Simms?" queried DCS Whitstable, "What's happening with these Chinese? Am I to understand they've claimed Diplomatic Immunity." He glowered at Simms, who glanced at Brown before turning back to the DCS. "Don't look at Brown," he snapped. "I'm asking you, and no, it wasn't Brown that told me, it was this morning's Custody Sergeant. Apparently as soon as the shift changed they started shouting at him, telling him to contact the Chinese Embassy. Plus we still don't know their names. When the sergeant asked them what they were on about, they said they told you last night. So why haven't you done anything about it?"

"I was going to come and see you about it this morning, Sir." said Simms, bridling slightly. "When we questioned them last night they would give us nothing, just something about this Lau Huang having something that belonged to China. The property of the Republic of China was how he put it. They have no diplomatic passports, in fact no documentation whatsoever. We made a thorough search of where they were staying. Nothing."

DCS Whitstable harrumphed, took out his pipe and inspected the empty bowl. "I must admit to some confusion over this case." he said, clenching his pipe between his teeth and sucking on the empty bowl. He strode over to his desk and sat down, the leather captain's chair creaking under his weight. "Give me the file, please Inspector." He pointed with the stem of his pipe at the folder Simms was holding. Simms handed it over. "You know I passed this down to you because I thought it would be just another of those bloody triad things. We'd waste time and manpower wading through treacle in Limehouse, and Chinatown, and getting absolutely nowhere. But this," he tapped the pages with his pipe, "is something else.

"DS Brown, I understand your Chinese informer virtually handed them over. How come the usually inscrutable and, let's face it, downright unhelpful and inhospitable Chinese rolled over for you?"

"I don't really know, Sir," said Brown. "He did say that this Lau Huang character, that's the victim, Sir, was sort of revered by the triad, so they wanted his murderer caught."

"So why us, Sergeant? Why not handle it themselves. They're normally very good at revenge. Why get us to do their dirty work for them. We normally find out about these things when a body washes up at Limehouse at low tide. Did this not seem strange to you? Or you, Inspector?" He looked across at Simms.

"I'm hoping I might find out a bit more when we question them this morning, Sir," said Simms, "after we leave here."

"I think I might join you," said Whitstable, flipping through the file. He came to the slip of paper, found in

Las Huang's attache case. Then scrutinised it thoroughly. "What's this?" he said, holding it up.

"It was found amongst Lau Huang's possessions. Sergeant Brown found it hidden in the lining of an attache case."

Whitstable peered at the note, frowning in concentration. " It's got some English writing. It says Swifts Bank." He sat back in his chair and looked upon at Simms, eyebrows raised in enquiry.

"Yes, Sir, it's in the report." Simms leaned over and pointed to the page in the file. "We spoke to the manager, who confirmed Lau Huang was a client. He also told us he'd deposited something large in their safety deposit vault. He didn't know what and wouldn't tell us even if he could. Client's absolute confidentiality."

"Can we get a warrant, Sir?" chipped in Brown.

Whitstable raised his eyes at the sergeant. "No, Sergeant," he said. "You can't. I'm not saying don't apply. But you won't get it. Simms, fill the sergeant in later on, will you.

"Now, let's go and have a word with our Chinese friends." He got up from behind his desk and marched out the office with Brown and Simms behind. Simms only pausing to collect the file from Whitstable's desk.

At Canon Row the bigger of the two suspects sat across from DCI Whitstable and DI Simms. DS Brown stood behind them. "I will tell you, as I have told your associates," his eyes moved to glance at Simms, then Brown, before settling once more on Whitstable. "Detective Chief Superintendent, I, and my colleague, have Diplomatic Immunity." He spoke as though to an ignorant child, in a calm voice gradually getting more tense. "Now will you please contact the Chinese Embassy, or I will make this most unpleasant for you."

"Really?" rumbled Whitstable, "You'll make this unpleasant for me, will you? Well let me spell it out for you. The only people in for something unpleasant around here are you and your friend. So don't give me any more of your Diplomatic Immunity. You've no passports, diplomatic, or otherwise. No paperwork, nothing. So stop messing us around." He slapped the table. Simms and Brown both jumped. The suspect didn't even blink. "Why did you kill Lau Huang?" shouted Whitstable going even redder in the face.

The suspect just smiled and leaned back in his chair, folding his arms. Whitstable suddenly stood up, picked up the folder and waved it at the suspect. "The one place you can be sure of going is the end of a hangman's rope." He snarled and stormed out, followed by Simms. Brown instructed the constable outside to take the suspect back to the cells before hastily following them.

In the main area outside the interview room, the three stood in a circle. DCS Whitstable clutched the file to his chest, unlit pipe in his mouth, his left hand in his pocket. "Leave this with me," he said. "I'll speak to the Commissioner. We may have to speak to the Home Office on this one."

"And the prisoners, Sir?" asked Simms

"Have them brought over to the cells at the 'Yard. Leave them to stew until I've seen the Commissioner. There's not a lot more we can do for the time being. They're not going anywhere."

"What if it turns out they do have immunity, Sir?" asked Brown.

"The Home Office can deal with that. Give them our humble apologies, pat them on the head, and send them on their merry way. Back to bloody China with any luck." With that DCS Whitstable turned and marched out to return to his own office, back at the 'Yard

DI Simms and DS Brown also returned to their office. "Wonder if our interpreter has shown his face?" said Brown as they got back.

"Well he's not here," said Simms, looking round the unoccupied office. "I'll see if he's downstairs." He picked up the phone and called down. After a brief conversation he replaced the handset. "No sign of him." He looked at his watch. "Quarter to eleven. I told you that would be the last we saw of him. Everything seems to hinge round that damn note. I wish I knew what the bloody thing said, even if it is in code." He plonked himself down behind his desk.

"So what do we do now, Guv'?" asked Brown

Simms blew out his cheeks in a mark of frustration. "Damned if I know, Tom," he said. "We'll just have to wait and see what the response is to the Chief Super. Meanwhile," he tossed a file across to Brown, "we've got all these to be getting on with." The pair settled down to their paperwork.

"By the way, Guv'" said Brown, "What did Whitstable mean, we wouldn't get a warrant?"

"It's called politics, Tom," said Simms, "Too many powerful people have secrets the'd rather no one knew, and they often keep them in safe deposits, like Swifts Bank. They're certainly not going to grant a warrant to let the likes of you and me go sniffing around. Deny the warrant, they keep their grubby little secrets safe. The bank's happy their reputation for discretion is unmarked. Everyone's happy."

"I'm not," said Brown. "Bloody stinks."

"You know that, Tom, and I know that. But that's the way it is. That, my friend, is the way of the world."

Chapter 18

The office in Whitehall would appear austere under some circumstances. However, the picture on the wall, a watercolour of Windsor Castle, the photographs on the filing cabinet of officers in dress uniform and on the desk, of the occupant's wife, made the place a little softer. The fire roaring in the grate made the place seem almost homely. The man seated behind the desk was 58 and had the bearing of a military man, even wearing civilian clothes. He had brown hair swept back from a wide, almost handsome face, with a clipped military moustache. He wore gold rimmed spectacles, which he was polishing when a young man came in.

He knocked on the door, whilst peering round it. "Sir John's on the phone for you Mr Kell. Something about that Chinese murder."

"Thank you, Tim," said Kell. "Put him through." This was Captain Vernon Kell, Director General of the British Security Service, just recently been given the sobriquet MI5, and Sir John was Sir John Simon, the Home Secretary. "Sir John," said Kell, "what can I do for you.

"I think I have something which is more your sphere than mine," said the Home Secretary. "You recall that Chinaman murdered at a hotel in Holland Park, the other day? Well, it's been passed to us. They caught the culprits within twenty-four hours, under very odd circumstances. Thing is, they're claiming Diplomatic Immunity."

"And do they have diplomatic passports?" asked Kell.

"That's the thing," said Sir John. "No, nothing, just the clothes they were arrested in. They're currently being held at the 'Yard. Something doesn't quite add up. Be a good chap and have a look into it. If there's the slightest chance they do have D.I. it could be a bit messy. You know how touchy the Chinese are. Well, you were there. Boxer rebellion and all that? Have a look, report back and we'll see what's what."

"Very good, Sir John, leave it with me." said Kell.

"Good man." said Sir John, and hung up.

"Tim!" Kell shouted through to his assistant.

Tim popped his head round the door. "K?" he asked, using Vernon Kell's unofficial title.

"Tim, can you get me William Bant, at the home office, please." Tim ducked back out of the room. A minute or two later the phone on K's desk rang. He picked it up immediately. "William," he responded good naturally, even smiling as he answered, "How the devil are you? Listen, I've just got off the phone with Sir John. He's tasked me with looking into this murder in Holland Park…..Yes, that's the one. They've got two Chinamen in custody at Scotland Yard, but they're trying to claim D.I. …..No, no passports, but Sir John wants me to take a look. I think he's a bit worried about stirring things up with the Chinese. Should be just run of the mill. We're a bit short handed, as you know. Wondered if you'd pop along with me, this afternoon? You know, two heads better than one, especially as we both speak the lingo…..I though if you could come here for about two thirty. Should have a bit more information by then. I can run you through it, then we'd nip round to the'Yard…Excellent, see you at two thirty." He replaced the receiver and called Tim through. "Tim, can you get on to Scotland Yard and ask them to send the file round on this Chinese murder ASAP."

The two prisoners were already seated side by side, when K and William Bant entered the interview room. Bant wrinkled his nose at the reek of stale tobacco smoke and sweat.

"Good afternoon gentlemen," said K, sitting down. "How have they been treating you?" He looked to the smaller one, "How's the old arm? Not to painful?" he placed a folder on the table in front of him.

"Perhaps we should introduce ourselves," said Bant. "I'm Mr Jones, and my colleague here, is Mr Smith. We're from the Home Office," he smiled across at them.

The larger prisoner placed his clasped hands on the table. "Mr Jones, if that is your name, as your stumbling police have no doubt told you, we have Diplomatic Immunity."

"Not that stumbling," chuckled K, "caught you two in less than twenty four hours."

The prisoners remained silent. The larger of the two permitted himself the smallest of smiles. The smaller continued to scowl.

"You say you are here to retrieve something you claim belongs to your Government," said Bant. "What, exactly is it, this thing you're here to get back for your Government?"

"We are not at liberty to disclose that." said the larger. "All I can say.."

His colleague interrupted him with a rapid torrent of Chinese. Effectively, "Keep your mouth shut, Chang, and follow your orders. I am the senior officer, and I tell you what you can and cannot tell them."

K and Bant looked at each other and with the briefest of nods decided to let their captives know they could speak Chinese.

"So you're the leader, are you?" K addressed the smaller captive in fluent Chinese. "And your name's Chang." he said, addressing the larger one. Both captives' mouths dropped open and a look of utter surprise crossed their faces.

"I can speak Chinese too.' Smiled Bant.

"So let's stop messing around." said K reverting back to English. "You're both fluent in English, and the remainder of this interview will be conducted in English. So don't bother any pretence of not understanding, we can always revert to Chinese. I would be very annoyed if we have to do that." K glared at them.

"Now," snapped Bant. "What is it you are so desperate to retrieve?"

"We will not tell you," said their leader. "So please retain your dignity by not continuing to repeat the same question. The answer will always be the same, and we will all soon become bored."

"So what's your name, then?" said K. "We know your friend, here, is called Chang. What are you called?" The captives both remained silent. "You see, you claim Diplomatic Immunity but you have no papers, and we've only just found out the name of one of you. You can see our problem, can't you. We contact the embassy and say 'excuse me, we've got two chaps here, murdered one of your countrymen, say they have Diplomatic Immunity courtesy of your embassy. No, sorry, we don't know their names and they haven't got any papers or passports'. You don't need me to tell you what their answer will be, do you?" He looked from one to the other. "What are your names, and what is it you are after?"

The smaller captive looked at his partner, then back at K. He seemed to reach a decision and looked back at

K. " My name is Cheng Yi, my colleague is Chang Su. If you contact the embassy, they will confirm we are who we say we are, and we have Diplomatic Immunity." He spoke in a resigned tone.

"So what is this item you're after, Cheng Yi?" asked Bant.

"I cannot tell you," repeated Cheng. He looked across at Chang Su, who kept his head bowed and stared at his hands. He looked back at Bant, "and besides, we don't know where it is."

K lent forward over the table and spoke slowly and clearly. Enunciating his words deliberately, and with a sneer. "Perhaps if you hadn't murdered Lau Huang, you would know." And he sat back.

Both prisoners had their heads down, avoiding eye contact. K looked at Bant and indicated for him to continue. "If this really is the property of the Peoples Republic of China, perhaps we could help recover it." He smiled across at them. Neither spoke. There was a long silence, finally broken when Bant said "There is still the matter of Lau Huang's murder. I think we should concentrate on that, then. We don't shoot people over here. You'll both be hanged."

The prisoners both now seemed somewhat subdued. Cheng took a couple of deep breaths, then let out a sigh. "Mr Smith," he said to K, "I assure you we have Diplomatic Immunity. Please contact the Chinese Embassy."

"Assuming you have Diplomatic Immunity," broke in Bant, "you've committed murder. It's likely our Home Secretary will demand your embassy rescind your immunity and your ambassador will acquiesce." He paused, then continued, "You will hang."

Kell stood up, followed by Bant. As they left the room the two prisoners looked at each other. They said nothing, but for the first time they each saw fear in the other's eyes.

In the corridor outside, K instructed the constable to take the prisoners back to the cells. "What now" inquired Bant.

"I'm not sure," replied K. "I'll have to speak to Sir John. I wonder what the hell it is they're after. It must be damned important to send two killers after it."

"There's that note they found in Lau Huang's room. May be that might shed some light on it." suggested Bant.

"Yes," agreed K. "I was thinking along those lines myself. Let's head back to the office and go through it together a little more thoroughly. Let's not forget, those two in there and the Chinese Embassy don't know we've got it."

K and Bant worked into the evening, using their knowledge of Chinese, China and Chinese culture to try and make sense of the note. The idioms and meanings of characters seemed totally at odds with each other.

"What about this reference in English, to Swifts Bank?" asked Bant, at one point.

"Lau Huang deposited something at the City Branch." said K, "It's in this DI's report." He looked at a sheet of paper. "A DI Simms. Seems to have his wits about him. Stroke of luck his sergeant having a useful contact in Chinatown, though."

"And Swifts Bank is where this thing our two chums are after is?" Asked Bant.

"More than likely," replied K. "Look, I think we've gone about as far as we can with this. We may as well call it a night." He took out his watch and checked the time. "Just gone ten. I'll give Sir John a ring at his club, he's usually there till gone eleven this time of the week." He reached for the phone and dialled a number. It was soon answered and he asked to speak to Sir John Simon, the Home Secretary. After exchanging pleasantries K came to the point about the prisoners claims of Diplomatic Immunity. Sir John paused, then asked K to give him a little while and he'd phone him back. Was he at his office?

Ten minutes later, William Bant had left and the Home Secretary phoned K back. "I'll speak to the Chinese Ambassador first thing in the morning. If these people do indeed have Diplomatic Immunity we'll have to play it carefully. I've issued a temporary 'D' notice to the press. Best keep it under wraps for the time being."

"About this object they're so desperate to recover. Bant, and I, are pretty certain this Lau Huang has deposited it with Swifts Bank, in the City."

"Do we have any idea what it is?" asked Sir John.

"No we don't," he said. "But we're one up on the Chinese. We know where it is and they don't. We could offer to try and recover it if they will tell us what it is. If we can get our hands on it without them knowing. May be of some use to us?"

"Hmm. Leave it with me," said Sir John. "I'll get back to you in the morning, after I've spoken with the Chinese Ambassador."

Despite the late night, K was at his office desk at half past eight the following morning. He sipped at the cup of tea his assistant, Tim, had brought him, and looked again at the coded note. It made no sense. Some of the characters meant 'flowing', 'smoke', or that could mean 'cloud', 'water'. Yet their seemingly random order made nonsense of it all. K looked at he sprawl of pencilled notes on his desk. He was no further on than when he started.

Ten thirty-five Sir John Simon knocked on his office door and popped his head round. "Not interrupting anything, am I?" he smiled.

"Of course not, Sir John." replied K, getting up and coming round his desk to shake the Home Secretary's proffered hand. "It's good to see you. I was expecting you to telephone." He showed his surprise at this personal visit by Sir John.

"Well, I wanted to get out of the office," said Sir John. "I tell you, talking to these blessed Chinese is like trying to knit fog. Turns out this pair in the cells at Scotland Yard, do indeed have Diplomatic Immunity. Their Chargé D'fairs is going to visit them, to confirm they are who they say they are. If that all goes well, they're gone. Back to China and out of our hair."

"How do the police feel about that?" asked K.

"Initially a bit peeved," said Sir John, "but they soon came round to the idea after they realised its a load of work off their shoulders. It helped, of course, it being a Chinese national murdered by Chinese nationals. Been a different kettle of fish if it was one of ours."

"Did you speak to them about this thing they were after, Sir John?"

"Oh yes. They were adamant it was the property of the Republic of China, and we were to return it immediately. I told them we had no idea where it was and asked them what it was. I even asked them to describe it. All they would say was, it was in an ornate bronze and gold chest. Other than that they flatly refused."

"So the mystery thickens," said K. "When are our friends due to leave?"

"All being well, they should be released to the Chinese Embassy this afternoon. There's a ship leaving Tilbury tomorrow morning for Shanghai. They'll be on that. Police escort from the embassy to make sure it's them, and we're really getting shot of them. Police presence remaining at the quayside until the ship sails."

"Well," said K, "that appears to be that." He lifted the folder from the centre of his desk, and let it drop into his 'out' tray. They both stood, shook hands and Sir John Simon, Home Secretary left.

K returned behind his desk and sat. He lent back in his chair and puffed his cheeks, then lent forward and picked up a buff folder from his 'in' tray. A red diagonal stripe across one corner denoted it was 'Top Secret'. Onwards and upwards, he thought to himself.

Part 3

Chapter 19

1934. A late summer afternoon in London. A cloudless sky, sunlight's dazzling reflections from windows of the many offices causing passersby to shade their eyes, or turn their heads. The doors to Swifts Bank, City Branch, opened and a large figure was silhouetted against the sunlight. As the doors swing shut behind him, those in the bank could see that he was a Chinaman, but immense. He was over six feet tall, and broad shouldered. A very powerfully built man. His head was completely bald and he was dressed immaculately in a light grey three piece suit made of silk. A pristine white shirt was offset with a deep royal blue silk tie with a diagonal stripe, silver, crimson, silver. A matching silk handkerchief adorned his breast pocket. The heels of his highly polished black oxfords made a measured click as he walked purposefully up to a cashiers position.

"I wish to speak with Sir Bernard MacIntyre." For such a large man his voice was surprisingly high pitched, and somewhat husky. As if it hadn't been used in a long time.

"Whom shall I say is asking for him?" asked the young man behind the desk.

"My name is Zhao Gao." he replied, "It concerns the affairs of one of my countrymen, Lau Huang." Throughout the exchange his face had remained expressionless. His head erect so that he was glancing down at his interlocutor, as if in disdain.

Sir Bernard came through the door into the main bank hall. A brief look of surprise crossed his face when he saw Zhao Gao. An imposing presence for anyone, but most unusual in a Chinese. The same height and if anything, even heavier built than Sir Bernard. "Mr Zhao," said Sir Bernard, extending his hand, "What can I do for you?"

Zhao Gao shook the proffered hand with a firm, strong grip. "I wish to speak with you about an important, but delicate matter. It concerns a fellow countryman, Lau Huang."

"Really?" Sir Bernard was both surprised and alarmed that this name should suddenly crop up after nearly three years. "Perhaps you'd care to come through to my office, where we can discus this in private." He gave a wary smile and ushered Zhao Gao through to his office. He offered tea, and was declined. Sir Bernard sat behind his desk and Zhao Gao sat opposite. "Now what is it you actually want?" he asked

"Just over two and a half years ago Lau Huang deposited an artefact with you, is that not so?" asked Zhao Gao.

"Mr Zhao," started Sir Bernard, in a resigned voice, "Unless you have some form of written authority that this bank can recognise, I cannot possibly discus the business of one of our clients with you. I can neither confirm, nor deny, that a Mr Lau Huang is, or was, a client of this bank."

"Sir Bernard," began Zhao Gao, "I know that Lau Huang came to this bank specifically, and deposited a valuable artefact within your vault. I know this because Lau Huang was carrying out my instructions. I represent the Changbai Shan Mountain Retreat. We are a Taoist monastery. We now call ourselves a retreat to avoid scrutiny from the present regime. The artefact that he deposited here has deep cultural and religious significance to us. It was brought here for safe keeping when the Japanese invaded. The reason for my visit is twofold. First of all I must personally verify that you have this artefact in your vault. After that I will contact Changbai Shan to ascertain the situation in Manchuria. It is possible I will need to collect the artefact to return with it to Manchuria."

"That's all well and good, Mr Zhao," responded Sir Bernard, "but, as I said before, I can neither confirm, nor deny, that Mr Lau Huang is, or was a client." Sir Bernard was starting to show annoyance. "Without the appropriate written authority, my hands are tied." He raised his hands, palms up, from the desk, as if to demonstrate the point.

"I have this." said Zhao Gao, taking an envelope from inside his jacket and handing it across.

Sir Bernard took the envelope and opened it, using a small letter opener from his desk. He withdrew the paper and read. After reading it he placed it on his desk. He lent his elbows on the desk, clasped his hands together and rested his chin on them. He looked down at the paper for a while, then sat back, placing his hands on the desk. "Mr Zhao, all this tells me is that you represent the Changbai Shan Retreat, that the retreat sent Lau Huang here to deposit something in our vault." Zhao Gao nodded gently as Sir Bernard was speaking. Sir Bernard continued, "I will need to check our files, to see what we have." He opened a deep drawer in his desk, and extracted a large, leather-bound ledger. He opened it and went through several pages. "1931, you say." he said without looking up.

"That is correct." said Zhao Gao. He sat upright and motionless watching Sir Bernard leaf through the ledger.

Sir Bernard seemed to find something, and with his finger on the page he reached across his desk with the other hand and picked up the phone. It was answered immediately by his secretary, in the outer office. "Miss Fern, could you bring me file M.V. 153 L.H. please."

In a matter of minutes a prim bespectacled lady of around forty came in and placed a file on the desk. "Here you are, Sir Bernard. Will there be anything else?"

"No. Thank you, Miss Fern." Miss Fern left, and Sir Bernard opened the file, "If you would just let me peruse the file?" Sir Bernard glanced questioningly at Zhao Gao. Zhao Gao merely nodded. Sir Bernard read through the papers, taking his time. Reading each document carefully. Finally he arranged the papers neatly and closed the file. Looking up at Zhao Gao, he said, "Mr Zhao, I am prepared to break with protocol slightly." Zhao Gao looked expectant. "I am prepared to confirm that Mr Lau Huang was a client of this bank, but I can say no more than that."

"But you have my letter of authority." snapped Zhao Gao.

"I'm afraid that bears no weight." replied Sir Bernard, adopting a sterner tone. "Nowhere, in any of the documentation we have on file, does it mention you, or this Changbai Shan Retreat or monastery. The only name is that of Lau Huang, both in the original instructions that accompanied the required funds, and in the confirmatory letter he presented when he came to the bank."

"That was for security purposes," barked Zhao Gao. "The forces aligned against us are sly and deceitful. It was imperative that any outside reference was kept to a minimum. But I assure you, he was acting on Changbai Shan's behalf."

"Be that as it may. There is nothing I can do. I would need a written authority signed by Lau Huang to allow you any further access, and I'm sure you are aware that is not possible. Lau Huang was murdered the night after he came here."

"I already know that, Sir Bernard. That is the reason for my visit. That and the changing circumstances in

Manchuria. You are saying you will do nothing more to help me?"

"It's not a case of me doing nothing." Sir Bernard was starting to show his annoyance. "This bank has very strict rules on confidentiality. Why that was one of the foremost reasons for choosing us in the first place. I'm sorry, Mr Zhao, but there's nothing more I can do for you." With that he stood up and went over to the door.

"In that case, Sir Bernard, I will bid you good day." With a stern look on his face he strode to the door. He paused and turned to Sir Bernard before leaving. "However, I will be consulting with my compatriots in Manchuria. This may take some time, but I shall return. Should you have a change of heart you can contact me at The Brompton Hotel, near Russell Square." With that he marched off, Miss Fern escorting him down the stairs and through the door into the main banking hall.

Sir Bernard returned to his desk. He opened the file again, and flipped through it, then sat for a while in thought. After a while he sat up and returned the ledger to his desk drawer. From another he withdrew a small black address book. He flipped through it till he found a particular entry, then reached for his phone, "Miss Fern, could you give me an outside line, please? Thank you." When he knew he was connected he consulted his address book again, and dialled a number.

Chapter 20

K was seated at his desk, quietly reading through a file. He was following the text with the tip of a silver propelling pencil. Every so often he would stop and make a note in the margin. A tap on the office door, followed by it opening and K's assistant, Tim, putting his head round. K looked up. "Sir John for you, K."

"Thanks, Tim, put him through." said K. A moment later the phone, on K's desk rang. He picked it up. "Sir John, what can I do for you?"

"K, you remember that Chinese affair, back in '31? Well, the damnedest thing's happened. It so happens a close colleague of mine is friendly with Sir Bernard MacIntyre, the manager at Swifts Bank, in the City. Apparently, this morning a large and very well dressed Chinaman came into the bank, insisted on speaking with Sir Bernard, and you won't believe this, demanded access to the item deposited by Lau Huang. You remember? He was the chap murdered in Holland Park after going to that bank."

" Most peculiar," said K. "Did he get it? The item, that is."

"No, he didn't. He was carrying some papers of authority from some Taoist retreat, or monastery. His name's Zhao Gao. He showed them to Sir Bernard. Thing is, there's no mention of this chap, or the monastery in any of the papers the bank has on file, and Sir Bernard's adamant that the original Chinaman, Lau Huang, made no mention either." Sir John paused, K waited. He wasn't going to immediately volunteer his department for any spurious enquiry. He had enough on his plate. A diminished department, that was small to start with. Now occupying just the top floor of the South block of Thames House. The rise of National Socialism and Herr Hitler, in Germany, was enough to be going on with, thank you very much. "Thing is," went on Sir John, "we don't want another incident like last time. The Chinese weren't best pleased then. We could do with talking to this Zhao Gao, find out what's what. I was thinking an informal chat? Somewhere comfortable. Use one of the rooms in Whitehall. Make him feel at home. He's staying at the Brompton Hotel, just off Russell Square."

Damn, thought K. Why now, when we have all this other stuff on. Still, if Sir John thinks there's something in it, we'd better pick chummy up and have a little chat. "Very well." said K. He looked across at the clock, noting it was late afternoon. "I'll get something organised for this evening. It should be nice and quiet, then."

"Good man." said Sir John, "Use one of the V.I.P. Rolls Royces from the diplomatic pool, that should impress him."

"Very good, Sir John. Leave it with me. Do you wish to sit in?"

"Thank you, K, but no. It wouldn't do for one of His Majesty's ministers to be involved, should things go awry."

The call ended, K called Tim into the office. He told him to organise the interview cum meeting room and lay on some refreshments. Tea and biscuits should suffice. He then picked up the phone and called William Bant, who now worked for K in MI5, and asked him to come over to his office. Then he organised the car.

Bant turned up a few minutes later and plonked himself on the leather Chesterfield, that K had acquired for his office. "So, K, what's this all about?" he asked

K looked up from the file he was reading. He had just been reacquainting himself with the details of the case from 1931. "Something's turned up concerning that murdered Chinaman, at the Goulbourne. You remember?

Chap called Lau Huang was murdered by two Chinamen who turned out to have Diplomatic Immunity."

"Good God, yes," responded Bant. "I thought that was all done and dusted."

"So it was. However, someone's turned up and caused a bit of a stir." He then went on to brief Bant about Zhao Gao, his visit to the bank and Sir John's subsequent request to have a chat. "So that's where we are. We'll drive the Rolls round to the Brompton and invite him round for a chat."

"What if he refuses?" asked Bant.

"Oh, I don't think there's much danger in that," said K. "He wants to get his hands on whatever this thing is. We just tell him we may be able to facilitate it for him. Spin him a yarn about wanting to improve cooperation and understanding between our two great nations etc. etc. He'll come."

The black Rolls Royce swished quietly through Russell Square. Bant was driving, K in the passenger seat. K suddenly leant forward. "That must be him." He indicated a large, bald Chinaman who'd just turned into Russell Square and was walking towards them. Bant brought the car to a halt. K got out the instant it stopped. He was a mere few yards in front of the man. "Zhao Goa?" enquired K, with a smile. "My colleague, and I are from the Home Office." Zhao Gao stopped dead in his tracks and looked warily at K, then at Bant, who'd just got out of the car.

Zhao Gao pulled himself up to his full height. "What is the meaning of this?" he demanded.

Bant came round the front of the car and spoke to him in Chinese. "Nothing to worry about. We'd just like a word." Zhao Goa's surprise was palpable.

"If you'd care to pop in the car," said K in English, "we can go somewhere more comfortable, and more private."

"Are you arresting me?" asked Zhao Gao.

"Good lord no." This time it was K speaking Chinese, "but I think you may find it to our mutual benefit for you to come along." As he said this he stepped back and opened the rear door of the Rolls Royce. Zhao Gao took a step forward and glanced into the car, then back at the two men. "I assure you, we wish you no harm and we'll happily drop you back at your hotel afterwards. Or anywhere else you wish to be dropped off."

Zhao Gao answered in English. "Very well, I will take you at your word, but I warn you. Should you try to play any tricks, you will find yourselves in serious trouble."

"I don't doubt it." said Bant quietly. K held the door while Zhao Gao climbed in, then got in the back beside him. Meanwhile, Bant went back round the front and got in behind the wheel.

"Where, exactly, are we going?" asked Zhao Gao. He sat in the back of the car, bolt upright, resting loosely clenched fists on his knees. "And please, I would prefer we spoke in English. Whilst both your Chinese is excellent, I find your accents a little difficult."

"Very well." replied K. "We're going to an office, in Whitehall."

"These are your Government offices.?"

"Yes, some of them. You'll find it quite relaxing, I assure you." said Bant.

"I will not be relaxed, but I shall remain calm." Bant looked at him in the rear view mirror. They continued their journey in silence.

The office was indeed comforting and relaxing. Two large dark green leather chesterfields faced each other across a large carved wooden coffee table, in front of a large ornate fire place. A small cosy fire in the grate. Just sufficient to keep the late summer evening chill at bay. Across from the chesterfields, facing the fire, was a large mahogany desk. As Zhao, K and Bant entered the room Tim got up from behind the desk, closing a manila folder as he did so. "Can I get some tea"? he enquired. Zhao Gao looked around the room, at Tim, at K and Bant.

"Thank you, Tim, said K, "that would be very nice." Tim left the room and K indicated the sofas. Zhao Gao walked round and sat at the end of the sofa nearest the fire. K and Bant sat on the other. each occupying opposite ends. Almost before they had sat Tim arrived with the tea things, placed them on the coffee table and sat down on Zhao Gao's sofa at the other end.

"Shall I be mother?" said Tim.

Zhao Gao gave him a curios look, "Mother?" he enquired, looking across at the other two. "He wishes to be a mother?"

"No, no." chuckled K. "It's an old English phrase. It means 'shall I pour the tea?'."

"You have not brought me here to have tea," said Zhao Gao.

"Indeed not," said K. "It's your interest in Lau Huang, and the article he brought from China, and placed in the safe deposit vault at Swifts Bank. You know, of course, that Lau Huang was murdered, here in London, and that his murderers were two of your fellow countrymen. Did you know they had Diplomatic Immunity, and they were returned to China by your embassy, here?"

"Yes, I did. I also know they were executed by firing squad within twenty-four hours of their return. That is of little consequence to me. I do not come here as a representative of the Chinese Government. I am a senior representative of Changbai Shan Retreat. We are essentially a Taoist monastery in the Changbai Shan mountains, in Manchuria. The artefact Lau Huang brought to this country is a vital and sacred possession of the monastery. It has been in our possession for over two thousand years. The Chinese Government wish to steal it for their own ends. That was why, when the Japanese invaded Manchuria, we felt it safer to remove it to safe keeping in somewhere more stable, far from our borders. We feared the Chinese Government would use the upset and confusion of war to attempt to steal the artefact from the monastery. We do not know how they came to know of the artefact's existence, or that we were bringing it to London. We must assume that there is a spy within the monastery. I am only glad it was placed in safekeeping before the Government's agents could lay their hands on it."

"So why have you come to London now?" asked Bant. "The climate in Manchuria is still very unstable. Surely you don't want to take it back there?"

"You are correct in both instances. However, the situation in my country decrees the need for the artefact's return. The effect of it's presence will be immeasurable."

"You make it sound as if it has some sort of power," said K. "What, exactly, is this artefact?"

"I cannot, and will not tell you," said Zhao Gao. "It is a sacred and highly guarded secret." He looked from one to the other of the two men seated opposite him. "I wonder," he paused, his face expressionless. "There was a piece of paper in Lau Huang's possession. It is in secret writing. We know the Government's agents didn't find it." K and Bant briefly glanced at each other. The move not lost on their guest. "I see you know of which I speak. This piece of paper is also vital to my mission and I must ask you to return it to me forthwith."

"Well, here we have a dilemma," said K.

"In what way?" queried Zhao Gao.

"In that you want the paper back, plus this artefact. But you won't tell us what it is. I feel that you must give us more, in order for us to reach some form of agreement. Why, for instance, are the Chinese Government so keen to get their hands on it? What can it do for them, and what has it done for your monastery, over the millennia, that makes them so keen?"

"I'm afraid I cannot possibly pass that information on."

"But you've admitted there's a spy in your monastery. He may pass that information on to others if the Government can't get their hands on it. What about these Triads, we're hearing about? Would they want it?"

"The Triads, as you call them, hold us in great respect. They would never countenance such a thing. They would kill someone who made such an approach to them."

"What about this spy?" Bant this time. "Isn't he still a danger in the monastery?"

"We have introduced a strict regime for communication outside the monastery. He is contained and we will find him in the very near future. He will, of necessity, reveal himself." Bant and K exchanged looks. "You do not believe me? We have not survived for over two thousand years without guarding ourselves very carefully. He is not the first to think they can enrich themselves by betraying us, and I have no doubt he will not be the last. But they all fail, and this one will, and so will those in future. But I must return the artefact to Changbai Shan. I must!" He leaned forward as he said this, slapping his hand on the coffee table to emphasise the point. He then pointed to Bant and K in turn. "And you must give me back that piece of paper."

K sat back in the Chesterfield. He looked thoughtfully at Zhao Gao for almost a minute. Bant, beside him, remained silent. "I have a proposition for you, Mr Zhao." He said finally.

"And what is that?"

"We will get you your artefact from the bank, and we will let you have the paper. But in return you must let us at least examine this artefact. Surely you can see your way meeting us on this?" K held up his hand as Zhao Gao was about to speak. "Don't give me your answer now. Think about it, sleep on it. even contact your monastery for advice. We can wait a little while, I'm sure." K stood up Bant following his lead. Zhao Gao also stood up. It was clear he was not pleased, not pleased at all. His so far expressionless, and inscrutable demeanour was starting to slip. A look of annoyance passed across his face. He ignored K's out stretched hand.

"I assure you I will not change my mind," snapped Zhao Gao. "But I insist on the return of the paper." He moved towards the door.

"Tim will drive you back," said Bant. "Tim?" He indicated the door.

"Of course," said Tim, then to Zhao Gao as he ushered him out, "This way, Sir"

The door closed behind Tim and Zhao Gao. K turned to Bant, who was lighting a cigarette by the fire. "Well, William, what do you make of that?"

"What indeed," agreed Bant. "I think that piece of paper deserves some further scrutiny."

"My thoughts entirely," concurred K. "I've done a translation of the characters, although they make no sense in themselves. We need someone with a more cryptic mind. Perhaps that new chap, what's his name?"

"Henly," said Bant. "Andrew Henly, without the second 'e' he tells everyone he's introduced to."

"Isn't he supposed to be something of a whizz with codes?"

"Yes, quite astonishing, apparently. First class honours degree, and a masters in mathematics from Oxford."

"Excellent. We'll have a chat with him tomorrow. Now, I know I've translated the Chinese characters correctly, as you, yourself have. But I can't help feeling there's something in there we're missing"

"Well, there's a chap at the Foreign Office. Chinese fellow that's fluent in some of the older dialects as well. I'll see if we can borrow him."

"Very good, William. If you can set them up in an office. See what they come up with. Could you oversee?"

"Not a problem, K, I can keep an eye. While they do that we can get back to the German problem. I think that's going to start hotting up soon."

Tim drove Zhao Gao back in silence. The evening streets fairly quiet now. The theatre goers seated and the late diners yet to emerge. Glancing in the rear view mirror, he saw Zhao Gao staring implacably ahead. As they entered Russell Square Zhao Gao said, "Would you stop me here, please. I shall walk the rest of the way"

"Of course, Sir" said Tim. He pulled into the kerb, and opened the door to go round and let Zhao Gao out of the car. But before he'd taken a step Zhao Gao opened his door himself, and got out of the car. He slammed the door shut. Tim stood by the bonnet, on his side of the car, unsure what to say, or do.

"Tell your masters," said Zhao Gao, facing Tim across the bonnet, "They are interfering in something they do not understand." With that he turned and walked off in the direction of his hotel. Tim watched him turn the corner, then he got back in the Rolls Royce and drove off, back to Whitehall.

They saw neither hide, nor hair of Zhao Gao ever again. He simply vanished into thin air. Enquiries established he never arrived at the hotel. The last person to see him was Tim, who was thoroughly grilled by K about the whole affair. They couldn't understand what had happened to him. Two days later the hotel received instructions to pack up Zhao Gao's belongings. Later that afternoon Carter Paterson arrived with a crate to pack his stuff into. The crate was marked up care of the Changbai Shan Retreat in Manchuria. The hotel said their instructions came over the telephone from Zhao Gao, himself. The receptionist was adamant it was him, there was no mistaking his 'high pitched, wheezy voice'. The man at the Carter Paterson office described the man who instructed them as a "bloody great Chink in a posh suit and a funny high voice". No doubt Zhao Gao.

Chapter 21

The office William Bant secured for his little decryption team was in a large Georgian townhouse in Bloomsbury. Ironically on Russell Square. After they had been there some time, the office there was simply referred to as The Square. Andrew Henly and his partner in crime, Woo Chan, soon settled into their new home, and set to with vigour. The office was actually the whole top floor. They each had their own medium sized room in which to work separately, a small kitchen and the usual offices, at the back and at the very front of the building, overlooking Russell Square, a large room that ran the width of the building. It was in here that they worked together, trying to put together their individual workings out. Their own rooms were fairly conventional offices, desk, chair, filing cabinets, couple of spare chairs. The doors to these offices were partially glazed, the top half having frosted glass. This was because these rooms were in the centre of the building, and thus had no windows. This upper floor originally had three rooms, one at the front, and two at the back, but was converted into offices when purchased by the Government at the turn of the century. The large room at the front was where all the exciting stuff happened. Here they would combine their efforts to see what they'd come up with.

Unfortunately, after just over twelve months, it was being used less and less. Henly was able to come up with all sorts of numerical interpretations, none of which seemed to show any relevance under close scrutiny. Woo Chan was generating reams of variations and interpretations of the Chinese writing.

One morning, in early September, 1935, they were having one of their now infrequent meetings in the big room, as they referred to it. The oversized table, in the middle, was strewn with papers baring figures, mathematical formulae and Chinese characters. Woo Chan had just come up with yet another interpretation, this time from a small group of characters. "Làngfèi shíjiān," said Woo Chan. "In this context seems to mean wastes, or waives cost of time, but I feel it's almost code for displaces time." His tone was curious, rather than the usual 'here we go again' as of late. "Also I have ascertained that these characters are for date and time." He showed Andrew Henly the characters on a piece of paper he was holding. He went over to a blackboard, used the rubber to clean off some older characters, then wrote the characters on the board.

"What date and time do they refer to?" asked Andrew.

"They don't indicate specific dates, or times," said Chan. "Rather they are like headings. Although here," he indicated a group of characters then drew lines connecting them to one another and a central character. "It shows the cycle of years. This is according to the Chinese zodiac. A cycle of twelve years. For example, we are currently in the Year of the Pig. Next year will be the Year of the Rat."

"OK," said Andrew, "I've heard of that. Like when they have Chinese New Year."

"Exactly," said Chan. "However, it gets more complicated with the months, and these are also given the names of animals. There are ten of them, and they're Lunar. However, they are divided into quarters of the year. Each quarter is named after an element. Wood, Fire, Metal and Water. So, for instance we are currently in the Year of the Pig, in the quarter that is Metal, the month of the Monkey."

"I see," said Andrew. "At least, I think I do. What about days and weeks? Don't tell me they're named after animals, as well."

"Oh yes," smiled Chan, amused at his colleagues bewilderment. "But it's always the same twelve animals of the Chinese zodiac. So some days have to double up. For instance Monday is always Goat, but Tuesday can be either Dragon, or Pig. Weeks are determined more by day number than a specific week, such as Second Goat of Monkey. Roughly, anyway."

"Right," said Andrew, "what's your thinking behind this? Are you thinking that this lanfi cheeshen refers to the artefact, itself?"

"Your pronunciation is almost correct. It's Làngfèi shíjiān." He spelled it out to Andrew. "But yes, I think it does."

"So, if what you're saying is correct, this artefact can displace time?" said Andrew, incredulously.

"I don't know," said Chan, "Possibly. I think this note was a sort of coded instruction manual."

"God Almighty!" exclaimed Andrew. "Do you realise what it would mean to get your hands on something like this, and know how it works?" He lit a cigarette, and drew deeply on it. Turned and looked out the window, onto Russell Square. Although it was still late summer, the trees in full leaf, it was a dull and overcast day. Andrew had felt a slight chill in the air on his way into work this morning. Chan joined him at the window. Stood beside him looking down on the square.

"So what do we do now?" he asked. "Would you like me to continue, or shall we speak to Mr Bant first?"

Andrew took another drag on his cigarette while trying to make up his mind. "This is the first thing we've come up with that makes any sense. No, doesn't make sense, but it's ..Oh, I don't know what I'm trying to say here."

"It's the first time we've come up with anything that fits together," filled in Chan, "no matter how ludicrous it seems. Perhaps we should let Mr Bant know what we've got so far, then carry on with it. See where this time displacement hypothesis takes us."

"You're right, of course," agreed Andrew. "At least we now have a starting point. As you say, let's see where that takes us. I'll give William Bant a call."

Kell's office was like a council of war. Kell behind his desk, William Bant and the Home Secretary, Sir John Simon sat in easy chairs. Andrew Henly and Woo Chan stood at a trestle table that had been hastily erected and was strewn with their files and papers. Beside them was a blackboard on an easel. This was covered with all sorts of figures and formulae. Chinese characters, with explanations, lines leading to symbols. The whole lot looked utterly confusing, and everyone looked exhausted after going over it several times, trying to digest what they had before them. Kell lit a cigarette, stood up and walked over to the open window.

"If what you two gentlemen have just explained to us is true then the ramifications are huge." It was the Home Secretary speaking. "I mean, just think what anyone equipped with this would be capable of. No wonder they wanted it kept safe and tucked out of the way."

"And no wonder the Chinese Government want to get their hands on it," added William Bant.

"These monastery people," Kell leaned over his desk to look at some notes, "this Changbai Shan Retreat, seem to have decided to leave it in the safe keeping of Swifts Bank. Mr Zhao Goa had obviously returned post haste, probably because of the situation in Manchuria."

"That's probably also the reason he decided to leave it where it was," put in Bant. "Ascertained it's safe keeping as far as he could, then back to China."

"Are you certain it will work?" asked Sir John, for about the fifth time.

"As certain as we can be without the actual artefact to compare it too," replied Henly. "We could only be 100% sure if we had the artefact."

A silence reigned for a few minutes, everyone seemed alone with their thoughts. They each realised the enormity of what they'd come across. The big question now, was what to do about it. At last Sir John stirred himself. "Right, gentlemen," he addressed Henly and Woo Chan. "Thank you very much for bringing this to us. We really do appreciate the time and effort you've put into this. Needless to say this is all very hush, hush. Not a word to anyone outside these four walls, and I mean anyone."

"Of course, Sir John," said Henly. Woo Chan modded in agreement.

"Now, gentlemen, I must ask you to leave us. What we now have to discuss is higher than Top Secret, and I'm sorry to say, not for your ears. If you could leave the blackboard as it is, and the papers, on the table. Thank you." As he said this, Sir John got up from his chair, went over and opened the door. Holding it open for them he shook each of their hands, in turn, as they left. "Thank you so much, again, for all your hard work."

After Andrew Henly and Woo Chan left the room the three of them went and stood by the table and blackboard. They looked at the papers, the board and each other.

"My God, K," said Sir John. "What have you stumbled on?"

"I did say you won't believe it," said K.

"Do you?" said Sir John, to K. "Or you?" to Bant.

"It all seems very compelling," said Bant. "They're both experts in their field, and were quite reluctant to admit to it themselves when they first broke the code."

"And in the past month or so they've done a hell of a lot more working out the detail," said K. "I, for one, believe them. This artefact can displace time and enable someone to move through time, at will"

"I have to say, it was damned convincing," said Sir John. He looked from K to Bant. "So" he paused. "What do we intend to do about it?"

"Could we get a warrant and seize it?" said Bant.

"I'm reluctant to do that," said Sir John. "And that's not for the reasons you're thinking. I don't want to show our hand. I'd rather, at this stage, keep it between just us three. Put your heads together, see what you can come up with. But I think we need to get our hands on it. Wouldn't do for some other foreign power to get hold of it." He made his way over to the door. "Wouldn't want anyone to break into the bank, one night, and steal the thing." He gave a little smile. "Good day gentlemen," he said, and left.

Bant and K looked at each other. "Did he just say what I think he said?" said Bant.

"Of course not," said K with a smile. "He's the Home Secretary. He couldn't possibly suggest such a thing... Whatever it was you think it was." He went over and sat down behind his desk. "Know any good safe breakers, by any chance?" He grinned across at Bant.

"It's funny you should ask," said Bant, with a smile, and flopped down in the easy chair facing K. "We have a young field officer, name's Paul Rivers, came to us from the Royal Engineers. Whilst a subaltern he undertook a couple of ops for us. Off the books as it were. Likes to sail a bit close to the wind, so thought it best to bring him in house. Permanent transfer to special duties for His Majesty's Government. Proved quite a useful chap, very resourceful, and has grown quite a wide network of contacts. Quite a few on the wrong side of the fence, so to speak."

"The name Rivers rings a bell, now you mention it. What do you propose?"

"I was thinking he could use his contacts put together a team to raid the bank"

"What!" exclaimed Kell. "We can't possibly sanction something like that. Put together a gang of known criminals and carry out a bank raid? Have you any idea of the repercussions should even the slightest thing go wrong? And involving criminals is one way of ensuring it goes wrong. No, William, the answer's no."

"Hear me out, K," said Bant. "We embed Rivers in the gang. He will be in command. He will recruit a suitable member of his network to set up the gang. This contact will ostensibly be the gang leader. He will do all the recruiting of the other members, he will be totally unaware of our involvement and the whole thing will be totally deniable."

"I'm still not convinced. We can't send a gang of armed men crashing into a bank, putting members of the public at risk, to say nothing of the bank's staff"

"No, no. Not an armed raid. We get into the bank when it's closed. Over a weekend, say."

"And how do you propose to do that? Climb in through a window? And then there's getting into the actual vault."

"I was thinking along the lines of tunnelling in. Find an adjacent empty property, take out a short term lease and use that as a base. Tunnel in from there."

"What, over a weekend? That's a bit of a stretch, and how would they get into the vault? It's probably got a steel floor."

"We wouldn't do it all over a weekend. We can take our time tunnelling through. Let it be known that alterations are being carried out to explain any noise. We can get right under the bank, then wait till the weekend, or a Friday night even, to actually break through."

"Okay, so say we get in, how are we going to ensure we get the artefact and the gang don't decide they want it?"

" We simply tell the gang Rivers' acting on behalf of an extremely rich and dubious character, with a collection of serious stolen art, and he wants this artefact for this collection. We could suggest he's American which would help in explaining why no one's met Rivers before."

"Won't they want a cut?"

"Their cut's whatever they can rob from the vault. A lot of it's going to be ill gotten gains anyway. And if it's not, it's probably insured"

"And what about stuff that isn't ill gotten, yet uninsured. People who think it's in such a safe place it doesn't need insurance."

"Collateral damage."

"There could be stuff in there that doesn't want to see the light of day. Things that should stay hidden, compromising things. Do you know what I mean?"

"It's a risk, I grant you. But we won't get anywhere if we're not prepared to take a risk"

"What if it all goes wrong, and Rivers is caught?"

"We cut him loose. We make it quite clear to him that if it goes wrong, he's on his own."

Kell sat back in his chair, rested his elbows on the arms and steepled his fingers. He took a couple of slow deep breaths. Looked across at Bant, looked down at his hands. He suddenly pushed himself up out of his chair and went and looked out of the window. Reaching into his pocket he took out a cigarette and lit it. He took a couple of deep drags then turned round to face Bant, breathing out a long plume of smoke. "Sorry," he said, taking his cigarettes back out and offering them to Bant. Bant got up and came over. Joining Kell at the window he took a cigarette from the pack. Kell gave him a light.

The two men stood in silence smoking and staring out of the window. Bant knew better than to push K. He'd said his piece, now he left it up to K to make up his mind.

"We'd need to make absolutely sure this doesn't come back to us," said K.

Bant smiled to himself. K was coming round to the idea. "Of course," he said. "We have a very experienced agent handler called Reginald Cockscombe. His agents only know him as Reg. He'll run the show. There will be no direct contact between us and Rivers. I'll brief Cockscombe, but won't tell him the whole story. Just something about it being highly secret that was stolen from HMG and we can't go through the usual channels to get it back."

"There is the question of getting somewhere to tunnel from," said K. "This is the city, not some local high street branch with a greengrocer next door. The buildings round there are all rather grand, about five stories high."

"Granted," replied Bant. "I'll have to have a look round, see what's available. If we could rent, say, the basement and the first two floors, we could pass ourselves off as, oh, diamond merchants, or bullion dealers. That way we have an excuse for all the work in the basement. Putting in a new vault, or some such. It would be rather ironic, in a way."

Kell smiled. "Yes, it would. Right, work something out in greater detail. I'd like some sort of feasibility study, but keep the intent vague. Nothing in there to actually mention the bank or what we're actually after. First of all you need to have a good look around the area. Get to know the place. I know it's London, and we're on its doorstep, so to speak. But you need to get the feel. See what buildings are available, access, that sort of thing."

"Does that mean you're 'green lighting' it then, K?"

"More of an amber," replied Kell. "Let's see what's what, the lie of the land. Take it one step at a time. I can't impress upon you how delicate this will be. For the time being it's between you and me. This doesn't go outside these four walls. No mentioning to Cockscombe or anybody else. Do your feasibility study and report back to me. If anybody asks what you're doing, which they shouldn't, given your job, just tell them it's security research."

"Very good, Sir" said Bant, grinning from ear to ear. He stubbed his cigarette out in the ashtray on K's desk and made his way to the door.

"Oh, and William," called K, as Bant was opening the door to leave, "Don't enjoy yourself too much, this is serious business." His grin was almost as wide as Bant's, as the latter left and closed the door.

Chapter 22

Bant walked leisurely past the City branch of Swifts Bank, its stone edifice towering up from the pavement. A wide set of steps led up to an entrance between two marble pillars. Two huge solid oak doors were open and fastened back to reveal the vestibule and uniformed concierge manning the mahogany and glass doors to the bank's interior. Bant took all this in with the barest glance toward the bank, and strolled casually on. His walk took him left, into St James's Square, then left again, into King Street. Reaching the part of King Street that was parallel to the back of Swifts Bank, Bant found what he was looking for. The small entranceway into Cleveland Place. Bant was clothed in the uniform of the city. Bowler hat, morning suit, rolled umbrella and a copy of The Times tucked under his arm. He had to control the grin that started to spread across his face as he approached the building adjacent to the rear of Swifts Bank. There is a God in heaven, thought Bant, and he's an Englishman. A six storey building almost butted up against the rear of the bank. By the large polished wood and glass front door was a board with brass name plates, the top three bore the names of an established stock broker, a commercial finance company, and a shipping broker. The bottom three were blank. Bant pushed on through the door into the vestibule. A large, spacious area with a door off to the right right. To the left an open area, on the rear wall two doors, the upper halves glazed with frosted glass. Front and centre a large staircase up to the first floor gallery, a narrower staircase to the left then leading up to the second floor. There was no receptionist, or indeed reception area. You only came here if you worked here, or had an appointment, and if you had an appointment here, then likely someone quite senior would meet you at the door and escort you up. Excellent, thought Bant. To the left of the stairs, and set back, was a lift, added as a later improvement to the original structure. Bant entered the lift and pressed the button for the fourth floor.

On the fourth floor there was, indeed, a receptionist, who seemed quite surprised to see William Bant standing in front of her. He gave her his best smile. She said, "Can I help you?" in a haughty manner of self importance.

"Oh, good afternoon," beamed Bant, "I wonder if you could possibly help me?"

"Oh Yes"

"Yes, you see my company is looking for premises in the immediate area. Particularly one with a basement in which we could install a vault. Some of our business involves storing extremely valuable, erm, shall we say securities on the premises. I notice the bottom three floors and, I assume, the basement are currently vacant. I merely wondered if you knew who the vendor is?"

"Oh, there's no vendor. All occupancy here is by tenants." She gave him a condescending look.

"In that case," he smiled again, "I wonder if you would have the name and address of the landlord, or their agents?"

And it was that simple. Bant stepped smartly out of the building, swinging his brolly, and made his way back to the office. Now if everything else in this enterprise went just as smoothly. But it wouldn't, of course, he knew that. These things never do. He knew that from here on in, things would become more difficult, more complex, more likely to go completely tits up

Reginald Cockscombe's office was at the opposite end of the corridor to K's and a smaller, far more modest room. He was reading through a report when Bant knocked on the door and entered without waiting for a reply.

"Hello, Reg," he said, with a smile. He did his customary manoeuvre when he was about to get a subordinate to do something a bit iffy. He went round to Reg's side of the desk and perched on the corner looking down at him. " Anything important on at the moment?"

"Bill," said Cockscombe, leaning back in his chair, "what a pleasant surprise. Just the usual at the moment. Bloody boring actually. Just a couple of the lads following various attachés from the German embassy around London." He picked up the report he'd been reading then let it drop back onto his desk. "Did you know, for instance, the Naval Attache's wife, Frau Von Gestner, has a thing about lunching at Derry and Toms. Or so young this young chap's expenses would imply. She certainly buys a lot of bed linen and soft furnishings there."

"Fascinating," said Bant. "Reg, tell me, how do you fancy robbing a bank?"

Cockscombe swung his chair round to face Bant and clasped his hands in his lap. "Do you have any particular bank in mind?" he asked. "If it's mine I'd like to move my account first."

"I think you'll be okay. It's Swifts Bank, in the City."

"That's alright, then. When do you want it doing? Are we talking armed raid or break in?"

"Oh break in. We need to be a little subtle. Can't go charging into a bank waving guns around then claim we're doing it for King and Country."

"I take it there's something specific we want to get our grubby little hands on. We're not doing this to boost the petty cash, in these financially straightened times?"

"Indeed, Reg. There is something we want and we need to, as you so eloquently put it, get our grubby little hands on it before anybody else."

"No chance of a warrant?"

"No. A number of reasons. Firstly we don't want to tip anybody's hand that we're after it, or know it's there, or that we are aware of it's presence in the country. Secondly, it is actually the property of HMG. However, there are certain powers that think they have it, and are determined to hang on to it. So they squirrelled it away in a safety deposit box in the vault at said bank."

"What?"

"It was loaned by us to a certain party. From whence it disappeared. Grovelling apologies at the highest diplomatic level, all very hush hush. But we were pretty damn sure they decided to hang on to it, and play the apologetic, much aggrieved party. But now we've found out where it is and we're going to re-appropriate it"

"Might I ask who the duplicitous party is?"

"The Chinese," said Bant with a smile.

"The Chinese?" echoed Cockscombe. "Why on earth would we lend the Chinese anything, let alone something they'd risk all to hang on to?"

"Don't ask," responded Bant, with a wry look on his face. He took a buff folder from under his arm. A somewhat doctored and diluted version of the original. He handed it to Cockscombe. It had a diagonal red 'Top Secret' stripe across the corner. However, above the red line, was a thinner violet one. This denoted 'Above Top Secret'. "I'll wait while you read it." Bant went and sat in the office chair across the desk from Cockscombe. He took out a cigarette case and offered it across. Cockscombe took one, took a table lighter off his desk, lit Bant's then his own. Bant blew out a stream of smoke. "You understand, this folder cannot leave my sight. I cannot leave it with you and you cannot make notes."

Cockscombe paused as he opened the folder and looked across at Bant. A certain firmness settled on his face, as if steeling himself inside for some noble quest. "Understood," he said, then fell to reading the contents of the folder. Almost immediately he shut the folder again, sat back in his chair clasping his hands over it. "You do realise that we can't just break in and open the vault. At the very least we'd have to tunnel in. This is a city centre bank. Where on earth are we going to tunnel from and, more importantly, who is going to do the tunnelling?"

Bant smiled across at him, "All in good time, Reg, all in good time. Now, you give that folder a good read. Take your time. Ask me any questions and if I can, I'll answer them."

Again, Cockscombe fell to reading, slowly turning the pages. At the end he went back to some of the sections and reread them, just to make sure he had it all in his head. Finally he closed the folder, sat back in his chair, folded his hands in his lap, on top of the folder, and gazed into space, "I think I have just the man for the job." he said, "Paul Rivers." He tapped the previous file he'd been reading. "Was an Engineer's miner in the war. Ideal man to run the show."

"Excellent," said Bant,."Was going to suggest him myself. You crack on with briefing him and get him started on choosing a team." He smiled inwardly, then had to stop himself. Cockscombe choosing Rivers without any prompting, this can't go on, he thought. Tread very carefully, Bant, old son, too easy to get complacent. He stood up with a big smile and reached for the folder.

Cockscombe passed it over. He was also smiling. "If nothing else, it should get me out the office."

"It will indeed, Reg," said Bant, "It will indeed."

The whole idea of an unauthorised bank raid had just added a frisson to Cockscombe's otherwise humdrum life, and he knew Rivers was just the man for the job. Not that there was much of a choice. Limited finances meant the service only had a handful of serving field officers, and this had to be kept in-house. At this level, anyway. The rest of the personnel on this operation needed to be totally disposable. He had no allusions, though. If it all went belly up his man would be cut adrift. And Paul Rivers was a man used to risky undercover work, who knew the risks, and understood deniability.

He'd arranged the meeting at one of their 'district offices'. In this case an office over a newsagent's in Fulham. The sign on the street door next to the newsagent's read "Willington Secretarial Services" in peeling gold letters, and the infrequent coming and going of different people was completely un-noteworthy. He was sitting behind the only desk in the office smoking a cigarette when the street door buzzer went. He looked at his watch. Ten fifteen a.m., bang on time. He went downstairs and let Rivers in. The pair of them clumped up the bare wooden stairs to the office. Through an inner door, at the top of the stairs, into an equally bare office. Apart from the wooden desk, with a plain wooden chair either side of it, there was a round paraffin heater, currently unlit, a four drawer filing cabinet, mostly empty, and two old and scruffy easy chairs. They dragged the easy chairs around, so they roughly faced each other, and sat down.

"So, what have you got for me?" asked Rivers. His southern accent still detectable under his well spoken, slightly deeper than normal, voice.

"You'll like this, Paul," said Cockscombe with a smile. "You're going to rob a bank."

Paul Rivers raised his eyebrows. "Really? Are we that short of readies?"

Cockscombe chuckled. "No, it's not cash we're after. We want you to tunnel into a vault and retrieve something rather important."

"What, all on my own? I know I was in mining with the Engineers, but even then I had help."

Cockscombe gave him a wry look. "Of course not. Use your contacts to recruit a small gang. We're currently looking for premises to rent that you can operate from. Work your way in, and bring the goods out."

"So which bank is it you want me to break into?"

"Swifts Bank, City Branch, in Pall Mall."

"What?" Rivers' surprise verged on shock. "How the fuck do you expect me to get in there! Have you seen the buildings around there? There's not some little corner shop we can lease. It's not like round here. They're all big buildings. Merchant banks, stock brokers, the odd diamond merchant that thinks he's a cut above Hatton Garden. Big buildings, big money. Then there's access. I think someone might notice a truck load of men carrying digging tools."

Cockscombe held up a hand and stopped Rivers in mid flow. "I know, I know. We've considered all these points, and can we moderate our language, please. We're looking for nearby premises where we can lease the basement and, at least, the first two floors. We have set up a front company that deals in precious metals. Gold, silver, that sort of thing. We will, of course, need to build, or extend a vault in the basement. That will excuse the coming and going of workmen, plus a perfectly reasonable explanation for the noise and mess.

"Now, do you have anyone in mind you can approach for this sort of job?"

"As a matter of fact, yes. A chap who served under me in '17 and '18. I've used him a couple of times for small jobs. Currently serving time for burglary. Not whilst working for me, I hasten to add. Due up for parole shortly. He could put a team together. He's done so in the past several times, for various jobs, and not been caught. The burglary he got caught for was a complete fluke, and he was working alone at the time. Came out of a back alley carrying a bag of loot, straight into the arms of two passing bobbies. I don't know who was more surprised, them or him."

"What's this chap's name?" asked Cockscombe, taking a notebook and fountain pen from inside his suit jacket.

"Eric Teale," said Rivers. "Age forty one, currently at His Majesty's pleasure in Wormwood Scrubs serving five years. Got sent down just over four years ago."

Chapter 23

William Bant came backwards into Reginald Cockscombe's office, barging the door open with his backside, his arms full of rolled up blueprints and documents. "Here we are, Reg," he said. "Everything you need to know about Cleveland House."

Reg jumped up and cleared space on a side table. "Is this where we're operating from?"

"It is indeed. Cleveland House, Cleveland Place. I could not believe it when I found the place. Backs right on to Swifts Bank. We have the basement plus the ground and first floors. Our fellow tenants will be impressed, and not the least bit surprised at our high level of security, for we are Hilditch Holdings, open brackets precious metals trading, close brackets and associates."

"Who are the associates?"

"Haven't the foggiest. It's one of our back stop companies. You know, one of our pre registered companies that has all the historical cover, should anyone be nosey enough to start poking around. This one was set up in 1899. We used it to move some gold out of SouthAfrica during the Boer War."

"So when do we start?"

"Now, dear boy, now," said with some excitement as he started organising all the papers and drawings he'd brought in with him. "Preliminaries first. Your team need to set up the shop, so to speak. Strong door to the basement, and security to the ground and first floor. We need to show any observers, especially our co-tenants, we mean business. Especially with security. It might be an idea to hire some front of house people, not many say three or four. They'll have no clue as to the real nature of our enterprise. They'll think they're employed by a bonafide company carrying out normal office duties. On no account are they allowed into the basement area."

"I'll get our man Rivers on to it straight away

Eric Teale stepped through the gate from His Majesty's Prison Wormwood Scrubs into the outside world. A big man, broad shouldered and muscular. He wore a working man's clothes. Dark reefer jacket, dark trousers and black, scuffed boots. As he stepped through he pulled a cloth cap on, tugging it forward to keep the rain out of his eyes. He tucked his bundle under his left arm, stuck both his hands into his jacket pockets and hunched off into the rain. He strode off purposefully. A man who knew where he was going. Only he didn't. His slightly early parole had come as something of a surprise, the sealed letter handed to him as he left added intrigue. He'd stuffed it into his pocket, where it currently rested, unread. At the road turn in he paused under a tree and pulled out the letter. A simple message, "Turn right on Du Cane Road towards Acton. You will be met." He looked around. A few people passing by on either side of the road paid him no heed, a blue Carter Patterson lorry ground past heading towards Acton. A horse and cart clopped past going the other way. He turned right and strode off down Du Cane Road.

As he walked under the railway bridge a raincoated and trilby hatted figure pushed himself away from the wall. " 'Morning Eric," he said.

Eric stopped and peered at the figure. A wry smile crept across his face, "Well, well. Mr Rivers. I should have known."

"I've found a place for you to stay," said Rivers, and led the way to a car parked just beyond the railway bridge. A train rattled its way over the bridge obliterating all other sound for the moment.

"And?" asked Eric, as they stood beside the car.

"What do you mean, 'and'?" asked Rivers, opening the car door.

"There's always an 'and'," replied Eric. "Early parole, you meeting me. It's not like we're bosom buddies. You want something."

"Well, there is a little something," said Rivers,. "Hop in. I'll run you to your digs and tell you about the little favour we need from you."

The car rocked as Eric settled his big frame into the passenger seat. He looked across at Rivers. "Got a fag?" he asked.

"Better than that," responded Rivers. He reached into an inside pocket and drew out a small packet of Lloyd's cheroots. "Never let it be said I don't take care of you." He passed the packet across, followed by a box of matches. With a smile Eric took one out and lit it. Took a deep draw then blew a stream of pungent, aromatic smoke. Rivers wound his window down a couple of inches.

The digs Rivers had arranged was a one bedroom basement flat just off the Commercial Road, in Whitechapel. Eric took a look round, while Rivers took a seat in a battered armchair. "It'll do," he said, "So, what's this little favour you're after?"

"You're going to rob a bank, Eric, and apart from one specific item, you get to keep everything else you get your grubby hands on. How does that sound?"

Eric lowered himself in to the other, equally battered, armchair. "You want me to hold up a bank and just walk away and no one's going to try and stop, or catch me? You're bloody mad."

"No, no." said Rivers. "We're going to be much more subtle than that. We're going to tunnel in to the vault."

"When you say we, do you mean you're coming in with me?"

"I am indeed. I will be part of, indeed head of our happy little band."

"You mean there are others involved?"

"There will be, Eric. You're going to recruit them. I recon five of us should be sufficient. So you need to find three more. Men you can rely on to keep their mouths shut and do as their told. I want no mavericks. No one who's likely to decide he wants a better share once we're in there. Men who are prepared to do the hard work, get the job done than disappear. Think you can do that?"

"Give me a few days," said Eric. "When do you want the job doing?"

"No great rush," replied Rivers. "What we're after isn't going anywhere anytime soon. We can use our mining experience to tunnel in. Your men will essentially be just labour for the most part, until we're into the vault. We'll use here as our HQ. You get on and get the team together, I'll see to all the other details. Contact me on this number when you've got the men and we'll meet up here so I can explain what's what." Rivers took a notebook and pencil from within his jacket, wrote down a number and handed it to Eric.

"Who shall I say is behind it, they won't believe it's some scheme I've just cooked up," said Eric.

"No, of course not. Tell them I'm representing a shadowy figure in the art world who has his eye on this particular piece of oriental art. Your payment is whatever else you can get out of the vault you get to keep. That way everybody's happy and, to a certain extent, it masks the reason for the raid. One other thing. If anyone gets caught, they're on their own. They'll face the full force of the law." He took a deep breath, "and that includes the two of us."

Eric gave Rivers a grim smile. "Fair enough." He held up the piece of paper. "I'll be in touch." Both men stood up and shook hands, then Paul Rivers left. Eric sat back in his armchair and thought about who he should recruit for this little job.

Chapter 24

It took Eric a little over a week to get his team together, calling at various doss houses, flats and pubs. Mostly in the East End and the occasional venture South of the river. He was careful who he spoke to, and what he said. Like any big city, London's criminal underworld had its own hierarchy. Certain families oversaw what went on in their own patch and if you wanted to pull something big, like a bank job, then they had to be in the know, and in for a cut. Eric Teale did not want them to know, or get in on the act, so he had to tread very carefully. The wrong word overheard in the wrong place and someone would be paying Eric a visit to impress upon him the importance of ensuring that a certain someone would be getting their share. He wanted to be in, out and long gone before anybody else decided they'd been done out of what they considered to be rightfully theirs.

So carefully and quietly Eric went about his business. His first recruit was one Charlie Cook, a 56 year old ex army captain, although he titled himself Major, his acting rank when he resigned his commission. Owner of a thriving antique business originally funded by the sale of antiques he'd liberated from France after the armistice. Major Charles Cook (Ret'd) would be the king pin in Eric's little team. Able to source virtually anything and a manner well suited to where they were going to go to work.

The next was Ernie Banks. A 39 year old giant of a man 6'4" tall and barrel chested. Known to both Eric and Rivers as he served with both of them as a miner/engineer at the front, during the war. Softly spoken, with a deep sonorous voice, he was the epitome of the gentle giant. Friendly and loyal, his criminal activities were limited to commercial theft. In some ways an honourable and honest man in difficult circumstances.

Lastly there came Norman Thomas, a wiry 37 year old man of average build and average looks. The sort to easily disappear in a crowd. Eric had to think hard about Norman. He could be difficult and bolshie. Quick to take offence and ready to start a fight. He was also homosexual, but tried to keep it under wraps. However, he was loyal, and the fact that he rarely, if ever, backed down and always pulled his weight meant Eric decided to include him.

So just eleven days after Eric Teale being released from Wormwood Scrubs, Paul Rivers parked his car two streets away from Erics flat, at 9:15pm, and made his way there. Eric let him in and introduced him to the others, "This is our principle's representative, Mr Smith." He'd already briefed Ernie Banks to not use Rivers' name, and he'd had a quiet word with him.

"Principal's representative?" sneered Thomas,. "Who does he think he is?"

"I'm the man that will make you very rich," said Rivers, with a steel edge to his voice, "and you will follow instructions and behave. If that doesn't suit you, there's the door. But know this, my principal's reach is far and wide. If you leave now, you never breathe word of this." Rivers indicated the room and it's occupants with a sweep of his hand. "If you do you will be hunted down and dealt with. Permanently. Do you understand?"

"Okay, okay," said Thomas, raising his hands "I'm only asking. I'm in. Just want it to be known I expect my fair share. That's all."

"Mr Smith," said Eric, addressing Rivers. "perhaps you'd like to tell everybody what we're about to do."

"Thank you, Eric," said Rivers. "Well, gentlemen, we're going to break into a bank vault. The safe deposit vault to be precise. There should be rich pickings for everyone. My principal is after the contents of one particular box. Everything else is for you to do with as you wish. If we time this right we should have plenty of time to sort things out. It may be a good idea for you to divide your spoils whilst in the vault so that we can each go our separate ways as soon as we leave."

"What about the bank staff and customers?" broke in Ernie,."Who's keeping an eye on them while we're in the vault?"

Rivers turned to Eric, "Have you not told them anything, Eric?"

"No," said Eric. "I wanted to wait until we were all together."

"Fair enough." Said Rivers, "Right, we won't be holding the bank up, we're going to tunnel our way in. We have a premises to work from and all the necessary plans. We do it carefully and slowly. If we do it right we should break through on a Friday night so we have the entire weekend to go through the vault."

"Oh yeah," chipped in Thomas. "and who's doing all the bloody digging? Does anybody here know about tunnelling through anywhere? This sounds too bloody risky to me. What if it all caves in on us? We'll be dead, and what for? Bugger all, if we're dead, that's what."

Ernie stepped forward, his massive bulk towering over everybody, "Eric and I were mining engineers, on the front line, we worked at Messines so we know what we're doing."

Rivers broke in. "As for the digging, we'll all be doing our fair share on all the tasks. Putting in the shoring as we go, moving the spoil; some may have to be taken off site, and at the coal face, so to speak.

"I will have some specific tasks for individuals. Mr Cook, to all intents and purposes you are the manager of our company."

"What makes him so fucking special!" snarled Thomas. "Why should he lord it over us?"

"He won't!" Snapped back Rivers, "He will appear to be the manager to anyone outside. Unwanted visitors, other tenants in the building. He will just be a front. Now has anyone else got anything to say, before I carry on? No? Right, I want no more arguing and bickering. You each carry out your tasks as you are instructed to, when you're instructed to. Is that clear? If you're not prepared to do that, there's the door, but remember what I said. Now, are we all in and on side?" A mumbled chorus of yeses and nodding heads, "Mr Thomas?"

"Yes, I'm in. Just wanted to know where I stand."

"Good," said Rivers. For the next hour he ran over the outline of what the task before then involved, and how they were going to go about it. There was little interruption except for questions about the logistics, and who was paying for it all. He managed to allay those by informing them that his Principle had deep pockets and there was no need to worry on that score.

Finally he took two sets of keys out of his pocket. He handed one set to Eric Teale. "These are to a dark grey Guy flatbed lorry, parked round the corner. You and Ernie can use that for all the heavy stuff, timber and heavy equipment and the like. These," he handed the other set to Charlie Cook, "are to the large navy blue Commer van parked behind the lorry. You and Norman use it to get some basic office furniture and signage for the front of house." He went into his brief case and came out with two large order books. You can use these when you buy stuff. This is who we are."

Charlie Cook read off the order form header "Hilditch Holdings (precious metal trading) and Associates. Sounds impressive. What happens if anyone checks up?"

"Oh, it's a quite bonafide company. It will check out. They will find it currently under reorganisation after the recent financial down turn. Soon to reopen in brand new premises in the city. That's us."

"What if someone actually tries to contact this company?" enquired Cook.

"Not a problem. I was about to run through this with you. Once the front of house is set up, and a strong door fitted to the basement we're working from, we will have a few front of house employees. They will be totally unaware of our actual task. They will believe that they are working for a bonafide company as receptionists and clerks. You are to have minimal contact with them. As far as they are concerned you are workmen involved in the construction of a new strongroom. Under no circumstances are any of them to go into the basement. No one, apart from us, goes past the basement strong door. Are we all clear on that?" Another chorus of nods and yeses. "Now, paying for material and equipment. You will use the order pads and pay for anything under £25 in cash. Anything over that sum will be by company cheque, here." He handed a cheque book each to Ernie and Charlie. They looked a bit dog eared and the first two or three cheques had been used, their stubs filled out with various amounts payable to various companies. "You're both set up as signatories, and best of all, they won't bounce. That account does exist at Martins Bank, and has ample funds for our venture.

"Now, if there are no more questions I suggest we all get a good night's sleep. We'll meet back here eight o'clock sharp, with the vehicles. I will have shopping lists for you, and the address of where to take it all."

"What's to stop us cashing a few cheques, ourselves?" piped up Thomas.

"Why would you do that?" responded Rivers, with a cold edge to his voice. "The pickings from the vault far outweigh a few cashed cheques, and I think I already mentioned the reach of our principal." He glared at Thomas.

Thomas put up his hands in mock surrender. "Okay, okay. Fair enough, just thought I'd mention it."

"Consider it mentioned," snapped Rivers. "Now let's go, we have a lot of work ahead of us." Cook, Thomas, and Banks filed out the door, leaving Rivers and Teale alone.

"Well," said Eric, once the door had closed, "what do you think?"

"Ernie I've known briefly. Cook I don't know. He comes across well, just the sort of chap to front us, but I'm not sure how trustworthy he is. Thomas is a mouthy little so and so, likes to stir things, but he's easily slapped down and kept in line"

"I can vouch for Ernie and Charlie," said Eric. "I've known them a while, and they're both solid. Thomas I had to think about, but like you said he's easily kept in check and he's a good worker and pulls his weight, even when things get tough. He's one of those that never give up."

"Okay," said Rivers. "Well, I trust your judgement. Now, I'm off. See you tomorrow and we'll get this show on the road."

Chapter 25

In just over a week Hilditch Holdings (Precious Metals Trading) and Associates had moved into Cleveland house. They furnished the ground and first floor offices quite opulently. A chairman's office, with attached boardroom and a manager's office occupied the first floor. The ground floor had an office manager's office and a general clerical office, which included a small typing pool. Fronting this was a reception area. Rather grand, as befitting a company dealing in precious metals. The area contained several oxblood red leather Chesterfield armchairs, the receptionist's desk sat between two doors each one mahogany, with the top half glazed with opaque frosted glass. On the glass, in gold leaf a stylised logo of the company's initial letters, H H, above the name of the company. The door on the left, as you faced the desk, opened into a corridor that ran toward the back of the building, then opened out to the service entrance on one side, and the door to the basement on the other. The door on the right led into a space behind reception. A very solid mahogany door to the left led into the other corridor. Facing the wall behind reception, two glass fronted offices. To the left the general office, to the right the office managers office. As Hilditch Holdings had taken over the first two floors, it meant the main staircase led up from their reception, so anybody coming in would go through their reception. No problem with the employees of the companies upstairs, and Hilditch Holding's receptionist merely directed callers upstairs. A large brass plaque next to the staircase and lift denoted which company was on which floor.

So it was that Paul Rivers sat behind the reception desk when the first of their potential office staff recruits entered the building. They had selected three, or rather three had been pre selected by an agency on their behalf. Paul Rivers told them exactly what they wanted. He also told them that if they proved satisfactory, then they would use them to recruit more staff once Hilditch Holdings opened it's doors for business in the not too distant future. The first to arrive was a Cynthia Goldsmith. A prim and proper woman in her late thirties that looked every inch the office supervisor. She entered the building and marched straight up to the reception desk. "Mr Smith?" she enquired.

"Indeed I am," replied Rivers. He would be known as Paul Smith to everyone in this enterprise. Even to the two that knew otherwise. He stood from behind the desk and held out his hand.

"Cynthia Goldsmith," she announced, giving his proffered hand a firm shake. "I have an appointment."

"Quite so, Miss Goldsmith," said Rivers. "Please come through, we're upstairs." He led Cynthia Goldsmith up the grand staircase to the first floor. "You will have to excuse us, at the moment," he said. "We've just moved in and have a lot of work to do before we open for business." He ushered her through the door to the office marked 'General Manager'. As they entered Charlie Cook rose from behind an imposing mahogany desk and came round to greet her. He was dressed immaculately, in a dark suit with pinstripe trousers, regimental tie, and handkerchief in his top pocket. "Miss Goldsmith, allow me to introduce Major Charles Cook, our General Manager."

"Delighted, Miss Goldsmith, delighted," effused Charlie Cook. Don't over do it, thought Rivers. "Please do have a seat." He settled her into a chair facing the desk. Rivers took another, to one side, and Charlie Cook went back behind his desk. "Now, the agency speak very highly of you. Please think of this more of a formality rather than a job interview. What we have here is a work in progress. We are gearing up to start trading in precious metals. This requires several things. Firstly all the initial paperwork needs taking care of, financial records, that sort of thing. I would also like a weekly report on the current market in precious metals. As office supervisor it will be your responsibility to ensure this is produced each week. The other thing is, as we will be dealing with precious metals, we will, of course be building a strong room, in the basement. This will require quite a bit of noise, I'm afraid, and people coming and going."

"Of course, Major Cook," interjected Cynthia, "When do you intend to start trading?"

"Mr Smith?" asked Cook, sitting back in his chair and looking across at Rivers.

"We are hoping three to four weeks," said Rivers. "As soon as the new vault is completed, and the security system installed."

"Mr Smith's my right hand man," said Cook smiling across at Cynthia. "My general factotum, so to speak. If you need any questions answering, he's your man."

"I noticed a chairman's office, when I came up the stairs," said Cynthia. "Is he here yet?"

"No, I'm afraid he's not," said Rivers. "Lord Balmuir is currently in America. He'll be joining us when we open for business." They'd decided on a fictitious chairman, currently abroad, to lend a little more authenticity to the sense of incompleteness of the company. Actually there was a Lord Balmuir, hardly anybody had heard of him. A minor Foreign Office official, and part time explorer, he had currently been missing for six months in the Hindukusch. No one expected to see, or hear from him ever again.

"Do you have any further questions?" asked Cook.

"Yes," said Cynthia. "you mentioned a weekly report."

"Ah, the weekly report," said Cook, "Yes, if you could go through the daily reports of precious metal trading, and collate them into a weekly report showing movement over the week and any trends. It's vital we are ready to be fresh off the mark when we open our doors. You will have a staff of two working under you, to begin with. One clerk and one receptionist. They can help collating the figures for your report, plus their other duties, of course. Now, if there's nothing else, Mr Smith will take you downstairs, and show you your office." He stood up and extended his hand over the desk. "I look forward to you joining us, Miss Goldsmith."

So, over the next couple of hours the rest of their innocent front of house recruits arrived. Firstly, a Miss Millicent Dobson, confessed that her friends called her Milly. A slim young lady of twenty one, with long wavy black hair and striking emerald green eyes, who informed Charlie Cook she had a steady boyfriend. She said this with a swing of the head, to move her hair from in front of her eyes, and a bright smile. She gave the impression of someone very pleasant and friendly, but could very well stand up for herself. Milly was their new receptionist.

Next was a slightly dumpy, jolly little blonde of nineteen. Miss Dorothy "call me Dot, everyone does." Harding. Their new clerk typist who proudly announced she was engaged to Walter. Walter was just a porter, at Waterloo Station, but destined for better things, they were informed.

They were all told of the work going on in the basement, to build the new vault. In fact, they had already started their preparations which accounted for the banging they could hear. Cynthia Goldsmith sat in on the other two interviews, and vaguely knew Milly Dobson through the agency. After they'd been shown their place of work, and their duties explained, they were told as it was Thursday, have a nice long weekend off and report for work at nine o'clock Monday morning.

Charlie Cook and Paul Rivers (aka. Smith) stood in the foyer of Cleveland House and watched the three ladies depart. They walked off, up Cleveland Place towards King Street, chatting together. Getting to know each other and looking forward to their new job.

"Right," said Paul, "let's see how they're getting on." They walked back through the door to the left of reception. Paul making sure it was locked behind them. In the loading bay area there was already a growing pile of equipment, a stack of timber and Ernie Banks just carting some of it through the door to the cellar. Norman Thomas was checking off some of the equipment against a list and Eric Teale stood aside to let Ernie pass as he came out of the cellar. "How are things going, Eric?" asked Paul.

"All good," was his reply. "I think we've got everything we need. We'll leave most of the timber up here, and take it down as and when we need it. We got some steel sheeting." He pointed to some six foot by four foot sheets of steel. "So it looks as though we really are building a vault, plus we need some to fabricate a strong door for here. We should be ready to get under way in about two hours."

"Can we get the strong door in place before we start?" asked Paul.

"Ernie and I will start on that once the gears all sorted," replied Eric.

"Excellent. You two press on with that, the rest of us can make a start downstairs. We can break through the floor tonight. Get that door in place. It's Friday tomorrow, the girls don't start till Monday, so we'll lock up and rest up tomorrow. Back here for, say, seven p.m. and we can crack on through the weekend." Nods all round then they all got stuck in to their various tasks. Soon the area was filled with the sound of industry. Sparks flying as Ernie and Eric used an oxyacetylene torch to cut up the steel for the door, then more as they welded and fabricated. Meanwhile, in the cellar, Paul and Charlie Cook had changed into overalls and boots and they were taking it in turns, with Norman Thomas, to dig through the concrete floor with pick axes. It was gruelling work, they were sweaty and filthy when at last Norman swung his pick and it broke through to the ground beneath.

They'd been hard at it, and it was now approaching five a.m. when Ernie came down the stairs. "Door's on," he announced.

"Very good," said Paul, rolling his shoulders to ease the aching muscles. "Have you got the lock on?"

"We have, indeed," said Ernie producing three complicated looking brass keys. "It's all complete. We've fitted a Chubb security lock, "Who's keeping keys?"

"You have one, Ernie, I'll have one and Charlie can gave the third. The girls will think Ernie's the foreman, and it would look bloody strange if Charlie and I didn't have keys to our own vault." He looked across at Norman, to see if he would say something.

He put a hand up, palm outwards. "Fine by me, I just want to crack on and get in there and away."

"Here, here," said Eric, coming down the stairs behind Ernie.

"Right," said Paul, "Let's call it a day. Lock it all up and we're back here at seven o'clock tonight, OK?" Nods all round. They slung their picks against the wall, filed up the stairs, put out the light and locked their new strong door. He turned and looked at the locked door. It couldn't have looked better if it had been professionally made and installed. "You've done a superb job there, gentlemen. Thank you." He and Charlie used a tap in the corner to rinse themselves off before quickly changing back into their suits while the rest of the gang went off into the early morning pre dawn. Then they left the building, making sure everything was locked up and went off for some well earned rest.

Chapter 26

One p.m. Friday afternoon Paul Rivers picked up Charlie Cook from his Mews house, in the Bentley the department had acquired for him. Someone, somewhere, in the civil service was both confused and annoyed that their staff Bentley had been requisitioned. They parked up outside Cleveland House, leaving the car on full display right by the front portico. They made a point of one or the other of them was always in the reception area or on the stairs for the rest of the afternoon. They bid a cheery goodbye and good afternoon to all the staff from the companies on the upper floors as they passed. Around six o'clock the whole building seemed quiet. Rivers and Cook went up the stairs to the top three floors, to see if anybody else was still in the building. The place was deserted, all the outer office doors locked. At the office doors Charlie Cook delved into the briefcase he was carrying, and produced an empty milk bottle with some stones in it, and lent it against the door. He looked up at Rivers and gave him a wink. "If anybody's still inside," he whispered, "when they come out we'll know."

"All the way down in the basement?" queried Rivers.

Cook shrugged. "You'd be surprised how far sound travels in an empty building at night," he said.

Seven p.m. on the dot the others came in through the back door. Cook and Rivers had already changed into overalls. Rivers was waiting by the open basement strong door and led them down. Near the wall closest to Swifts bank was a hole in the concrete floor roughly a yard across. The chunks of concrete, that had been removed were stacked in the corner. The actual basement was huge, occupying the entire area of Cleveland House. It was divided up into a number of rooms with just an archway as entrance to each one. Most of the tools they needed were in the room with the hole in the floor. Next door was the oxyacetylene cutting equipment they would need to break into the bank vault. It also held a large trestle table, on which were the plans of both Cleveland House and Swifts Bank's basements and other drawings of the distance between the two and the placement of any pipes and services they needed to avoid.

Straight away they set to digging down into the earth beneath Cleveland House. As the earth was shovelled up, it was wheelbarrowed into the farthest room. As they went down they shored the sides up with the timber they brought down. Past the concrete of the basement they opened out the shaft so that as they reached the level they wanted, they had a chamber in which to operate. The spoil, from the tunnel, would be brought into here, then hoisted up into the basement.

All weekend they worked. The chamber under the basement completed and a good section of tunnel. Sometime on Sunday afternoon they hit London Clay. A thick smelly clay layer that came a good eighteen inches up from the desired floor to the tunnel. Work halted and every one retreated back to the basement and had a confab around the table with the drawings. "God, that stuff stinks," said Ernie Banks. "You can smell it up here. What if it gets upstairs, what will we say is the cause?"

"We tell them the truth," said Eric Teale. They all looked at him. "Well, a half truth. We say we had to sink some foundations for the new vault through the basement floor and we hit London Clay."

"Fair enough," this from Charlie Cook. "But what are we going to do about it? It'll slow us up considerably having to dig through it."

"No," broke in Ernie. "Look," he spread out a section drawing of the ground showing both the basement of Cleveland House, the vault under Swifts Bank and the ground in between. "We have enough headroom to raise the rest of the tunnel by the hight of the clay. We just need to dig enough out to make a ramp, so the tunnel floor slopes up for the spoil trollies to run." These were the small wheeled trucks they used to carry the spoil back to the basement as they tunnelled through.

Norman Thomas, usually the complainer, surprised them all by saying, "Right, then, lets's crack on." And headed back to the tunnel.

Around midnight, with the ramp almost complete and the clay dumped in the corner of the basement room furthest from the stairs, Paul Rivers and Charlie Cook left to get themselves cleaned up and ready to greet their new work force at the start of the day.

At 9am Monday morning prompt the three girls came up the steps and through the imposing front doors of Cleveland House. Both Paul Rivers (aka Smith) and Major Charles Cook were in the reception area to greet them. There was a small pile of bogus correspondence in the tray on the reception desk. In Cynthia Goldsmith's office there was a stack of newspapers from the previous week, plus some more specialists publications pertaining to stocks and shares and tradings in precious metals. In the general office there were a stack of invoices. Some from all the equipment they'd purchased for their tunnelling in the name of Hilditch Holdings. Other more spurious purchases from office equipment to shipping invoices for travel to points all over the globe.

"Lovely to see you all," beamed Major Cook. "As you can see, things are starting to pile up. Let's get you settled in, then we can get down to business. Miss Goldsmith, let me show you your office and what needs doing. Mr Smith would you be so kind as to help these two young ladies take up their positions?" With that he ushered Cynthia Goldsmith through to her office, where he explained how he wanted her to compile a report from the newspapers and journals on her desk.

"Well," said Paul, "Miss Dobson, Milly isn't it? If you'd take a seat behind the reception desk while I take Miss Harding through to the main office. Hold the fort, so to speak. There's a list on the desk that tells you which other companies are in the building, and where they are, if anyone asks. If the phone goes, just answer as Hilditch Holdings, ask them to hold and fetch me. I'll just be through here." He led Miss Harding through to the main office and showed her the stack of invoices. "Well, now, Miss Harding, Is it Dorothy, or Dot? I can't remember."

"Dot, Sir," she replied, reddening slightly.

"Dot it is, then. Good, now. These invoices all need filing. The usual thing. In alphabetical order, by company, and date order therein. Is that alright?"

"Yes, Sir, that will be fine, I can do that. Is there any other filing?"

"Ah," said Paul, with a slight grimace, "Now you mention it. The stuff already filed may need a bit of a sort out. Quite a lot of it got a bit mixed up in the move. May be worth going through that first. Get it sorted."

"That's okay, Sir. I'm a bit of a dab hand at filing." She smiled at him, proud of her skill.

"Wonderful," responded Paul. Not too much of a dab hand, he thought, we need to string this along for at least a week. "I'll leave you to it then." With that he went out into reception. Milly Dobson was just directing an elderly gentleman, in frock coat, pinstripes and a bowler hat, to one of the companies on the upper floor. She'd obviously done a good job, for as he departed for the lift he smiled, touched the brim of his bowler and declared, "Thank you very much, my dear."

"Any Calls?" asked Paul.

"Nothing, yet," she replied. She held up some envelopes. "These are for Major Cook," she said. "Shall I take them up?"

"No, that's okay, thank you." Paul took them off her, "I'll take them up in a minute. Now, the telephone." He showed her how the reception phone worked, how to put calls through to Major Cook, to his own office, to Cynthia Goldsmith's office and the general office. After he was sure she had the hang of it he went up to Major Cook's imposing office.

As Paul shut the door behind him, it was all he and Charlie Cook could do to stop laughing out loud. "Ah, Mr Smith," said Charlie, in a loud imperious manor, "I see you have my correspondence."

"I do indeed, Major." Replied Paul, in an equally imperious booming voice, and handed said correspondence over with a flourish. Charlie Cook went and sat behind his desk and used an ornate letter opener to open the envelopes. Paul flopped down in a leather armchair and let out a long sigh. "I'm bloody shattered," he muttered.

"Me too," said Charlie, as he sorted through the meaningless leaflets and made up financial reports that had come in the post. Stuff made up by Reg Cockscombe and posted at various post boxes around London. He'd even sent a package to the British Embassies in Washington and Paris, for the attention of the Cultural Attaché, the cover position of the Secret Intelligence Service's man at the embassy. These contained a series of envelopes, of various size, to be posted to Hilditch Holdings over the next week, or so. No one asked any questions, they just assumed Hilditch Holdings was a cover company for some intelligence gathering operation.

Chapter 27

Wednesday, just after lunch, Paul was in Charlie Cook's office. They'd been checking the plans of the bank vault. Charlie behind his desk, Paul perched on the corner. For some reason the conversation had turned from the vault to one of Charlie's anecdotes. It had something to do with an 18th century dresser that Charlie had acquired by dubious means. There was a knock on the door. Before Charlie could say 'enter', the door opened and a complete stranger stood there. Paul stood up, Charlie casually closed the folder containing the plans. Before they could gather their wits, the stranger spoke.

"Good afternoon," he said. A slightly florid man of mid to late fifties, pinstripe suit, guards' tie, a shade under six foot, well clipped military moustache and slicked back dark hair, greying at the temples, "William DeVere," he walked into the room with a broad smile. When he noticed their confused look he continued, "DeVere Cummings?" He pointed upwards, "Top floor."

"Of course," said Charlie, coming round the desk, beaming his winning smile and extending his hand, "Charles Cook, and this is my right hand man, Paul Smith." He indicated Paul. They all shook hands and Charlie bid them all take a seat and proceeded to pour three large whiskies from the decanter on the side.

Downstairs, Dot thought how hard those men were working in the basement. She though it might be a nice idea to offer them some tea. Three days on the job, she had the way of things and was already starting to feel at home. She got on really well with Milly, and Miss Goldsmith seemed quite nice, too. She asked her if she would like a cup, then stuck her head round the door into reception and asked Milly. "I'm going to pop round and see if the men fancy a cup," she said.

"Do you think you should?" asked Milly. "the Major seemed quite strict about the new vault."

"It'll be fine," said Dot, confidently. "I'm only going to ask them if they fancy a cuppa." With that she went through the other door, from reception, that led to the back.

Ernie Banks was just taking some more lumber down to the basement, for shoring up the next stretch of tunnel. He left the strong door wide open, intending to pop back up and shut it once the lumber was stowed. Norman was just helping him stack it when a voice echoed down the stairs.

"Cooee!" And the sound of hesitant steps on the stairs. Norman and Ernie looked at each other wide eyed. "Do you boys fancy a cup of tea?" Norman shot to the bottom of the stairs, to head her off.

"You can't come down here, miss," he shouted up to her. Starting ups the stairs, himself. "I'm sorry, miss, but if you're caught down here, we'll both be for it." In more ways than one, he thought to himself. "It's special security," he bluffed. "And there's lots of dangerous equipment." By now he was up the stairs and ushering Dot back into the service area. "It's very kind of you." Her face had dropped, and he thought she was about to cry. "Honestly, we're fine. We have our own tea making things down there." He pointed back down the stairs. He walked her to the door leading to the front. "No harm done, though," he reassured her. "though perhaps best if you ladies stayed out of this part of the building, eh?"

"Yes, sorry," she forced a tiny smile as she went back through to the front. Norman watched the door close behind her and let out a deep breath.

Ernie had come to the top of the stairs and was standing in the doorway to the basement. "That was close," he said

"Too bloody close," said Norman. "You left the bloody door open."

"I had my bloody hands full," he retorted, "in case you hadn't noticed."

"Okay, okay." He held his hands up. "Sorry, just a bit jumpy after her nearly walking in on us."

"Fair enough," replied Ernie. "From now on when someone's bring stuff down, one of us goes with them to shut the door behind them. That door stays shut as much as possible."

In the tea making area beside the office Dot clattered about making tea for herself, Milly and Miss Goldsmith. The sharp rebuke from that workman had unsettled her. He'd been alright afterwards, but the way he shouted at her when she was only going to go down those silly stairs had given her quite a start. She still felt a bit shaken, and as a consequence was making more of a clatter than usual, with the tea things.

"Is everything alright, Dot?" Cynthia Goldsmith stood behind her.

Dot turned quickly. "Oh, yes Miss Goldsmith," she flushed. "Just making the tea. Didn't know you was behind me." She tried a half smile and turned back to the job in hand.

"Just so long as you're alright," said Miss Goldsmith, and went back into her office.

"Told you not to," said Milly, when Dot took her tea through. "What happened?"

"Who said anything happened?" responded Dot.

"Come on Dot," said Milly, with a smile. "You've not taken any tea through to them, and you were crashing about out there, like a bull in a china shop."

Dot relayed what had happened, and that Cynthia Goldsmith had asked what was up. "You won't say anything to her, will you?" she implored Milly.

" 'Course not." said Milly. "My lips are sealed."

Chapter 28

About 11:45pm, Thursday night, they felt it safe to have both the basement door wedged open, and the big door into the side alley half open to get some air into the place. The stink from the London clay was cloying and nauseous. Plus it was stifling in the tunnel. They hadn't given ventilation too much thought as it was going to be fairly short, but working at the face was strenuous and in such a confined space quickly became overly stuffy. The movement of the spoil trucks gave some movement to the air, but not much. While these doors were open someone was always up in the loading bay area, keeping watch. Norman Thomas was slouched against the inside wall when he heard slow, measured steps coming up the alley. Quickly he ran over to the basement, and half way down the stairs. In a loud whisper he told them someone was coming. Charlie Cook immediately shot up the stairs, past Norman, and into the loading bay. He slowed to a stroll toward the outer door just as a patrolling constable came into view. He shone his torch onto the loading bay, and into Charlie's face. Although it was somewhat unnecessary due to the electric light illuminating the area.

Charlie put a hand up to shield his eyes from the light. "Good evening, constable," he said. "could you lower your torch, please?"

"Yes, sorry sir," said the constable lowering and extinguishing his torch.

"I believe you've been made aware of us working here at night?" he asked.

"There was some mention of it when I came on duty, yes sir. Just checking everything is in order."

"It certainly is, constable, as you can see."

"Yes, Sir," responded the policeman, moving over to the open basement door. "What, exactly are you doing down there that causes this stink?"

Charlie headed him off at the top of the stairs. "We're installing some rather complex, not to say secret security equipment. It means digging through the basement floor, in certain areas, to reinforce the foundations. That smell is the clay."

The policeman tried to edge round Charlie as if they were engaged in some sort of slow dance. "Mind if I have a look, then?" he asked.

"I'm afraid not," said Charlie, with a smile. "Security is very tight. Only those that need to know, and are involved in our vault's construction, are allowed down there."

"Perhaps if you asked your boss," suggested the policeman.

"Actually, I am the boss," said Charlie. "Major Charles Cook, I'm here supervising the installation of part of the security measures." He pulled himself up to his full height, which was about the same as the policeman, and looked him steadily in the eye. "And I'm afraid a visit downstairs is out of the question." Charlie's heart was pounding. What had started out as a simple fob off to a passing bobby, was rapidly turning into something altogether more dangerous. What would they do if he insisted, and forced his way downstairs? His mind was in overdrive trying to work out any number of scenarios involving the discovery of what they were actually doing.

"Of course, Sir," said the constable. Charlie almost let out a sigh of relief, but he maintained his composure and gave him a brief smile. The constable turned and walked out through the loading-bay. He half turned as he left. "Good night, Sir."

"Good night, Constable, and thank you for your diligence." Then, after the constable disappeared, and just the sound of his boots faded down the alley, and only then, did Charlie Cook let out one huge sigh of relief. He walked over to the basement door. "It's okay, he's gone," he called down. Everybody appeared at the bottom of the stairs, the look of relief plain on their faces.

"Best shut the outer door," called up Paul. "We could do without some other conscientious bobby sticking his nose round the door to check up on us."

"Right," said Charlie. He walked over and pulled the big wooden door across and shoved the big bolt down into it's receiving hole in the floor. He reached up and did the same with the long handled top bolt that slid home into its iron bracket on the lintel. He came back down into the basement. Everybody was still hanging around in the room at the foot of the stairs.

"Okay, everybody," said Paul. "Excitement over, let's get back to work We're nearly there, but there's still plenty to do."

Friday afternoon Ernie carefully pushed a steel bar up through the tunnel roof. Very gently he eased it up though the earth roof just past the last piece of wood shoring up the tunnel. Soil and grit trickled down over his arms. He blew some away from his face, and shook his head to keep it out of his eyes. Pausing now and then to rub the sweat off each hand, in turn, on his trousers. Dragged a forearm across his forehead, then continued his push. Slowly up, an inch at a time. Suddenly it stopped. He shoved against it, but it moved no further. He pulled it back down less than an inch, then pushed it back up. He looked back over his shoulder with a big grin on his face and gave Eric, crouched behind him, the thumbs up. Eric scuttled back out of the tunnel and stood up in the void below the basement floor of Cleveland House. Norman Thomas peered down at him. "Well?" he said.

Eric smiled up at him. "We're there." He climbed the ladder out of the chamber. Ernie wasn't far behind him. They went over to the table with the plans spread out on it. They looked down at the plan of the vault in Swifts Bank.

Ernie tapped the plan with a muddy index finger. "By my reckoning, we're just about there." He indicated a spot just short of dead centre.

"By your reckoning," said Norman, with a slight sneer.

"Yes, by my reckoning," snapped back Ernie, with an unusual display of anger. "Reckoning that got me smack under the German line HQ, at Messines. Why do you always have to have a dig, Thomas? We're all in this together. If you think you could do this better, you should've spoken up."

"Okay, Ernie," interjected Paul, who'd just joined them. "Let's just calm down. Norman, lay of the smart remarks."

"What did I say?" pleaded Thomas.

"Just can it. Everybody," said Paul, firmly. "We're almost there. All we have to do, now, is widen out the tunnel end up to the underside of the vault floor. Then cut our way through and we're in."

"In and out by Monday early hours seems pushing it." Cut in Eric.

"We won't," said Ernie. "We'd be lucky to cut through by Monday morning, which is obviously out of the question." They all looked at Paul, who was leaning over the plans. They turned at the sound of Charlie Cook coming down to the basement.

"How are we doing?" asked Charlie.

"We're there," said Ernie.

"We need to dig out the end, up to the vault floor," said Paul,."Then it's just a matter of cutting through."

" So, this is it," said Charlie, brightly.

"Not quite," said Ernie. "It'll take us all weekend to break through."

"Oh." Charlie looked crestfallen.

"Not to worry," chipped in Paul. "We use this weekend to widen the tunnel and get everything ready to break through. Then we rest for a week. We break through next Friday night."

"Good idea," said Charlie, perking up.

"Could do with some rest," said a fed up looking Norman Thomas. "I'm bloody knackered."

"Right, " said Paul. "Let's crack on."

"One thing," interrupted Eric. "Ernie and me'll need to pop out in the truck tomorrow." Paul looked quizzically at him. "I know where I can lay my hands on a couple of large baulking timbers to shove against the vault floor during the week."

"Why, it's not going to bloody collapse on us, is it?" said Thomas, in alarm.

"No, no," laughed Paul. "Good thinking, Ernie. We jam them hard up against the vault floor. It eliminates the risk of that part of the floor suddenly sounding hollow when somebody walks across it." Everyone smiled and nodded. It made perfect sense. They didn't want to take any unnecessary risks of being discovered. "Right, back to work. We've got a tunnel to finish."

Chapter 29

Monday morning Charlie Cook was sitting in a leather armchair, in Paul's office, when Cynthia Goldsmith walked in carrying a large folder. "Oh, hello, Major." She seemed slightly surprised. "I have your report, here." She indicated the folder in her arms. "I was going to bring it through to you."

"Don't worry, Miss Goldsmith," said Charlie, giving her his winning smile. "I've saved you a journey."

"What was it you wanted to see me about?" asked Paul.

"Well, Mr Smith, it's just that the workmen don't appear to have turned up. It's all locked up, and their lorry isn't there, or their van."

"It's alright," said Paul, with a smile. "We're at a bit of a hiatus. We have some lock mechanisms being made especially for us, in Switzerland. Unfortunately some technical hitches have delayed them, somewhat. We won't be getting them now, till the end of this week, beginning of next. And until we get them we can proceed no further."

"Oh that's alright, then," she said, and handed the folder to Charlie.

"Oh, bye the way," said Charlie, as he took the folder from her,. "Mr Smith and I may be away from the office a good deal, this week. Meetings you understand."

"Of course, Major. But I've got nothing in my diary for you this week," said Cynthia querulously.

"It's alright, Miss Goldsmith," interjected Paul, "I've been dealing with these appointments. They're a little on the delicate side, to be dealt with in the strictest confidence. Besides, they were arranged before we even moved in here, so there was no need to bother you, really."

"Very good, Sir," replied Cynthia. With what seems like a somewhat forced smile she turned and left the room.

As they heard her footsteps descend the stairs they turned to each other and just stopped themselves from bursting out laughing.

"Good thinking," chuckled Charlie. "I love the idea of the Swiss locks. I almost want to see them."

"And I like your meetings, to get us some time away from here and rest up."

"Well mollified with the prearranged, highly confidential aspect. I'd completely forgotten about sorting any meetings with her. I may have to get her to put one or two in her diary, to allay suspicion."

"Set a couple up for next week" winked Paul.

Mid afternoon, Friday, Charlie and Paul arrived at Cynthia Goldsmith's office. Charlie put his head round the door. "Miss Goldsmith, could you make a note? I have an appointment at Coutts Bank, with Sir Arnold Waverly, at 12:15 pm, next Tuesday afternoon."

"Certainly, Major," said Cynthia. She repeated it as she wrote it in her desk diary. "Tuesday, at 12:15. Sir Arnold Waverly at Coutts."

"Thank you Miss Goldsmith."

Paul stuck his head round the door, as Charlie retreated. "We're just going to see if our Swiss locks have arrived. We could be in for a busy weekend."

"Yes, Mr Smith." She responded with a quick smile, then got back to whatever pointless task she was currently engaged in.

When they came through to the loading bay they found the outer doors open, and the van backed half way in. Ernie Banks and Eric Teale were manhandling a large wooden crate from the back.

"What on earth have you got there?" asked Charlie.

"This," announced Eric, proudly, "is a heavy duty electric quarry drill. Almost as good as a pneumatic drill, but without the need for a bloody great compressor"

"Very good," said Paul, sardonically, "but aren't you forgetting something?" Ernie and Eric straightened up and looked at Paul. " How do you propose to power it at the far end of the tunnel?"

"Already thought of that," said Eric. "There's a cable drum in the van. I noticed the other day, there's a three phase outlet on the wall over there." He pointed across to a large grey cast-iron junction box on the wall. "It's the inlet junction box for the lift. I can hook up to that and run the cable down and through the tunnel."

"Why three phase?" asked Paul

"Like I said, this is a heavy duty drill. It's an industrial one. There's a rig it sits in, on the back of the truck."

As if on cue, Norman came round the sides of the van from outside. "Afternoon gents, how do you like our new toy?"

"Where did you get it?" asked Charlie.

"Used our noddles," said Eric. They noticed Ernie had a broad grin on his face. "We bought it."

"Bought it!" exclaimed Paul. "Who the hell from?"

"Finchet Industries Limited, in Clapham. Well, I say bought it. We've actually got it on trial. We just paid a deposit, told them we wanted to check out one of these new drills with a view to using them in our mining division, in South Africa."

"That's damn good thinking," said Paul.

"Yeah, we've still got a few of those order forms you signed for us, Charlie," said Ernie. "Or should I say Major Cook." They all had a chuckle, then got to work lugging the equipment down to the tunnel. The drum of cable was left by the junction box on the wall, the van parked outside and the truck reversed until it was up against the loading bay entrance. It was just that bit too big to fit in. Norman dropped the tailgate and jumped up. He drew back a tarpaulin to reveal a metal framework and large wooden box with rope handles at each end. Together they got everything off the lorry, and down into the basement. Eric set to work at the junction box, to fix the cable. Everybody else was in the basement getting the equipment through the tunnel into the chamber beneath the vault at Swifts Bank.

They used the spoil trollies to haul the drill and associated crates through the tunnel. Then they hit a snag. The drill's framework wouldn't fit in the tunnel, or more precisely, there wasn't enough room to get it on to the trolly. Ernie was at the far end, ready to haul the truck through. Paul, Charlie and Norman were trying to wangle the frame onto the trolley. It was very heavy and awkward, and Paul had to continually remind them all to be careful every time the caught the roof, or sides of the tunnel. Ernie appeared, crawling along the tunnel. "What's the hold up? I've been waiting ages for you to call me to pull."

"Fucking thing won't fucking fit," swore Norman, in exasperation.

"What if we take the truck out, and manhandle it through?" They turned at the sound of Eric's voice. "I'm all hooked up out there." He jerked a thumb over his shoulder. "Untie the truck and take it out, then see if the frame fits."

"It will, just about," said Ernie, eyeing it up from inside the tunnel.

With Ernie at the front, shuffling backwards, and Eric and Norman at the back, they heaved and jiggled it through the tunnel. "Watch it doesn't snag the shoring," said Eric between grunts, as the slowly moved it along.

"At least we won't have to bother about bringing it back out again," said Norman.

As they started up the ramp, over the London clay, they were so busy concentrating on getting it up the incline they failed to notice as the top of the frame rose up towards the roof. A particularly hefty shove and pull slammed the top of the frame into the roof boards, knocking one to one side. A creak was followed by a small avalanche of earth from behind the shoring. Amid shouts and cries they managed to free the frame and get it out of the way while Norman attempted to stem the flow of earth. Coughing and spluttering at the soil getting in his mouth he tried to push the board back, a sense of panic building inside him. He didn't want to be buried alive. Eric scrambled back to help. Ernie, stuck the other side of the frame, could only shout at them to get a lump hammer and hammer it back into place. Meanwhile he watched with growing horror at the steadily growing mound of earth beneath the gap in the tunnel roof. Paul scrabbled down the tunnel to see what all the fuss was about, then scrambled back out to reappear just a minute later with a lump hammer. Norman held the board in position, trying to force it against the weight of falling earth. Eric started to hammer at it. Awkward in such a confined space, he couldn't get the swing he wanted, but slowly the board moved back into position. Finally it was back and the flow of earth stopped. Eric and Norman flopped back against the side of the tunnel, gasping for breath. Ernie heaved a sigh of relief. All those times tunnelling under enemy lines and the comrades he'd lost in cave-ins, being buried alive had always been a fear uppermost in his mind. It would be something of an irony for him to end up being entombed beneath the streets of London. Paul reappeared again, pushing a spoil trolley in front of him.

"Best get back to it," he said calmly.

"We nearly got fucking buried, then," snapped Norman

Eric put a hand on his arm, "It's okay, Norm, we're okay. We got it sorted, but we do need to push on and get this thing," he jerked a thumb towards the frame "Up and running ASAP."

"Suppose so." Norman pushed himself away from the wall. They managed to get the frame through to the chamber, under the vault, without further incident. Eric went back and unrolled the cable. Fortunately the cable drum fitted into the tunnel, with room to spare, and Eric merely had to roll it through, laying the cable as he went. Ernie went back out of the basement, while Eric and Norman assembled the drill and frame. They angled the frame so the drill pointed vertically upwards and was advanced upwards by turning a handle that turned a screw drive.

Ernie, Charlie and Paul were looking over the plans of the Swifts Bank vault. Eric was just finishing off wiring up the control box for the drill when a loud bang, followed by a crashing sound, came from the tunnel. They dashed to the tunnel and called through. Silence. They called again, Paul going into the tunnel. "For God's sake be careful," said Charlie.

Paul got to the start of the ramp. The hastily repaired roof had given way, with a side shoring board as well. "The fucking roof's come down," he shouted back, "The whole fucking tunnel's blocked." Ernie came scrambling through and squeezed up beside him.

"How far does it go?" he asked, more to himself, than Paul. Paul would have no more of an idea than him. "We need to get this cleared as soon as we can. There's no air getting through to the other side for Norman and Eric."

They'd been digging for about a quarter of an hour. Paul and Ernie in the tunnel, one digging, the other shoring up as they went. Charlie filling the trolley with earth, dragging it back out, emptying it and pushing it back for the next load. Suddenly something started moving at the top of the mound blocking the tunnel. "Back!" shouted Paul. They both scrabbled back expecting another fall. Instead a hand reached through, then the other hand and a sizeable whole appeared.

"Hello!" shouted Norman.

"You okay, in there?" called Paul

Norman made the whole bigger and pushed his face up against it. "Yeah, we're okay. Thought we were done for then."

"How far back does it go?" asked Ernie

"About another foot or so. We dug out a couple of feet before we heard you digging. The roof and sides seem intact our side. Eric had just finished setting the drill up when the roof came down."

"OK," said Ernie. "We'll dig the rest out from our side, and make sure all the shoring's okay."

Chapter 30

In the early hours of Saturday morning they started drilling. A chalk circle had been drawn on the concrete vault floor, and Eric started to drill holes along the chalk line. Although not as noisy as a pneumatic drill, it was still deafening in the confined space they were working in. As the drill completed the first hole, it suddenly shot up, with no resistance. Eric looked at the rest of them with a broad grin. "There's no steel floor. We won't be needing that lot." He nodded towards the oxyacetylene cutting equipment they'd dragged through earlier.

It took three hours to drill around the circle, plus two lines of holes inside the circle forming an X across its diameter. They heaved the drill and its framework out of the way, pushed it into a corner against the small spoil heap from Norman and Eric's digging out of the roof fall. They all shuffled back into the tunnel, except Ernie. He needed all the room to swing a sledge hammer up at the concrete circle. The first few strikes didn't seem to be having any effect. Then a few chips fell from the spaces between the drill holes. Then cracks appeared. "Nearly there," gasped Ernie, the sweat pouring off him as he swung again.

"Here, I'll spell you," offered Eric, coming into the chamber while Ernie took a breather.

Ernie handed the sledge hammer to Eric. "Cheers, Eric." Ernie crawled into the tunnel on his hands and knees, then slumped back against the wall. Eric got a grip on the sledge hammer, positioned himself and started swinging at the concrete. Each strike increased the cracks. Then a segment fell free, narrowly missing Eric. A small cheer emanated from the tunnel. Eric kicked the chunk out of the way and swung again. Four more swings and the hole was complete.

Paul came into the chamber and shone his torch up into the vault. A quarter of the way across the hole was the bottom of a steel cabinet of some sort. "Shit," he muttered. The others stood around him peering up at the obstruction. A ladder was propped against the side of the hole and he climbed up, squeezing his head and shoulders past the cabinet. Norman, Charlie and himself might be able to squeeze through, but there was no chance Ernie and Eric could. He shone his torch around the vault. The light reflected back off the many steel safe deposit box doors. He tried to push the cabinet, but it wouldn't budge. He squeezed further in, finally getting to his feet inside the vault. Someone called up were they in the right place. Paul swung his torch around the room. On the far wall were some larger deposit boxes and in the middle one very large one, about a yard square. He leant on the cabinet above the hole and peered down at the ring of expectant faces. "No, we're in the gents," he called down. Then laughed at their expressions. "Only joking, we're spot on. We need to shift this damn cabinet, though. Charlie, if you and Norman can squeeze up here we'll try and shift it."

"I'll try and push from down here," said Eric.

"Try this," said Ernie, and handed him up a large crow bar. Paul got the end jammed under the cabinet. With he and Charlie heaving on it, and Eric pushing from below, the cabinet slowly shifted. At last the hole was clear, Eric squeezed through followed by Ernie. Finally they all stood in the vault, shining torches around the room. "We did it," said Ernie. "We only fucking did it."

"Right," said Paul, interrupting their enjoyment of the moment. "Let's not hang about. These boxes aren't going to open themselves."

Norman went back down and passed up tools to them. Lump hammers, large cold chisels and crow bars.

They immediately started to lever and hammer open the boxes. Soon there was a growing pile of loot on the floor.

Paul, meanwhile, was trying to open the large deposit box, which was proving to be tougher than it looked. The corners were bent out and gouges around the lock, but still it remained stubbornly shut. Eventually he stood back. "Can somebody give me a hand over here?" He shouted to make himself heard over the excited noise of the others. The crash of hammer on chisel and doors being burst open. The clatter of goodies being emptied on to the ever increasing mound beside the hole in the floor, and the excited shouts as they discovered the various treasures other people had squirrelled away. "After all," he said, as the hubbub subsided, "this" he used the hammer in his hand to indicate the large door, "is the reason we're here."

"We've got loads here," responded Norman. "Still plenty for all of us."

"No!" growled Paul. Their greed seemed to be about to jeopardise the whole enterprise. "I told you, our principal, may I remind you, financed this job specifically for what's in here," pointing at the large door. "Do I need to remind you of the consequences if we come away empty handed."

"But we won't be, will we?" snapped Norman. " he'll have share of this little lot."

"He doesn't want a fucking share," snarled Paul. "That share's my pay off. He just wants what's in here. Now. Let's get this fucking thing open. Yes? Before we do anything else."

"Okay, okay, keep your hair on," said Norman ambling over. Eric pushed him out the way. Jammed a pry bar into the gap by the lock and started to lean on it. Then he turned and started pulling. Veins standing out on his neck as he strained. Ernie came over and lent his weight on it. Suddenly the lock burst with a bang, sending Eric and Ernie into a heap on the floor. The pry bar clanging onto the floor beside them. The door flew open and crashed against it's neighbour. There was a hush as five pairs of eyes gazed at the artefact within. An ornately carved and chased bronze cylinder, hexagonal in cross section, about two feet long and eight inches across, rested in a felt lined wooden cradle. Two felt lined iron bands wrapped over the cylinder, and were padlocked to the base.

"Good God," said Charlie, quietly. "What is it?"

"It's very rare," said Paul, "and virtually priceless. Which is why you get to keep all the boodle." He straightened up and turned to them all. "This is the only thing our principal wants. Everything else is ours." With smiles on their faces they went back to work on the other boxes. Except Eric, who produced a set of heavy duty bolt cutters and sheared through the padlock shanks like a knife through butter.

"So that's what this is all about," he said quietly.

"It is, indeed," replied Paul, equally quietly.

"What is it?"

"Virtually priceless, and the only one in the world." He leaned in, moved the iron straps out of the way and lifted it out. Or tried to. It was so heavy he could barely lift it. "Christ Almighty, it weighs a ton."

Eric leaned in to assist him. "Perhaps it's solid gold," he suggested and helped Paul lift it out. They carried it over to the cabinet and placed it on top.

"I don't think it would be that heavy even if it was solid gold." He looked at it in puzzlement. The others had come over to have a look when they saw Eric and Paul carry it between them to the cabinet. He inspected the cylinder, looking at the designs. He grasped the ends, intending to roll it over to the next flat side to have a look underneath, but he felt something move under his left hand. On that end was a small symbol of a dragon embossed on the surface. Paul gave it a push. There was a click, then a whirring sound. The cylinder split in half, lengthways, the top half hinging slowly upwards. It was obviously under some sort of control, as it didn't just spring open. It stopped when it was perpendicular to the bottom half. What nestled within defied belief. Every one of them gasped and stepped back. Inside, without any means of visible support, lying along the centre axis of the outer cylinder was a smaller cylinder, again a bronze colour, a foot long and about four inches across. The ends of the cylinder were slightly wider than the body, and four equidistant golden rods ran the length between the ends. Along its flank were several small oblong windows, behind which were numbers. Just to the right of each window the edge of a knurled brass wheel protruded just proud of the surface. What caused them to gasp was the eerie blue glow coming off the cylinder, and the fact that the numbers in the windows seemed to be turning. The ones in the far right window advanced rapidly, the others less so. The ones on the left not moving at all. Paul reached in and touched the knurled wheel by the spinning numbers. He felt a kind of detent, so that he could depress the wheel slightly. When he pressed it in, all the numbers froze . He looked round at the others. They seemed motionless, absorbed in what he was doing. He turned towards them. They weren't motionless, they were frozen. A diamond bracelet, that Norman was in the process of tossing on to their ever growing mound of loot, lay suspended in the air. He took his finger off the brass wheel and let it come back up. Immediately the numbers restarted their movement, the diamond bracelet continued it's journey to the mound. The air seemed to change.

"How did you manage that?" asked Charlie

"Manage what?" said Paul, in some confusion himself into what just happened.

"One second you're leaning over the thing, the next you're standing sideways on and I didn't even blink."

"Oh I was just quick," he blagged. "Got a bit of an electric shock." He reached over to pull the lid shut. As he did so it seemed to take control itself and whirred slowly closed, shutting with a click. The others went back to the boxes and continued their pillaging. Paul looked at his watch. It was late Saturday afternoon. They'd been working round the clock, with barely a break for the odd sandwich and one of them going through to the office to make some tea. They were now just running on adrenaline. "Listen up, everyone," he called. They all paused in what they were doing and looked at him. "It's nearly half past four, in the afternoon. I suggest we take a rest. Get a couple of hours sleep, then crack on. Get back on it about seven, if that's okay?"

"Good idea," said Ernie. "I'm feeling a bit knackered, as it is." They all mumbled their agreement and made their way to the hole, clambering down and returning to the basement. They'd brought sleeping bags with them and they spread out in the basement.

"Here, how we going to wake up on time?" queried Norman.

"Have no fear," said Charlie, producing an alarm clock from his bag. "I come prepared for all occasions."

While they settled down Paul went back through to the vault with a heavy duty canvas holdall. One of several they'd brought to carry their loot away. In the vault he heaved the cylinder off the cabinet. It didn't seem quite so heavy, now. He thought it was probably because he had room to move it, rather than reaching into it's resting place in the safe deposit box. Strapped into the holdall, he carried it through to the basement, and plonked it down next to his sleeping bag.

Chapter 31

Very quickly, exhausted with their work, and excitement, not to say terrified at being almost buried alive, everyone was asleep. The basement was quiet, just the sound of breathing and snoring. Quietly Paul sat up. He carefully opened the canvas bag, and opened the cylindrical box. He put his hand in and grasped the inner, glowing cylinder. He felt a weird tingling run through his body. It was like being both there, yet outside himself. Lifting the cylinder out, it felt weightless in his hand. He turned it over. On the opposite side were many more windows with knurled brass wheels. Through these windows were Chinese characters and symbols. Along with this strange sensation, Paul felt he understood the symbols, and what they meant. He realised that while holding the cylinder he knew exactly what it did, and how to operate it.

He turned the wheels and suddenly the sleeping bags where rolled up in the corner. Then everybody came out of the tunnel, collected their sleeping bags and got in. Heard the faint echo of Norman and Charlie, and Charlie producing his alarm clock. Paul pushed another wheel and everything slipped back to the now. He was sitting on his sleeping bag and everybody else was sound asleep. Putting the cylinder away, closing it up and strapping shut the canvas holdall, he mulled things over. Sliding down into his sleeping bag he realised that what he had was more powerful than he could have imagined. He could actually slip through time. Slip through bloody time. The possibilities were endless. No wonder his bosses wanted to get their hands on it. He listened to the steady breathing and snores of his accomplices. There's no way I'm letting on to them what it does, he thought. Then another thought struck him. I don't have to give it to my bosses either. Reggie Cockscombe can go fly a kite. I get out of here with a bag jam packed with cash and precious stones, like the others, then with my magic cylinder I disappear. As he thought about it, the better it seemed. This - the term Làngfèi shíjiān popped into his mind - can make me impossible to catch.

Seven o'clock, and Charlie's alarm clock had everyone yawning and scratching, but eager to get on with the job. Eric sent Norman upstairs to the office, to make some tea. He didn't know about anybody else, but his mouth tasted like something had died in there. He'd disconnected the cable from the three phase junction box as soon as they'd finished with the drill, so that they could shut the basement strong door. It would be good to get some fresh air down there.

Back in the vault they set to. By midnight they'd opened and emptied all the safe deposit boxes in the vault. They brought the canvass holdalls up and started dividing up their spoils. Papers and documents they discarded into a pile in the corner. Charlie advised them on what to do with the jewellery, mostly to break it up and sell the stones separately. Two items he looked at very carefully, with a wistful look in his eye.

Paul said, "What's up, Charlie?"

Charlie looked up from the piece he was inspecting, "We'll have to leave these two."

"Leave them? Why?" demanded Norman.

"Because they're too well known," answered Charlie, "Even the individual stones. If you tried to shift them you'd have your collar felt before you got a hundred yards down the road."

"Bollocks to that," was Norman's response. "I'll shift them, give them here."

"They stay here," said Paul, sternly. "Nothing jeopardises this job." He took the two items off Charlie and put them in the large safe deposit box that previously held Làngfèi shíjiān. Norman shrugged and carried on sorting through the pile.

"Anyone know what these are?" Ernie held up a large sheet of paper. It looked like some sort of certificate, with the sum of one hundred thousand pounds on it. He had a whole pile of them in his lap.

Paul took it and inspected it. "It's a bearer bond. Whoever holds it owns it. How many have you got there?"

All eyes were on Ernie as he put the pile of bonds on the cabinet top and counted them. "Including that one, twenty five."

Norman let out a whistle. "Wow! two and a half million. Five hundred grand each."

"Hang on," said Paul. "You march into a bank with these, someone will contact the police. There's just been a big bank raid, and suddenly someone like you, no offence Norman, walks in with half a million in bearer bonds. Although, with bearer bonds it should be no questions asked, someone will speak to someone, and someone will call the police."

"What do you suggest?" said Eric. "We can't just leave them."

Paul was thinking quickly to himself. They wouldn't ask any questions in Switzerland. With Làngfèi shíjiān in his possession and the bearer bonds he'd be set up for life. "I'll take them. I know how to shift them, no questions asked. I just give you my share of the boodle, equivalent to their value. How's that sound?"

Norman looked around. They all nodded in agreement. "Fair enough. Lets go through your stash and share it out"

By Sunday evening they were through. Canvas holdalls full to bursting they passed them down out of the vault and dragged them through to the basement. Paul was last up with his holdall containing Làngfèi shíjiān, the two and a half million pounds worth of bearer bonds, and ten thousand pounds in cash. That was his share. Also, the bag did definitely seem lighter. He made a last sweep of the basement, then switched off the lights. He stood in the darkness, looking up at the rectangle of light that was the basement strong door and thought to himself, this is it, this is the start of a whole new life. He went up the stairs, swung the strong door closed and locked it. "Keys." he called. Charlie gave him the other two sets, having got the other one from Ernie and put them in his pocket. While he'd been locking up, the others had opened the loading bay doors and Norman had backed the van in. They all slung their bags in the back. Norman gave up his driving seat and joined Paul and Charlie in the back. Eric got into the driving seat and pulled forward while Ernie closed the loading bay doors. He climbed in the passenger side and the van seemed to sag under the weight of the two large men, and the loot in the back. I just hope no-one thinks a heavily laden van, late on a Sunday night, looks suspicious, thought Paul. As they pulled out into King Street Eric remarked it seemed to be getting foggy. From the junction with Cleveland Place their tail lights blurred by the thickening fog, then disappeared. All was quiet in Cleveland Place.

At about three o'clock, Monday morning, a solitary bobby walked up Cleveland Place, the sound of his footsteps muffled by the now thick fog. By chance it was the same policeman that had caused them a bit of a flap earlier in the week. He walked down the side alley, wondering if they'd be working through the weekend. He found everything in darkness, the loading bay doors closed and securely locked. A brief look round with his torch, and he was on his way. Silence descended on Cleveland Place, the yellow glow from the street lamps barely penetrating the thickening fog.

Chapter 32

4pm, Friday afternoon, and Vernon Kell was leaving his desk and contemplating a large scotch at his club, when the phone on his desk rang. He paused for a second, he could ignore it and pretend he'd missed it. He often thought that, when the phone rang at the end off the day. He never did, though. Generally minor in importance, occasionally they were vital; a matter of life and death. He picked up the phone, and gave his customary response. "K".

"Bant, here," came the reply. "Our friends are having a party, this weekend. Just thought I'd let you know. Could be the odd hangover on Monday." Kell immediately knew he meant the actual break-in to the Swifts Bank's safe deposit vault was about to happen. "We're all gathering at Reg's," continued Bant.

Kell said, "In that case, I think I might join you. I'll see you shortly." He hung up and rapidly left the office.

When Vernon Kell arrived Reg Cockscombe was sat behind his desk leaning back in his chair, legs stretched out underneath the desk, cigarette in hand. William Bant was in one of the two armchairs.

"K" exclaimed Reg, sitting up. Kell shut the door and took his place in the other armchair. Reg needed no prompting to brief K. "Got a call from Rivers, at fifteen forty-five. They're breaking through tonight. They intend to spend the weekend in there, emptying the safe deposit boxes. Rivers will contact me early morning Monday. He'll tell us where to pick him and our item up."

"Very good," said K. "Will you be standing by to monitor, over the weekend?"

"We'll both stay here," interjected Bant. "There's a camp bed in the other office. Overnight we can spell each other on telephone watch."

"So," K stood up and went to the door. "I can leave it in your capable hands." He left and shut the door behind him. Bant stood up and looked at his watch, then strolled over to look out the window behind Cockscombe's chair.

"Tell you what, Reg. I've a couple of things to attend to. What say I get those out of the way. I'll be back by about half past six. Fancy some fish and chips for tea?"

At the mention of fish and chips Reg visibly brightened. "Sounds a very good idea, William. See you later. Bags of salt and vinegar, on mine."

"A man after my own heart," said Bant, and left.

Cockscombe went out to his secretary's office. She was in the process of putting the cover over her typewriter. She seemed mildly surprised that he was still here. "I'm stopping late, this evening," he informed her. "Agent in the field." She took this to mean that one of cockscombe's agents was either in trouble, or about to bring him some very important and secret information.

"Very good, Mr Cockscombe," she said. "See you Monday."

"See you Monday, Miss Jones. Have a nice weekend."

"Thank you, Mr Cockscombe. You too." During this exchange she'd put her scarf and coat on. She picked up her hand bag, and with a cheerful " 'bye" she was gone. As Reginald Cockscombe wandered back to his office he noticed how quiet everything was. There was the clicking of heels disappearing down the stairs, a few farewell calls echoing up from the front vestibule and then silence. Apart from security, at the main entrance, he was alone in this vast building. It always amazed him how quickly the building emptied on Fridays. It started at lunch time. The more senior chaps having lunch at their clubs, then off to their country houses for the weekend. By mid afternoon most of the other senior men had left. Often to join their seniors at their country estate to enjoy a house party, or just getting off early to avoid the evening rush at the end of the week. Five o'clock most evenings the building was still a hive of activity, although starting to quieten down. Five o'clock on a Friday it was like the Marie Celeste.

He shut his office door behind him and lit a cigarette. Going over to the window he looked down into the street, blew a stream of cigarette smoke against the glass. This is going to be a long weekend, he thought to himself. He turned and rummaged through his desk draw, finally disinterring a deck of playing cards and a cribbage board. He plonked them down on his desk top and put his box of Swan Vestas beside them. He wondered which William Bant preferred, brag or cribbage?

3am, Monday morning. Cockscombe's office was a fog of cigarette smoke and nervous expectancy. There was still the faint whiff of fish and chips through the smell of cigarettes and sweat. On the top of the filing cabinet were several dirty tea cups. Their close attention to the silent phone was broken by Vernon Kell opening the door. " 'Morning, gentlemen," he said, then waved a hand if front of his face. "Good lord, would one of you open a window? What's happening, has he been in touch?"

Cockscombe opened the window. Both he and William Bant looked rumpled and tired. "Nothing, yet," he said. "I was hoping he might have been in touch late last night."

"Did you give him a time to call?" asked Kell.

"No. Just to get in touch as soon as he could once they were out."

"Surely they're not still down there?"

"I'd hope not, unless something catastrophic has happened.

Bant maintained his silence. Kell looked across at him. "You're very quiet, William. Any thoughts? This was your endeavour, after all." Bant's lips remained closed in a grim line. He merely shook his head. "Ah, well." He glanced at his watch. "Still time."

As a grubby yellow grey, foggy daylight started creeping through the office window all eyes were either on the clock on the wall, or the stubbornly silent telephone. Seven o'clock came. They were all on there feet smoking. One, or other of them pacing the short distance from wall to wall, or glancing briefly out the window before their attention swung back to the phone.

Eight o'clock Miss Jones put her head round the door. One glance and she knew better than to ask any questions. "Would anyone care for some tea?" she asked, gathering the dirty cups from off the filing cabinet.

"Thanks, Miss Jones," said Bant. "A cup of tea would be wonderful."

Ten minutes later she backed into the office carrying a tray of tea things. "General notice has just come out of Scotland Yard," she said, as she came in and put the tea things down on Cockscombe's desk. "There's been a bank raid." Straightening up she turned and as she walked to the door said "Somebody tunnelled into the vault at Swifts Bank, over the weekend. Took everything."

As the door closed behind her it was as if the temperature in the room had dropped ten degrees. Cockscombe was visibly paler. Bant felt sick.

Kell looked from Bant to Cockscombe and back. "One of you had better get over there and liaise, if that's the right word. It may well be a question of putting out a major fire. William?"

"It had better be Reg. I'm known to Cleveland House, spoke to people in there when scouting for suitable premises."

"Fair enough. Reg, you'd better get over there as soon as you can." He glanced out the window. "Not that anybody's getting anywhere quickly in this fog. If anything it's thicker than when I came in earlier."

"On my way." Cockscombe grabbed his hat and coat and left.

"William, you'd best stay here in case he does call. I'm going to my office. Let me know the instance anything happens." Then he was gone. Bant was on his own with the silent telephone.

William Bant slumped behind the desk. What the hell had happened? Although Reg had been the point man, Rivers' contact, provider of all they needed; money, property, front company, it was his, William Bant's operation, his bright idea. They may have complete deniability, enough cut-outs to prevent anybody connecting this to His Majesty's Government's more secretive offices. Yet he still felt a sickness in the pit of his stomach. He'd initiated a highly illegal, very expensive operation, raiding a highly respected bank, just a stone's throw from where he now sat. The telephone remained silent, almost mocking him.

Chapter 33

DI Simms had barely got into his office, let alone taken his coat off, when the phone on his desk started ringing. He leaned across and picked it up. "DI Simms," he announced.

"Whitstable," said Simms' superior, by way of introduction."You remember that incident with the Chinese and Swifts Bank?"

"I'm hardly likely to forget it, Sir," replied Simms.

"Well, they've been turned over."

"What, the Chinese?" Simms smiled to himself.

"No, you fool, Swifts Bank. Someone tunnelled into their vault over the weekend. Sounds as if they emptied everything. You and Brown get over there. You're officer in charge ."

"Can't DS Brown deal with it, Sir. I've got a million and one things to be getting on with."

"Well, now it's a million and two. It's not just the where, it's the who."

"Sir?"

"The people who keep their stuff squirrelled away in safe deposit boxes, at Swifts Bank. It's Pall Mall, not the Clapham branch. There will be people who know people, very important people. Some of them won't want their grubby little secrets falling into the wrong hands. It won't just be diamond tiaras and bearer bonds. Now get to it."

"Yes, Sir." At that moment DS Brown came into the office. "Don't take your hat off, Tom, we've got a job. I'll explain on the way."

As DI Simms and DS Brown crossed the pavement, from their car to the front portico of Swifts Bank, a black Humber appeared out of the fog and pulled up behind their Wolesly. Reginald Cockscombe got out and joined them at the top of the steps. He interrupted them as they were talking to the constable at the front door.

He produced an identity card, "Cockscombe, Security Services. Which of you is in charge?" He looked from Brown to Simms.

'I am, Detective Inspector Simms, Scotland Yard. This is my sergeant DS Brown." They all shook hands and went into the bank. The banking hall was deathly quiet. The staff were standing together, behind the counter, but no one was speaking. After the immediate excitement of the break-in's discovery there now came the lull. Nothing to say. They'd said, and speculated, all they could. The day to day just didn't seem appropriate right now. Another constable stood by the door to the rear of the bank. Simms walked over, "Where is the manager?" he asked.

"Through here, Sir, down the stairs." He held the door open for them pointing to the staircase leading to the vault.

Simms briefly turned to the constable, nodded at Cockscombe and said, "This gentleman is with the security services."

"Yes, Sir," said the constable.

At the bottom of the stairs a uniformed sergeant stood in front of an open vault door. By his side stood the bank's general manger, Sir Bernard MacIntyre. "Inspector Simms." he said. "This is a damnable business." He glanced past Simms and nodded at DS Brown, "Sergeant," then he looked at Cockscombe, then back at Simm. " Who's this?"

"My name's Cockscombe," he said, taking his ID card out and briefly showing Sir Bernard. "Security Services," he announced putting the ID card away again before Sir Bernard even had a chance to read it. He walked past everyone, and stepped into the vault.

"Sir," said the sergeant, looking from Cockscombe to Simms, "The fingerprint people."

"It's alright, sergeant," said Simms following Cockscombe into the vault. "We'll be careful. Besides, the forensics chap will be ages in this fog."

The vault was a mess. All the safe deposit box doors were hanging open, a good few hanging off their hinges. The actual boxes were scattered about, but mostly tossed in a heap in the corner, along with loads of spurious papers. Certificates, births, deaths, marriages and God knew what else. Cockscombe's eye was drawn to what was by far the largest box, it's bent and battered door hanging open. He walked over and peered in. An empty felt lined wooden cradle, two felt lined iron straps thrown back and two sheared padlocks. Resting in the bottom were two exquisite pieces of jewellery. Simms was peering over his shoulder, "Now why would they leave those behind?" he wondered out loud.

"May I?" said Sir Bernard, leaning in to take a look. "Ah, The Tollemache Diamonds and the Earlheim Rubies. There's a very simple reason they didn't take them, they're too well known."

"Which means whoever did this knew their stuff," chimed in Brown.

"Indeed they do," mused Simms. "Couldn't they have just taken the stones out, and fenced those?" He turned toward Sir Bernard with his eyebrows raised in question.

"No, no" Sir Bernard gave a thin smile. "Historical and famous jewellery pieces happens to be something of a hobby of mine. Even the individual stones are too well known. No one would touch them, they're too easily traced. They would need an expert cutter to change them, which would dramatically reduce their value plus take time to arrange."

"I see," said Simms. "Do you know what was in this particular safe?"

"As a matter of fact I do. That unfortunate Chinaman who was murdered, placed the item he brought to the bank in there. It was in a large wooden box. It took two of my staff to carry it down here for him."

"Did you see what it was?" broke in Cockscombe.

"No, I didn't. He demanded to be left alone in the vault so naturally we left him to it. Left us the wooden box and it's packaging to get rid of. Mind you he had paid a substantial amount, for the safe. It was paid up to the year two thousand and thirty one."

Suddenly all eyes were on him. "Till when?" said DS Brown, incredulously.

"Two thousand and thirty one, sergeant," replied Sir Bernard, smugly. Then a look of horror spread across his face. "He's going to want this money back, isn't he?"

Cockscombe had wandered over to the hole in the concrete floor. "I doubt it, Sir Bernard, he's dead, isn't he?" He peered down the hole. "No steel floor, I see, just good old fashioned concrete."

Sir Bernard flustered. "Well, I...I...we...We didn't think anybody would be tunnelling through the floor in Pall Mall," he finally said, indignantly.

"Well, you were wrong there, weren't you?" said Cockscombe, looking over. Sir Bernard glared at him. A stoney silence descended on the vault.

Then Sir Bernard asked Cockscombe, "Why exactly are you here, Mr Cosman?"

"Cockscombe, the name's Cockscombe. Well, a Chinese national deposits something very big, in your vault, for the services of which he's paid you a silly amount of money. The very same day he's murdered. Then another Chinese National comes here and demands you hand over whatever it is. But he has no credentials that allow you to hand it over. Now, it's been nicked, along with everything else of value." Cockscombe stopped himself. Had he said too much already. He just prayed they didn't think he was putting too much emphasis on it. Concentrate on the Chinese nationals aspect. "Our concern is the Chinese Government. If they think we've allowed one of their treasures to be stolen, it's not just the Bank that's in for a rough ride.

One of the constables came running down the stairs and addressed the uniformed sergeant. "There's a crowd gathering outside, Sarge, some of them are getting quite heated. I think they've got stuff down here."

"Oh God, it's started," groaned Sir Bernard and made for the door. As he got to the sergeant he said, "Sergeant, could your constables let in just those who have safe deposit boxes here. Tell everybody else we're closed for business, today. Come back tomorrow."

"Very good, Sir" he replied

"And get him to take a note of all their names," added Simms.

"Some of them might not want to." Sir Bernard said, with concern in his voice.

"Then they don't come in. Pure and simple. You've got that Sergeant?"

"Yes sir," he said, then spoke to the Constable, who ran back up the stairs to carry out his orders, followed by a somewhat disturbed Sir Bernard. But for all that, when he walked through the door into the banking hall he had the air of confidence and dignified calm.

The men and women coming in through the imposing front doors were greeted by a calm and reassuring Sir Bernard. He assured them everything would be sorted out and there was nothing to worry about, but the questions came thick and fast. He knew he wouldn't be able to fob them off for long. Two men, carrying attache cases, fought their way through the throng. Informed Sir

Bernard they were from the police forensic department, and went on through.

As the two men approached the vault, the sergeant called through to Simms that the fingerprint boys were here. Once Simms spoke to them and got them sorted out, he went and joined Brown and Cockscombe by the hole.

"Shall we go down and have a butchers, then?" asked Brown.

"Of course," said Simms. "We need to find out where this goes, and see what they've left behind." He turned to Cockscombe, "You coming?"

"Lead on McDuff," was his reply. In fact he was getting quite worried. With having heard nothing, it wasn't inconceivable Rivers, and his gang were trapped, or worse, buried under a fall-in.

He followed Simms and Brown down the short ladder, into the chamber underneath. They both had torches and lit the way, Cockscombe using their light to follow on.

Brown swung his torch around, and lit upon the industrial electric drill shoved to one side. "Well they certainly had the kit for it." He commented. Then they crouched down and scrambled through the tunnel. No fall-in, but cramped and dirty. By the time they emerged into the chamber beneath the basement they were filthy, hands and trouser knees covered in mud. Simms shone his torch up into the basement, then clambered up the ladder to stand beneath Cleveland House. Though at this time he hadn't a clue as to where they were.

"Where the hell are we?" asked Brown, of no one in particular.

"Good question," said Simms. He found a light switch and the basement was brought into stark view. They went through the rooms. Sleeping bags piled in a corner, an empty table that had held the plans. In the farthest rooms heaps of earth, and the smelly London Clay. Simms went up the stairs to the strong door. It was locked. He looked for a handle or some such. Nothing, just a brass keyhole, with Chubb stamped on it. He banged on the door a few times. Silence. He banged again and shouted. They waited. Nothing. "Right," said Simms, "Altogether, let's make a racket." He and Brown battered at the door. Brown had even found a hammer to bash it with. All three of them started shouting at the tops of their voices.

About 10 am Dot asked her two colleagues if they fancied a cup of tea. She then went into the little kitchenette to make it. As she went through she heard a noise, but put it down to the workmen arriving. She was in a cheerful mood, and sung to herself as she got the tea things ready and waited for the kettle to boil. As the whistle, from the kettle, died down she thought she heard someone shouting, so after warming the pot and filling the teapot she went into the corridor. There it was again. She went down to the door that led into the loading bay. It was locked, but she could hear it clearly now. Someone was shouting for help and banging loudly on something. She ran back into the office to get Cynthia Goldsmith.

"What's going on?" asked Milly, sticking her head round the door from reception.

"Nothing for you to worry about, Miss Dobson," said Cynthia.

"Someone's stuck out the back," said Dot. "They're banging and shouting."

"Let's not get over excited, Miss Dobson," responded Cynthia, "It could be something and nothing." She went down the corridor to the loading bay door and rattled the handle. She also heard the banging and shouting. "My goodness," she exclaimed, coming back to the other two. "Something's definitely wrong. Have the Major, or Mr Smith come in yet?"

"No, Miss Goldsmith," replied Milly.

"Well the doors locked," said Cynthia. "Do either of you have a key?" She received a double negative. "Very well. It's an emergency, I'll go up and see if Mr Smith, or the Major have any keys in their desk."

"Oh that'll take too long," said Milly. "Here." She pulled a hair pin out of her hair and got a paper clip off her desk. "It's a trick I learned off an old boyfriend. Just don't tell anyone." She went and knelt by the loading bay door, fiddling the pin and paper clip in the lock. After about ninety seconds there was a click, and she pushed the door open. The three of them went into the loading bay. It was empty. They looked around. Suddenly the cacophony started again, making all three of them jump out of their skins.

"Someone's stuck in the basement" said Cynthia, stating the somewhat obvious. She went over to the strong door and, at a pause in the noise, knocked on the door shouting "Who's there!"

"It's the police," came a voice, muffled by the steel door. "Open the door."

The three girls looked at each other in complete bewilderment. How on earth did the police manage to get themselves locked in the basement.

"We haven't got the key," shouted Cynthia.

"I'll check the Major's and Mr Smith's offices," said Milly, and rushed off back into the offices.

"Hang on," cried Cynthia at the steel door. "One of us is going to see if there's a key in either of the manager's offices."

"Okay," came the reply. "By the way, where are we?"

Dot and Cynthia looked at each other in puzzlement. "You're in the basement," shouted Dot with a frown. Cynthia gave her a look.

"No, which building?" They looked at each other wide eyed.

"Cleveland House," shouted Cynthia. "In Cleveland Place, off King Street."

The other side of the door Reg Cockscombe had gone back down the stairs. "I have to make a call." he informed them.

"I'll come with you."said Simms. "Tom, you wait here for them to let you out, and get their details."

DS Brown turned and sat down on the top step. "Righty oh."

Simms and Cockscombe were under the basement when Brown came trotting up. "They can't find a key, Sir," he called down.

"Okay," said Simms. "Come back through with us. When we get back to the bank, give the 'Yard a ring and get them to send the duty locksmith round to Cleveland house. Let them know it's a Chubb security lock, on a basement steel door."

The three of them scrambled back through to the bank, their dirty appearance drawing surprised looks from uniforms and bank staff alike.

"Good God!" exclaimed Sir Bernard when he saw them . "What on earth happened?"

"We just went through the tunnel. Let's just say it's functional, not wall to wall fitted carpet."

"Where does it lead to?"

"Cleveland House."

"Good God." You just said that, thought DS Brown, to himself. "There's that new precious metals trading company just moved in there, something Holdings ..." Sir Bernard's voice tailed off as the penny dropped.

"I'm going on round there," said Simms. "I'll walk, it'll be quicker in this fog." Through the glass of the front door he could see it's yellowy grey swirl obscuring almost everything. At least it's keeping the sightseers away, he thought.

"I need to make a call," said Cockscombe, to Sir Bernard.

"Certainly, just through there." He waved at an employee who opened the door through to behind the counter. He then went back to firefighting with his distraught customers.

Cockscombe dialled his own office. It was answered before the first ring had time to finish. "Yes?" It was a frantic William Bant.

"It's Reg," said Cockscombe. "I take it you've heard nothing."

"Not a dicky bird. I hoped it might have been Rivers just then."

"Right, I'm coming back to the office. Nothing here. No bodies, no one trapped. The policeman in charge is a DI Simms. He was in charge of the Chinaman murder case."

"Is that good or bad?" Bant was beginning to doubt his own judgement. This whole episode was causing him more upset than he cared to admit.

"Don't know" replied Cockscombe. "I'll be back shortly, which may be longer, with this fog." He hung up, thanked Sir Bernard as he passed him, and left.

Chapter 34

DI Simms came through the front door of Cleveland House, bringing a swirl of yellowy grey fog in with him. There was a group of people gathered round the reception desk. They all looked over as he came in. He realised he must still look bit of a sight, although he'd managed to clean up a bit. He still had marks from the tunnel on his coat and the knees of his trousers.

"Who the hell are you?" demanded a florid faced man wearing a guard's tie.

"Detective Inspector Horace Simms, Scotland Yard, Sir, and who are you?"

"Oh, I'm William DeVere, DeVere Cummings. We're upstairs." He sounded little flustered, yet maintained his upright, and somewhat belligerent manner.

"So what is the company, on this floor?" asked Simms, looking around at the rest of them.

"Hilditch Holdings, Detective Inspector." This was Cynthia Goldsmith. "To be exact, Hilditch Holdings, brackets precious metals, close brackets, and Associates." She turned and picked a sheet of headed notepaper off the reception desk. "Here" she handed it to Simms.

Simms glanced at it, folded it and put in his pocket, "Thank you, Miss?"

"Goldsmith, Miss Cynthia Goldsmith, Office Manager" she gave a nervous smile.

"Right," said Simms. "Who works here, for Hilditch Holdings?" Cynthia, Dot and Milly raised their hands. Apart from William DeVere, there was another man in a pinstripe double breasted suit, and a middle aged woman in a quite formal white blouse and straight, dark grey skirt. "So who are you two, and where do you work?"

"I'm Fiona Randle," said the woman.

"And I'm Simon Ducket," added the man. "We both work for James and Partners. We're on the fifth, just below William." He indicated DeVere.

"Who's on the other floors?" Simms enquired, scribbling rapidly in his note book.

"On three and four it's Pollard Wilson," added Ducket.

"And we're on ground, first and second floors," said Cynthia.

"Not to mention the basement," said Simms, partly to himself.

"Yes, of course," Cynthia blushed slightly.

"Now, then," announced Simms. "I'd like you all to return to your offices, and remain there. My sergeant and I will be up to talk to you in a while. Thank you." He'd no sooner spoken when a portly gentleman with a large handlebar moustache, wearing a grey overcoat and bowler hat barged in through the front door.

"Have you heard?" He almost bellowed as he came through the door. "Swifts Bank have been robbed. Some scoundrels tunnelled into their safe deposit vault over the weekend. Got away with millions, I'll be bound. Glad I'm with Coutts."

Dot fainted.

As they fussed round her, the portly gentleman looked at them with a bemused look on his face. "What? What's wrong, what did I say?"

"They tunnelled in from the basement here, Sir. I'm Detective Inspector Simms, from Scotland Yard. I'm in charge of the case."

The portly gentleman stood there wide eyed and open mouthed. Then, after a fair impression of a goldfish, managed a "Good God!"

"Could I have your name, please Sir?"

"Sir Robert Prestbury. They tunnelled from here, you say? How did they do that without anybody noticing?"

"That's what I'm hoping to find out, Sir Robert. Can I ask your business here?"

"Certainly, Detective Inspector. I have an appointment with William, here."

"Thank you, Sir." Simms made a note in his notebook. "I've asked that nobody leaves the building until we've spoken to them."

"Well I don't know what I can tell you," he said, indignantly.

"It's okay, Sir Robert," said DeVere, ushering him towards the lift, "It's been a shock for all of us. Best let them get on with their job. They know what they're doing."

"Yes. Yes, quite so." He let himself be led off. Simon Ducket and Fiona Randle followed them.

As they went off to the lift a car pulled up outside. Then Detective Sergeant Brown came into the building, followed by two uniformed constables. "I've brought Stubbs and Hacket along, Sir. They can cover the front door, and the basement. Make sure it's secure."

"Good thinking, Sergeant," said Simms. He turned to the three ladies remaining in the foyer. Dot was sat on Milly's chair, behind the reception desk, dabbing her eyes with a hankie. The other two stood beside her. "Well then, ladies, shall we go on through. I need some answers, and I think we could all do with a cup of tea. As they went through he hung back slightly to speak quietly with Brown. "I don't think they have a clue."

"Either that," added Brown, "or bloody good actors." A still tearful Dot, and Cynthia were in Cynthia's office while Milly made some tea. Simms took his pipe out and started fingering tobacco into the bowl from a worn leather pouch. Brown cleared his throat. "Sir."

He gave the pipe and tobacco pouch a meaningful glance.

"It's quite alright, sergeant," said Cynthia. "I rather like a man with a pipe." She smiled at Simms. Then blushed when she realised how that seemed. "Well, you know what I mean."

Simms smiled to ease her embarrassment. "Yes, and thank you Miss Goldsmith." He looked across at Brown with a triumphant smile that was almost immediately hidden behind a cloud of smoke.

Milly came through with a tray of tea things. "Best leave the door open, Miss," said Brown with a sardonic edge to his voice, aimed squarely at his boss.

"So," said Simms, once they were all settled, "if you could give me your names and position. Starting with you, Miss Goldsmith." Cynthia gave her position as office manager, then the others, in turn. Millicent Dobson, receptionist and Dorothy Harding, clerk and typist. DS Brown duly noted them all in his note book. "Who's in charge then?" he asked.

"Well Major Cook is the general manager," Cynthia replied.

"And Paul Smith, his personal assistant," added Milly.

"Though they're not in, yet, this morning," said Cynthia,

"Probably this horrible fog," put in Dot quietly.

"I don't think you'll be seeing either of them anytime soon," said Brown.

The three girls looked from one to the other, then Cynthia said, "That can't be right, Major Cook has an appointment at Coutts tomorrow."

"Yes, and the Chairman, Lord Balmuir, is due soon." Milly said. It was as if they were trying to deny to themselves the truth that was staring them in the face. They'd been duped into the cover for a bank robbery.

"Lord Balmuir?" Simms enquired. "Have you met him?"

Cynthia said, "No, Major Cook said he was in America and would be joining us once we were up and running."

"There is no Lord Balmuir, is there?" said Milly, gloomily. "No Hilditch Holdings, no new vault in the basement." She looked up at DI Simms with a combined look of sorrow and disappointment.

He looked at her with a grim smile. "I think you're probably right, Miss Dobson. This whole set up seems to have been for the sole purpose of gaining access to the vault in Swifts Bank."

A silence descended on the room. While there was a pause in proceedings Brown popped into the other office to use the phone. Simms finished his tea. "Miss Goldsmith," he said, "Would you be so kind as to show me the other offices, please? If you two could remain here, for the moment."

As they were about to leave the office a short stocky man in blue overalls, and carrying a tool case came through the door. "Arthur Griffiths, duty locksmith," he announced, in a strong South Wales accent. "I believe you need a door opening. Somebody mentioned a Chubb?"

"Ah, Good. If you could wait here a second, Miss Goldsmith. Follow me Mr Griffiths." He led Griffiths through to the back.

Arthur Griffiths placed his tool case at his feet and closely inspected the outside of the Chubb lock on the basement strong door. "Hmm, normally, with a lock like this, I'd cut round it. However, a steel door's a different kettle of fish. How soon do you want to get in there?"

"Oh we can get in there," replied Simms, drawing an old-fashioned look from Griffiths. "Via the vault in Swifts Bank," he added.

A light of realisation went on in Griffiths' eyes. "Oh, I see. So this is…?" He left the question trailing.

"Indeed it is," confirmed Simms. "So speed isn't necessarily of the essence."

"Right oh. I'll need to pick the lock. These are quite awkward, and may take some time."

"Can you do it?"

"Can I pick it, indeed. There's not a lock on God's earth I can't pick. Just leave me to it, boyo, I'll give you a shout when it's open."

"Fair enough. Once it's open, don't go in. Don't want you messing up any evidence."

"I'm not a complete amateur, boyo. This isn't the first time I've had to unlock a place that's had a crime committed in it, if you get my drift." He crouched and started rummaging in his tool case.

"Sorry," said Simms, "Didn't mean to sound rude, but this is something rather big."

"Right oh," said Griffiths, without looking round. He produced a canvas roll from his case and unrolled it. It contained a whole series of strange looking implements, gleaming dully in the loading bay's light. They resembled a set of dental instruments, more than anything else. He selected two that had long, thin, bent ends to them, and set to work on the lock. "You can leave me to it, now, boyo." He said over his shoulder.

Simms returned to the others, in the front office. He and Cynthia Goldsmith went up the stairs to inspect the other offices. Cynthia hardly spoke all the time Simms was going through the offices. He rummaged through paperwork on desks, in particular Major Cook's office, looked in drawers and cabinets. Finding them mostly empty he realised the lengths the gang had gone to to set up this sham. Cynthia merely told him who's office it was, then stood just inside with her arms folded, watching him root through everything. Finally they stood in the boardroom. "Did they ever have any board meetings, Miss Goldsmith?" Asked Simms.

Cynthia looked grimly at the floor and shook her head, "No, Detective Inspector. They didn't have any meetings. Major Cook and Mr Smith were the only two here." There was a slight catch in her voice as she said, "Lord Balmuir was supposed to be arriving next week." She looked up at Simms. "It was all a sham, wasn't it? What happens to us now? Will we be charged with helping them?"

"I doubt that, Miss Goldsmith," Simms smiled and spoke kindly to her. "The three of you will have to come to Scotland Yard, with us, to be interviewed and give a formal statement. But I don't think you need to worry about any charges." Simms felt genuinely sorry for her, and her two colleagues. Duped into taking what they thought was honest work, only to be left high and dry as soon as the gang carried out their raid. Sergeant Brown's voice shouted up from the floor below, that the door was open. Simms glanced round the boardroom. He'd gleaned all he could from here. He'd send the fingerprint boys over to give it all a more thorough going over, but there was nothing more for him. "Come," he said gently to Cynthia, ushering her out of the room. They went downstairs and were greeted by Griffiths enjoying a cup of tea. "All done, then?" asked Simms.

"Yes indeed boyo," said Griffiths. "Took me just over twenty minutes. Must be a personal best for me, on that type of lock."

"Thank you," said Simms. He got the uniform constable to stay with the girls while he and Brown went out to the back. They looked round the loading bay. There was some unused shoring timber, but not much else. All the tools were in the basement, or the space they'd dug out under the vault at Swifts Bank.

Sergeant Brown was looking around and noticed the three phase junction box. On closer inspection he could see marks around it where Eric Teale had hooked up the power cable for the drill. "Look at this, Guv'," called Brown. "This must be where they got the power for that drill down there. The cable's that jumble at the foot of the stairs."

Simms came over and had a look. "Must be," he said. "No other electrical source down here. This is a three phase junction box. Must be some drill they got themselves."

"Three phase?" puzzled Brown. "Why's there phase in an office building?"

"It's probably where the power comes in for the lift," replied Simms. "The lift was put in some time after the place was built, so this is the logical place to bring the power in."

"Lucky them," muttered Brown.

Simms went over to the basement door and looked down the steps. "Uniform can go through this lot," he said. "Let's get the ladies over to the Yard, and see what we can get out of them. Not much, is my guess."

"They were completely taken in," added Brown. "The Harding girl keeps bursting into tears and Milly Dobson has a face on her like thunder. She was hoping this would be a nice secure job for her, looking to get engaged soon. She thought this Paul Smith was a very nice man, and Major Cook was, and I quote, 'A real gentleman'. Can't believe she was taken in by them."

"They have my sympathy," said Simm. "Before we go, get on to Whitstable, see if he can let us have some DCs to interview the other tenants. We can't do it all ourselves."

Chapter 35

The three of them were in Kell's office, the air so thick with cigarette smoke it was as bad as the fog outside.

"What the hell's happened?" snapped Kell. "I thought this was all organised. Everybody had there instructions. Where the hell is Rivers?" Neither Bant, nor Cockscombe had seen K this angry before. "What if, unlikely as it now seems, Rivers tries to get in touch?"

"Miss Jones is monitoring the phone and will contact me here," said Cockscombe.

"And his flat? What's happening there?"

"I checked it on the way back from Swifts. Empty. He appears to have flown the coup. Wardrobe virtually empty, shaving gear and toiletries gone from the bathroom. That's not the worst, though."

"Go on."

"He's licensed for a fire arm, a revolver. It's missing, along with his legend box."

"Jesus Christ! Has he gone rogue on us?"

"I'll get on to Back Office," put in Bant. "Find out what aliases he had, and what false documentation." and hurriedly left.

"Good man," said K. "Reg, are we watching the flat?"

"Yes, K. I sent a couple of men there as soon as I got back."

"Very good, Reg, Get back to the Yard, find out where they're up to. Make a nuisance of yourself, stick a rocket up their arse. We need to put a lid on this PDQ."

"What reason shall I give?"

"Oh, feed them some guff about diplomatic documents of a friendly nation were taken. You know, the usual stuff. If it gets into the wrong hands. Potential damage to international relations. You could even throw in something about Germany rearming. Just keep the pressure on. Oh, and use your out of office name. What is it currently?"

"Wilson," said Cockscombe, "but the DI in charge already knows me as Cockscombe."

"That doesn't matter," replied Kell. "Keep them on their toes, and they won't think either of them are your real name. Bit more distance, if you follow."

"Yes, 'K' . And the more distance the better," said Cockscombe with a grim smile, and followed Bant from the room. Kell went and stood by his window, lit another cigarette and stared out at the fog. How quickly, what at first seemed a jolly good idea, can turn into a complete crock of shit, he thought to himself. He tried to think of the upside to all of this. With a sigh he realised there wasn't one and turned back to his desk.

At Scotland Yard Reg Cockscombe sat across from an irritated DCI Herbert Whitstable, who was taking his frustration out on his pipe. Digging out the charred remains of tobacco and tapping it out angrily into a heavy glass ashtray on his desk. "So, Mr Wilson?"

"Yes, Wilson," said Cockscombe.

"You want the Yard to keep a lid on this for diplomatic reasons too confidential for my delicate ears, is that right?"

"We would be most grateful, Chief Inspector. Some of the papers stolen from Swifts Bank's vault are highly confidential, the property of a friendly power. Should they fall into the wrong hands the results could be catastrophic. I don't need to tell you the concern over what's happening in Germany."

Whitstable harrumphed and muttered something about Herr Hitler might be on to something.

"Sorry, Chief Inspector, did you say something?" asked Cockscombe, with a slight sarcastic edge to his voice.

"No, no." said Whitstable. "We'll do as you wish. I'll inform DI Simms the need for discretion and we'll keep you informed of developments."

"Thank you. I don't need to tell you that we need a speedy resolution to this mess. No resource spared, use everything at your disposal."

"Thank you, Mr Wilson, but I do know how to do my job, and DI Simms is one of my most competent and experienced officers."

"Well thank you again, Chief Inspector," said Cockscombe, standing up. He offered his hand across the desk to Whitstable, who also stood and, with a certain amount of reluctance reached across and shook it.

"Mr Wilson," said Whitstable, as a dismissal. After Cockscombe had gone he stood for a minute or two at his office window. Standing with his thumbs hooked into his waistcoat pockets he pondered the conversation he'd just had with Reg Cockscombe, his Mr Wilson. He took his watch out and checked the time. Less than seven hours since they'd first been notified about the break-in and bloody Home Office were all over him. Diplomatic this, confidential that. Christ Almighty, why isn't coppering straight forward anymore? He went back to his desk, picked up the telephone and dialled the outer office. "Are DI Simms and Sergeant Brown back in the building yet?" he asked. He received an affirmative and asked they be sent up to his office.

Five minutes later a knock on his office door and Simms and Brown entered. "Ah, there you are," said Whitstable. "Please, both be seated. How are we getting along, have you got any leads yet?"

Simms sat up in his chair and took out his pipe, noting that Whitstable was filling his. Whitstable nodded his permission, with a wry smile at Brown's look of resignation. "We've spoken to the employees, the three ladies and I'm fairly convinced they know nothing. They were duped into being an effective front for the gang. To be frank, they're quite upset by the whole thing. They've lost their jobs, obviously, and now they'll be in the papers as part of the story. The other companies, in the building, likewise know nothing. They passed the time of day with the two men running the show. Sergeant?"

Brown took out his notebook and flipped through it, "A Mr Paul Smith and a Major Charles Cook."

"I see," said Whitstable. "The reason I've called you in is I've had a visit from the Home Office." Both Simms and Brown looked surprised. "Chap calling himself Wilson, though I doubt that's his real name, paid me a visit."

"If it's the chap we saw heading for the front door as we came up, he told us his name was Cockscombe when he turned up at the bank, this morning. Had a Security Services pass."

"Really?" Now it was Whitstable's turn to be surprised. "That's interesting. He want's it kept out of the papers, put a lid on it, as he put it. Apparently some highly sensitive papers have been stolen, along with everything else. What else have you got?"

"Well," said Simms, "Whoever they are, they're highly organised and well financed. I've got men going through all the office paperwork, with the help of the women. They've actually got invoices and cheque stubs for the equipment and materials they used to break in. We're contacting the various suppliers, to see if they can give us anything, but I don't hold out to much hope."

"Any other evidence? Clothing, personal belongings, anything like that?"

"No, Sir," replied Simms.

"What about fingerprints?"

"Loads of them, all over the place. Looks like they didn't care. Either they're not on record, which I think is unlikely, or they had their escape well planned in advance. It'll be a couple of days, at least before we get any results. Even longer if they're not on record as they'll have to check everything to make sure."

"Lean on them, Simms. Use my authority, tell them about Home Office pressure. They must prioritise the fingerprints from this case above everything else."

"Very good, Sir." Simms and Brown got up to leave.

"And don't forget, keep it quiet. Have a word with the ladies that worked for them. Tell them not to speak to the press. Might be an idea to spread the word among the other companies in that building, and have a word with your team. I'll issue an interdepartmental bulletin telling everybody to keep quiet, no unofficial press briefings etc. I'll have a word with the Commissioner once you've gone. Don't know why that Wilson fellow, or Cockscombe, as you called him, didn't go straight to him in the first place. Cut out the middle man, I suppose."

Chapter 36

Friday morning saw Simms and Brown back in Whitstable's office. Both men had their notebooks out and were standing. "We've been to all the companies the gang dealt with. Nothing. Paid on time, cheques didn't bounce. As far as they were concerned Hilditch Holdings was a dependable, reputable company. Sergeant Brown checked them out at Companies House, and they're a bona fide, registered company. Sergeant?"

"Yes, Sir. Hilditch Holdings, open brackets, Precious Metals, close brackets, and Associates. Registered in November 1897. Only one current director listed, a Lord Balmuir, current whereabouts unknown. Disappeared a couple of years ago up the Amazon, or into Darkest Africa, depending who you speak to. No one's seen hide nor hair of him since." Brown looked up from his notebook, "That's it, Sir."

"This whole thing's starting to sound fishier and fishier," said Whitstable. "This seems far too sophisticated for a bank robbery. I think friend Wilson, Cockscombe, or whatever his bloody name is, knows a damn sight more than he's letting on." As he finished speaking the phone on his desk rang. He picked it up, "Yes? He's here. Just a moment." He held the handset out to Simms. "It's the fingerprint Johnnies, they've got some results."

"Excellent," said Simms taking the receiver. He listened, making notes in his notebook, as they spoke. Finally he hung up. "They've identified four sets of prints. Earnest Banks, Charles Cook, Eric Teale and Norman Thomas. They're sending the details over. There's one set they're still checking, but it doesn't look as if he's known. I wouldn't mind betting it's the one calling himself Paul Smith"

"You're probably right. I bet our Mr Wilson knows," said Whitstable. "You didn't hear me say that." He gave them a meaningful look. "Right, off you go. If we can get hold of them, or at least one of them, we can start making headway."

Brown turned to Simms as they were heading downstairs to their office. "That name Charles Cook rings a bell. Charles Cook, Charlie Cook! Yes. Got him. If it's who I think it is, being their Major Cook would suit him down to the ground. In fact, if I remember correctly, he used to refer to himself as Major Cook. Was involved in some dodgy antiques fiddle a while back."

As they reached their office they intercepted a uniform constable on his way to them with an armful of manila folders. "The fingerprint results, Sir."

"Thank you, constable," said Simms. Brown relieved him of the folders and they went on in.

"So," said Simms, taking the top folder, just as Brown dumped them on the desk. "Let's have a look see." The top folder contained a synopsis of the fingerprint department's results. "It says here they've identified four out of five sets of prints. That's these four here." He tapped the pile with the stem of his pipe. "Friends Banks, Cook, Teale and Thomas. Let's pay them all a visit, see if they're where they're supposed to be and if they can shed any light on their anonymous colleague." They quickly went through the folders, making notes of their addresses, and places they were likely to be. "Right," said Simms, "I want four teams. You head one and I'll head another. We'll each take two uniforms with us. Set up two more teams of two uniforms and a DC. We'll try and hit them all at the same time, give them no chance to warn the others."

"What if they're not in?" asked Brown. "'cos they probably won't be."

"Then we chase them down, Tom, we chase them down," he said with a gleam in his eye. "I'm not letting these bastards get away. Let's go."

Chapter 37

DCI Simms and DS Brown were both feeling frustrated. They'd tried to catch Banks and Teale respectively to no avail. Neither were at their home addresses, which was to be expected, but there was no sign of them at any of their known haunts. By chance they both arrived at a snooker hall in Peckham at the same time. Arriving from opposite directions hoping to each catch their respective quarry at a shared meeting place. Again they were unlucky. All enquiries met with shakes of the head and open hostility. Most claimed they'd never heard of Banks or Teale. Those that grudgingly acknowledged they knew them swearing they hadn't seen them for weeks.

Outside, on the pavement Simms lit his pipe and Brown lit one of his rare cigarettes. "I'll call in, see if the others have had any luck," said Brown, going over to his car, the two uniformed constables already back inside. Brown climbed into the passenger seat, leaving the door open as Simms followed him to the car. Brown lifted the radio handset and called in, "Bravo one to control, over."

"Control to Bravo one. Receiving, go ahead, over."

"Bravo one, any reports from Charlie One, and Delta One? Over."

"Control, Delta One has just reported in. They have apprehended Cook and Thomas at Cook's premises. They're bringing them in now. Over."

"Roger that, Control. Contact Charlie One and tell them to call off the hunt. We're on our way back. Out." As Brown slammed his door shut, Simms was already jumping into his car. Simms' driver executed a neat, hurried three point turn in the narrow road and they both sped off back to the 'Yard.

When they arrived back, Cook and Thomas had just been processed and put in separate cells. Simms and Brown hung their hats and coats up, on the stand in the corner of their office. "Shall I take Cook, while you have a crack at Thomas, Sir?" asked Brown.

"No, I think we'll both see them, one after the other," said Simms, "Let's start with Cook." He picked the folder up from his desk as he spoke.

Cook was already in the interview room when they arrived. Brown nodded the uniform constable out and they sat down across the table from Cook. It was a bleak room that stank of stale sweat and staler tobacco smoke, its ceiling stained yellow from the nicotine. The battered wooden table was empty apart from a cheap tin ashtray, the tabletop scarred by numerous burns from cigarettes left perched on the edge, or even stubbed out on it. Simms opened the folder in front of him and Brown opened his notebook. "I'm Detective Inspector Simms, and this is Detective Sergeant Brown. You are Charles Raymond Cook?"

"Yes," came the monosyllabic response.

"We'd like to ask you some questions, Mr Cook, or can I call you Charlie?"

A shrug.

"We know, that you know you don't have to say anything, but it would be helpful, and you'd be doing yourself a favour by answering a few questions."

Cook gave a small chuckle. "You're right, I don't have to say anything. Plus, I'd like my brief present. I've not been given my phone call yet."

"Plenty of time for all that malarky," said Simms. "You know why you've been arrested." It was more of a statement than a question.

"Do tell," said Cook with a sneer.

"The Swifts Bank job," said Simms. "You and your friend Thomas, plus others, tunnelled your way into the vault, last weekend, and made off with." He paused and paged through the folder. "Over a million pounds in cash and jewellery."

"So you say, what?" said Cook, his officer accent and mannerisms starting to fall back into place after the shock of capture.

"Come off it Charlie," broke in Brown. "We know damn well it was you, you left your fingerprints all over the damn place. In the offices you rented in Cleveland Place. In the basement, the tunnel. All over the tools, and most importantly, all over the safe deposit vault in Swifts Bank. Why on earth didn't any of you wear gloves, for Christ's sake?" He took out his cigarettes and offered them to Cook before taking one, himself then lighting both.

"To make your job easier, gentlemen?" blowing out a stream of smoke.

"Come on, Charlie, a big job like that and a school boy error."

"And you were caught red handed," broke in Simms. "You and Thomas had a load of jewellery identified as stolen on the raid."

Cook looked up at the ceiling and heaved a great sigh. He seemed to slump in his chair, "That bloody Thomas. Stupid bastard. Told him it was a bad idea."

"What was a bad idea, Charlie?" asked Brown.

"He persuaded me to fence some of the jewellery for him. We should have been away in the wind, but my buyer couldn't make it till today. Insisted he came to me and Thomas wanted to hang around while the deal was done." He let out a wry chuckle. "I bet he wished he'd cleared off when I told him to."

"So where are the others?" asked Simms.

"What others? You've got me and Thomas."

Simms scanned the pages in the folder, again. "Earnest Banks, Eric Teale and one other."

"One other?"

"Yes, we haven't identified his prints, yet. Only a matter of time, though."

"Good luck with that, old chap"

"What do you mean by that?" added Brown

Cook looked down at the table, heaved another sigh, seemed to come to some sort of decision and sat up straighter in his chair. It creaked slightly as he moved. "I mean I think it highly unlikely you'll find his fingerprints on record."

"Why's that, then?"

"It was his show. Whole thing was his idea. Got Eric Teale to get us all together."

"How do you know that?" asked Simms

"I was contacted by Eric, and the first meeting was at his flat, when we all met up for the first time."

"And this chap was there?"

"Correct, Eric introduced him as Paul Smith. No prizes for guessing it's not this real name."

"What did he say?"

"Laid out the whole shooting match. Said he was acting for what he called his principal. This person was, according to Smith, a very rich art collector who wished to obtain a piece of art in the vault at Swifts Bank."

"So how much was he paying you?"

"That was the beauty of it. He wasn't paying us a bean, himself, we just kept all we could get out of the vault, just so long as he got his piece of art, and he was financing the whole thing. Rented the offices, paid for the equipment. Even paid the wages for those young girls we took on for the short time we were there. How are they, by the way? You do realise they had nothing whatsoever to do with the actual job. Do give them my best wishes when next you see them, won't you?"

"Did you get to see this piece of artwork this Smith character was after?"

"I did, yes. It was in the big safe in the vault. A long hexagonal box, looked oriental, possibly Egyptian. There was a smaller thing inside, had this odd sort of blue glow to it, covered in symbols and little windows with numbers and symbols behind them. Damndest thing. Devil of a job getting it out, but once he got it, it never left his side."

Simms and Brown glanced at each other. "Okay, Charlie," said Simms. "We'll take a break, there. Would you like a cup of tea?"

"Milk, two sugars," replied Cook.

Brown put his packet of cigarettes and a box of matches on the table. "Help yourself, Charlie."

"Well, well," said Charlie. "such treatment. Must be something I said." Reaching for the cigarettes he smiled them out the room and the uniform came back in.

In the corridor Brown said, "Bloody hell!"

"What the hell have we walked into, Tom? Let's go and see Whitstable." The pair virtually ran to DCI Whitstable's office. Simms rapped on the door and went in without waiting. A uniform sergeant was standing by the desk giving Whitstable some papers.

"I take it there are developments, DCI Simms." He turned to the uniform. "That will be all sergeant, thank you." He waited for the sergeant to leave before he turned to Simms. "This had better be good for you to come bursting in here like that, Inspector."

"Oh there are developments, alright," said Simms. "I don't know whether you'll think they're good, though." He recounted the interview with Cook.

"Bloody hell!" said Whitstable, when Simms had finished.

"I said that," said Brown, quietly.

Whitstable glanced over at him, then reached for his phone. "I'd better give our friend in Whitehall a ring. What's his name, again, Cockson?"

"Cockscombe," said Simms. "although I think you're supposed to know him as Wilson."

"God preserve us from the Security Service." He said the words Security Service with a certain amount of disdain and started dialling.

Chapter 38

Kell was standing looking out of the window in his office. The Home Secretary had left about five minutes previously. He'd first called in when news of the raid broke. "Just passing, K. Heard about this break-in at Swifts Bank? Quite a job, by all accounts." A fishing trip? Then he was just popping by on Wednesday. Today he actually said what was on his mind. "Are they getting anywhere, do you know? Should we be concerned?" Kell assured the Home Secretary it was nothing to do with them, he could rest easy. To which he replied, "Jolly good, keep me posted. I'm off to Chequers with the P.M. for the weekend." A pause, as if deciding to leave it there, or not. Then, "let me know of any developments, won't you. The P.M.'s taken quite an interest for some reason," and left.

Kell was roused from his staring out the window by a knock at his door, and said door opening. William Bant almost burst into the room. "They've caught two of them," he said breathlessly. "Reg just phoned me. He's on his way to the yard as we speak,"

"Which two?" enquired Kell.

"Cook and, er, what's his name? Yes, Thomas."

"Cook and Thomas, eh?"

"Quite, or Thomas Cook, like the travel company," said Bant with a grin.

Kell gave a short laugh, "I think the only travelling they're likely to do is to His Majesty's prison."

"We need to handle this very carefully, though," he continued. "Is Reg up to this? He's got to try and keep things very low key. This is still Headline news, we don't want it to get of hand."

"I'm sure Reg knows what he's doing, he'll take care. Don't forget he's closer to this than anyone else."

"Still no sign of Rivers?"

"No, K, we're hoping this pair can shed some light on it."

Reg Cockscombe stood in DCI Whitstable's office, along with DI Simms and DS Brown, having just explained the name change to them.

"So which is your real name, Cockscombe, or Wilson?" demanded Whitstable.

"Neither," came the airy reply. "Let's just say I'm Wilson for the duration, eh?" This bought a harrumph from Whitstable. "So, I'd like to interview these two men, myself. On my own."

"Impossible," said Whitstable, glaring at him. "We have strict procedures. You will be accompanied by DI Simms whilst conducting your interviews."

"With all due respect, both to you and DI Simms," he turned and gave Simms a brief smile, "This is a matter of national, and international, security. I don't give a damn about your procedures, I will see them alone. Feel free to speak to the Commissioner, I'm sure Sir Philip will be pleased to confirm my authority."

DCI Whitstable glared at him even harder. It was the sort of glare that had junior ranks trembling in their boots. "Detective Sergeant Brown, would you escort our guest to the interview room and provide him with every assistance." He all but spat the words every assistance.

Wilson smiled inwardly. The assignment of the most junior rank in the room, to assist him was noted. However, with his position in the Security Service automatically came a certain animosity from other branches of the security services. This was water off a duck's back. "Thank you for your co operation, Chief Inspector." Brown held the door open for him and they left.

DCI Whitstable leaned back in his chair, gestured for Simms to take a seat. Then he stood up and started pacing, left thumb hooked into his waistcoat pocket. His right hand held a pipe, which he inspected. "You can light that bonfire of yours, if you wish." Simms gladly took out his pipe, filled it and lit it. As clouds of tobacco smoke filled the room DCI whitstable arrived back behind his desk. He stood a second, then pointed the stem of his empty pipe at DI Simms. "There's something fishy here, Horace, you mark my words. This whole thing stinks to high heaven. I've not been involved with the Secret Service, much. I believe they're calling themselves MI5 now, for some reason. As I say, I've not been involved with them much, but every time I have it's when something of their's has gone wrong. I'd put good money on this missing chap Smith and his work of art to be at the bottom of this." He put particular emphasis on the phrase work of art. "Important documents and diplomatic relations my eye."

"Hello. Norman Thomas, isn't it? Shall I call you Norman, or Mr Thomas, or just plain Thomas? My names Wilson and I'd like to ask you a few questions." Wilson said this while the uniform constable vacated the room when he entered. Norman Thomas was already seated on the far side of the battered wooden table with it's obligatory tin ashtray, equally battered. Wilson pulled out his chair and sat down.

"You can call me what you want," said Norman Thomas. "I ain't saying nothing without my brief."

"Oh dear, Norman, that's not very co-operative. Now here's what's going to happen. You're going to answer my questions, fully and completely, Then we might see about getting your solicitor."

"I know my rights, and I'm not answering any of your fucking questions, got it?"

"Ah, yes, quite. Let me explain a few things, before we go any further. Firstly, I'm not a policeman, so the normal police rules go out the window. I'm from His

Majesty's Government, and your refusal to answer my questions could be seen as an act of," Wilson paused considering his words, then he looked at Norman and smiled, "utter stupidity. You see, cooperating with me could see your sentence drastically reduced. Not cooperating, on the other hand, would see any sentence dramatically increased, along with all sorts of reasons why you're not suitable for parole, when the time comes." Wilson smiled and sat back in his chair.

"You can't do that,"said Thomas.

Wilson sat forwards, resting his forearms on the table, hands clasped. "Oh yes I fucking can, sonny Jim," he snarled. "Now, Question, your illustrious leader, one Paul Smith, where is he?"

"I haven't a clue," he replied, his voice going up slightly with nerves. He'd been questioned by the police before, obviously. Some of them were nasty bastards, and didn't always play by the book. But this was something different, and it made Norman Thomas not only nervous, but also a bit frightened as well. Wilson just looked at him and raised an eyebrow. It was Norman's turn to lean forward. "Honestly, I haven't a clue. We deliberately didn't tell each other where we were going, just in case."

"In case of what?"

"Well, this. If we got caught we wouldn't be able to grass them up."

"So where did you last see him?"

"We dropped him off on the Edgware Road, that was it, that was the last time we saw him."

"Which way did he go, towards the tube station?"

"No, that was the strange thing. We dropped the other two off right by there, so it was just him, Charlie and me left in the van. We'd only gone on for half a minute when he says pull over. When we do he says "Thanks for all your help, gents." or something like that, jumps out and is gone."

"Was he in the front, or back of the van?"

"Does it matter?"

"Just answer the question. Front or back?"

"The back. Just jumped out and slammed the door shut."

"If he was in the back didn't one of you have to go round and open it, so he could get out?"

"No, he opened it himself. I think he must of held it partly open when we dropped the others off and Charlie and me got in the front."

"Who was driving, you or Cook?"

"Charlie was, I got in the passenger seat."

"Did you see which way he went? Up the street,? Across the road? Was someone waiting for him? Did he get into a car? What?'

"I don't know, I didn't look."

Wilson heaved a sigh and leaned back in his chair, then he made some notes on the papers in front of him. More doodles than anything else. Nothing really to write down, but it always seemed the right thing to do. Make notes, keep the other side thinking that everything is going to plan. Let them know you're in charge. Inside Wilson was thinking Bloody hell, Rivers has gone rogue and it's my head on the line, my Joe that's fucked off with the goodies. "Let's go back to the actual raid. You've broken in, you're all in there opening deposit boxes and helping yourselves. What did you do, divide the stuff up as you went, what?"

"No, we put it all together, in a heap. Cash, papers and jewellery." He had a little chuckle, "I can tell you, there was some tasty tom, there." Then the smile went from his face. "It was trying to shift some of it got Charlie and me collared."

"What did your Mr Smith do? Join in with you all. Or concentrate on a particular box?"

"Oh he was all for getting his piece of art. Made a right song and dance about it. Biggest box in the room, by far, and he couldn't get the bloody thing open. Had a right go at me when I suggested we leave it and share out everything else."

"What did he do? We know he got it open."

"Yeah, Ernie and Eric jammed a big jemmy in by the lock and pried it open. Took all their strength. When it burst, it sent the pair of them in a heap."

"Did you see what was inside?"

"Yeah, we all did. This ornate hexagonal sort of box. Long thing about so big," he held his hands about eighteen inches apart. "covered in carvings and stuff. Ain't see nothing like it. It was padlocked to the bottom of the safe. Eric chopped the padlocks with some bolt cutters and the pair of them lifted it out. Looked blooming heavy, whatever it was. I reckon it was solid gold, under all those jewels and things. Then he opened it and had a look at the thing inside." He stopped suddenly. A concerted, serious look on his face. He put both hands flat on the table and looked Wilson square in the eye.

"What is it?" asked Wilson, seeing Norman's expression.

"What I'm going to tell you is the God's honest truth, so don't say I'm lying, or trying to trick you just for a lighter sentence."

"Fair enough, Norman, just tell me what happened."

"There was this weird blue glow from inside, like there was some sort of lamp in there. Then he lifted out this thing like a dumbbell, only covered in weird symbols and stuff, with what looked like thumbwheels, and little windows with numbers and pictures behind them."

A thrill went through Wilson, but he kept it hidden. "Then what happened?"

"He put it back. Charlie made some comment about he did that quick, but that was it. He shut the lid and put it in his holdall."

"And that was it? Nothing else odd happened?"

"No, that was it. No, tell a lie. It was when we were divvying up the goods. Ernie found a great wedge of these bearer bond things. Smith reckoned we couldn't use them as the police would be looking for them. If we went into a bank it would be as good as putting our hands up.."

"That's true. So, what, you left them?" Wilson was frantically wracking his brain, trying to remember if there'd been any bearer bonds anywhere in the vault or the cellar, or if any were reported missing from the safety box holders.

"Christ no. There were loads. Two and half million quid's worth. Smith said he could off load them and swapped most of his stuff for them. The four of us had all the tom. He had his piece of art, about ten grand in cash and his bearer bonds. Seemed happy with that."

The earlier thrill was replaced by an awful sinking feeling. Two and a half million in bearer bonds. One place he could bank them, no questioned asked. Switzerland. Plus ten grand in travelling expenses. Shit, even he would be tempted. What had they been thinking. "Then what?"

"Nothing, that was it. We divvied up the boodle and left. Like I said, we dropped him off on the Edgware Road."

"Thank you Norman." Now came the blind. He didn't want Norman Thomas thinking this was all about the art object. "Now tell me, Norman, and think very carefully. Did Mr Smith take any documents? They would have been in a maroon leather folder, with a crest on the front. This is very important."

"No, that's it. I think we went through every box in the room. I don't remember seeing anything like that."

"Did you go through any of the papers and documents in the vault?" He remembered seeing quite a few documents scattered about.

"'Course we did, we're not daft. Only quickly. We were only after stuff we could shift fairly quickly. No time for any of that blackmail malarky. None of us did. Strictly the tom and the dosh."

"And no maroon leather folder?"

"No. Like I said we checked through everything."

"Well, thank you, Norman, you've been most helpful." Wilson got up from the table and called the constable in to take Norman Thomas back to his cell. As they were leaving he asked the constable to bring Charlie Cook up. Christ, what are we going to do? he thought. Looks like Rivers has definitely gone rogue. He went out into the corridor to find a phone. The nearest was the custody sergeants office. He reached there just as the constable and Cook came out of the cells, the Custody sergeant locking the door of iron bars behind them. "Thank you, constable, if you could just wait with Cook in the interview room. I have to make a short phone call."

"Very good, Sir," said the constable

Wilson had already turned to the sergeant. "Sergeant, I need to make an important call in private."

"Certainly, Sir, use the phone in my office." He lifted the flap in the custody counter for them both to go through. He let Wilson into the office behind, then closed the door to give him the privacy he's asked for.

Bant answered before the second ring "Reg?"

"Yes, listen, we've got a real problem on our hands. Rivers has definitely done a runner. Gone rogue."

"What?! Are you sure?"

"Sure as I can be. He's got the artefact and two and a half million quid in bearer bonds, plus change. We need to put out an all ports warning."

"Bit late for that, don't you think?"

"Yes, but we can trace which port he went through, and where he was going. Use his real name, plus any other known legends."

"What reason?"

"We can say it's in connection with the Swifts Bank job. I've no doubt they're doing the same for Banks and Teale. Tell you what, I'll get DCI Whitstable to do it."

"Okay, keep me posted."

Wilson left Cook to stew and went up to DCI Whitstable's office. As he suspected, Whitstable had already sent out an all ports warning for Banks and Teale.

"We're not going to get very far with Smith," scorned Whitstable .

"Also goes by the name of Rivers," said Wilson, and gave Whitstable a brief description.

"How come you suddenly know so much?"

"Thomas was quite helpful. Turns out he's somebody we've had our eye on for some time. International art thief and spy."

"Spies for whom?" queried Whitstable, with a voice laden with scepticism.

"For whoever pays the highest. Gets secret information from God knows where, and sells to the highest bidder."

"So you've had dealings with him before, then?" Whitstable leaned back in his chair and sucked on his empty pipe.

"You could say that," said Wilson, with a sigh. "But I can't possibly tell you any more than that."

I bet you can't, thought Whitstable. "Very well, Mr Wilson, consider it done." He reached for his telephone, then paused, hand outstretched. "It's funny we've never heard of him before. Him being an international art thief and all."

"You probably have," bluffed Wilson. "but it won't have been under these names. Thank you, Chief Inspector." He left the room as Whitstable started dialling.

Charlie Cook, Charles Cook, Major Charles Cook, sat at the battered table looking every inch the retired major. His response to Wilson's preamble was, "My good man, I have said all I wish to. Now, unless you are prepared to let me have my solicitor present, kindly lead me back to my cell."

"Mr Cook, Charles, Charlie? How would you like me to address you? Major?"

"Major would be nice," he replied urbanely. "but as I said, no solicitor, no speaky."

"Well then, Major, let me explain. I'm not a policeman." Wilson then went on to broadly explain to Charlie Cook that same situation and consequences he'd given Thomas.

"Well, if it's for King and country, you should have said. Would you have a cigarette, by any chance? I suppose it would be too much to expect a cigar."

"It would," replied Wilson, offering his cigarettes across, then taking one himself and lighting both with a silver cigarette lighter.

"A nice piece," commented Cook, nodding at the lighter.

"So, Thomas told me your leader and guiding light was one Paul Smith."

A nod.

"What was his intent?"

"His intent was to rob a bank."

"Shall we drop the sarcasm, Major. This will be a lot easier for both of us if you just answer my questions."

A brief smile from Cook. "His intention was to steal a piece of art, on behalf of his principal so he said."

"And did he? Get his piece of art?"

"Oh yes."

"Where did you last see him?"

"Oh, on Edgware Road. We'd just dropped Banks and Teale off at the underground." Slight surprise at this sudden jump.

"You were driving?"

"I was."

"Did you see where he went?"

"He disappeared."

"In what way, disappeared? Into a doorway? Across the road? How did he disappear?"

"He literally disappeared. 'Poof'" he raised both hands, "he just disappeared."

"I'm not with you."

"I think it had something to do with the piece of art he was after."

"How so?"

"Well, curious thing. He'd just got his hands on it - this was in the vault, you understand - opened this rather exquisite box and there was this blueish glow from inside. He lifted out whatever it was from inside, then suddenly he's closing the lid."

"What's so unusual about that."

"No, you misunderstand. From lifting it out and closing the lid happened in the wink of an eye. It would be like you coming through the door, then you're sat in your chair without the intervening walk to and sitting in said chair."

"I see. Did you say anything?"

"Yes, I said that was quick, or something similar."

"What did he say?"

"Just that he moved quickly, but I knew it was more than that."

"But you didn't comment further."

"We were rather busy at the time."

"Quite. Now, when you dropped him off, on the Edgware Road, did you know where he was going, had he said anything to you?"

"No, none of us knew where any of the others were going. Safety in ignorance, you know, what? Need to know and all that. You'd know all about that, no doubt," said with a knowing smile.

Wilson ignored the comment. "So he just disappeared? Why do you say it was connected with the piece of art?"

"I was watching him in the rear view mirror. It was fairly quiet, at the time, not many people about. He looked around, stepped into a doorway, so that he was semi hidden from the road, reached into the bag containing it, and disappeared."

"You sure he didn't just quickly go in the door?"

"Quite sure. I could still see him, more so when he bent to reach into the bag, then bang, gone. Just as if he'd been switched off like an electric light. That's the only way I can describe it. I didn't even blink and he was gone in an instant."

"Did you say anything to Thomas?"

"Good God, no. Firstly I didn't want to know. I had this horrible feeling we'd got into something a whole league away from what we we're given to believe."

"What do you mean by that?" Wilson was beginning to worry that this Major Cook was a bit too quick on the uptake.

"That this was more than just a piece of art, it was something technological. There could be, you know, governments involved. Foreign governments, and I don't want to hang for treason. Robbery's one thing, I'll hold my hands up to that, and take what's coming. But breaking into a bank, on The Mall of all places, for Johnny Foreigner, not on you life."

"You said 'firstly', why else didn't you tell Thomas?"

"The man's a weasel and a fool. I didn't want to get into a discussion with him about something he wouldn't comprehend."

"Yet you met up again, at your place, some five days after the robbery. Why?"

Cook spread his hands, palms upwards, in a sign of admission. "Greed, pure and simple greed. The buyer I'd set up I'd done a deal with. He was going to buy the jewellery off Thomas at a lower price than the going rate. He would then sell it on and we'd split the profit. It's just that bit took a few days to set it up. Honour among thieves, what?"

Wilson moved onto the subject of the documents in the maroon leather folder, with the same expected, and obvious results.

Chapter 39

"Well, at least we know it does what we thought it did." Bant was trying desperately to be positive about the catastrophe they found themselves in. The three of them were gathered in Kell's office. Cockscombe nervously smoking a cigarette.

"If we didn't think it worked, we wouldn't have embarked on this whole enterprise in the first place," said Kell. "I've had to lie to the Home Secretary."

Bant gave him an old fashioned look. "We're the Secret Service, it's expected. He doesn't want you to tell him the truth. Deniability and all that."

"True," said Kell, "true."

"Never mind all that, what the hell are we going to do?" Cockscombe was looking more desperate by the minute. It wasn't just this. Unlike Kell and Bant, he had no club to go to, to unwind with the like minded. The Service, as far as he knew, were unaware of his failed marriage. His wife currently in the country, helping to look after her poorly mother. He was in his miserable flat, in Tooting, scraping along. If this all fell on him, and if things got any worse it inevitably would, he'd be out of a job; maybe worse, and that didn't bear thinking about.

"Cheer up, Reg," said Bant, "things could be worse."

"I don't see how?"

Kell just scowled at Bant. This wasn't the time for glib comments. Even he couldn't see how it could possibly be worse. "We need to think out our next move." They were all seated, and all now smoking, filling the room with a fug of tobacco smoke. "If he can use this thing to just disappear like that," he snapped his fingers. "Then how do we catch him? How do we even track him, should we get a lead?" The room fell silent as they all contemplated the implications.

It was Bant that broke the silence. "Then we don't waste our energy looking for him. It will be like looking for a needle in the wrong haystack. This chap Cook needs to be persuaded to keep very quiet about what he knows." This was Bant doing what Bant did best, thinking on his feet. "We scale back our involvement. These documents you invented, Reg, we simply say we found them; dumped in an alleyway. Meanwhile we just keep a watching brief, to see if Rivers surfaces anywhere."

"I'll have a word with Sir John. See if we can sort out substantially reduced sentences for Cook and Thomas, for their generous cooperation when caught," said Kell. "Reg, I need you to adopt your Wilson persona one more time. Visit our friend Major Cook. Impress upon him the importance of keeping his mouth shut."

"Yes, K. What if the other two are caught. Banks and Teale?"

"I think we should worry about that if, and when it happens. I've a feeling they're well away. If they let Rivers walk away with two and a half million, in bearer bonds, you can bet they've all got similar value takings. They'll not be back. And that's a good point to put to both Cook and Thomas, Reg. How much stuff did the police get from Cook's place?"

"Just jewellery, to the value of a shade under fifty thousand pounds"

"No cash, or any thing else, gold bars or what not?"

"No, nothing at Thomas's place, or any of the other premises."

"Good. Drop a hint that as long as they're not stupid enough to try moving anything recognisable, I'm thinking jewellery, and they're discrete when they come out, we won't be looking too hard to get everyone's money back." Bant looked at him wide eyed. Kell just shrugged, "We won't mention that last bit to the police. If you don't want to get caught, don't go robbing banks."

"Even if we put them up to it?"

"But we didn't. They were never told of our involvement. As far as they were concerned they were just robbing a bank to line their own pockets. Anything else was secondary." They all looked at each other. "Right, let's crack on. Reg, you know what to do. William, set up some sort of watching brief on Rivers. All embassies, that sort of thing. I'm off to see the Home Secretary."

Eric Teale and Ernie Banks were never caught. It was rumoured they'd both gone to live the easy life in America. Teale in Florida, Banks somewhere in California. Though no-one was encouraged to look too hard.

Rivers was never seen or heard of again. Although that's not strictly true. Andrew Henly, cryptologist extraordinaire, progressed though the ranks, spent a fruitful war at Bletchley Park. Always kept an eye open, and an ear to the the ground. Alert to anything that might give a hint to the whereabouts of Paul Rivers and, more importantly, Làngfèi shíjiān.

And, of course, it did.

Chapter 40

"And that is it." Andrew Henly sat back, the leather Chesterfield creaking. "Now you know as much as I do. More importantly, anyone else, and the fewer people you share it with, the better."

Mark Hill pressed 'stop' on the cassette recorder, removed the cassette and wrote 'A. H. 7 ' on it, then snapped out the record tabs. He placed it with the other six tapes on the coffee table. He used the few moments doing this to compose his thoughts, but his response was still, "Bloody hell!"

"There's one other thing, Mark." He got up and went into his study, returning with a slim folder. He handed it to Mark. "This cropped up. Just once when cross-referencing some money transfers in the early sixties. Didn't think much of it at the time. Still not sure if it's relevant. A hotel on a small island just off the British Virgin Islands. Not sure who's jurisdiction it came under, at the time. Hotel Zanzibar. The thing that caught my eye, as you'll see when you read through. A boat carrying the entire workforce, that had been working on the hotel, including the architect and all his documentation, sank with the loss of everyone on board, in 1952. The reason given was it struck an old World War Two mine, that had come adrift from a minefield laid to protect Tortola. I checked, and there were no mines laid anywhere near Tortola during the war. Maybe something and nothing, but an exclusive hotel on an island just off the British Virgin Islands? And all those involved killed? Hang on to it, see if it crops up anywhere in your searches. Didn't have the resources, or technology, back in my day."

"So you see," went on Henly, going back to the matter in hand. "that's why I kept watching all those years. The thing that every one worried about, after the war, was someone finding out about the Service organising a bank raid that resulted in the eventual collapse of the bank. Well, it's having to be taken over by Martins Bank. Once 'K', Bant and Cockscombe were gone, no one paid much attention to the actual physical article, Làngfèi shíjiān. Dismissed it rather. However, if we'd had it, we would be in an entirely different future."

"Really?" Mark sounded a little incredulous, himself.

"Of course. Don't you see? With Làngfèi shíjiān it's entirely likely the Second World War would have been over in a matter of months. We wouldn't have needed to crack the Enigma code, we wouldn't have had to go cap in hand to the Americans. In all probability, we would be the world's number one super power, with the Americans hanging onto our coat tails." He leaned back again into the sofa, the leather gently creaking, and looked off into space as if imagining what might have been. He then seemed to come back into the room. He sat forward, a steely glint in his eye. "Find out what happened to that treacherous bastard, Paul Rivers and bring Làngfèi shíjiān back for Britain's sake." He paused, then, "And if Rivers is, by some chance, still alive, kill him." He spat the words out with real venom. "Even if he's now some doddery old fart, kill him. Shoot him. Make him look down the barrel of a gun and know why. Bastard!"

Mark Hill started to put his stuff away. The copious notes he'd made, the tape recorder and the carefully labelled cassettes. "Well, I shall do my very best to find him, and Làngfèi shíjiān." Henly's final statement had rattled him a little. "As for dispatching, that's not up to me, that would have to be sanctioned at a far higher level.

"But thank you so much for your time, Andrew. That, and the information from your files has, I think, made quite a difference. Would you like me to keep you abreast of progress?"

"Thank you, Mark, but no. Just let me know when you catch him, and get it back." As Mark finished putting his stuff away Andrew telephoned for a taxi to take him to the station. At the door to Andrew's apartment they shook hands. "Good luck, Mark, you're going to need it." Mark left and Andrew went over to a side console table and poured himself a scotch, then went over to the window and watched Mark get into his taxi and go. He raised his glass in salutation then took a mouthful. "Go get the bastard, Mark. Bring the goodies home."

He looked out at the English Channel. Cold, grey and foreboding. A coaster was heading into Shoreham harbour just a few miles along the coast. Standing with one hand in his pocket, the other clutching his whisky tumbler he smiled to himself and muttered a couple of lines of Masefield's "Cargoes" to himself. "Dirty British coaster with a salt caked smoke stack, butting through the Channel in the mad March days."

He didn't take much notice of the two men across the street. They watched Mark get into his taxi, and Andrew Henly at his window raise a glass whilst gazing out at the sullen sea, then they turned and walked away.

Part 4

Chapter 41

Mark Hill, now Dr Mark Hill, head of Money Laundering and Financial Irregularities section at MI5, often jokingly referred to as MILF, sat in Secure Conference Room 2 (SCR2), second basement level, Thames House. The only other occupant was Derek Coverdale, Deputy Director of MI5. A large man with a shaved head and piercing blue eyes. He'd reached his position through the ranks, unlike the current Director, a political appointee. Derek Coverdale was known for his almost uncanny capacity for patience and calm. At some of the tensest moments in some of the most dangerous and extreme operations he remained cool. A characteristic that inspired confidence and reliability, not just from his colleagues, but from his superiors as well.

It was early 2019. Ever since his meeting with Andrew Henly back in 1986, Mark Hill had kept a dogged watching brief on all things Harlequin, and any hint he could find of Làngfèi shíjiān, despite all the other current work he had to carry out. However, over the past few months, since autumn 2018 up until two days ago he'd managed to unpick a whole web of back doors from Harlequin through to a whole raft of offshore shell companies. They all led to one source, Hotel Zanzibar. The place Andrew Henly told him about, all those years ago. The final proof that that's where he would find the answers and possibly, Làngfèi shíjiān. Over the past two days he'd put a comprehensive file together, and sent a copy up to Derek Coverdale. Coverdale had called this meeting. One on one, no minutes, in a secure conference room.

Coverdale took his black rimmed reading glasses off and placed them on top of the folder in front of him. "To be honest, Mark, when I read the covering memo I was surprised you were still looking at this. I thought the whole thing had been on a back burner for so long everyone had forgotten about it. But this new stuff you found out puts a whole new spin on things. It's almost as if Harlequin were embedded in our financial systems."

"In a way, they are," said Mark. "They've had such an influence on the financial markets, not just London, but worldwide, that they've had a direct effect on everyone's lives."

"The banking crisis?"

"Yes. The most cynical, pernicious piece of manipulation I've ever seen. They instigated the whole idea of the sub prime market. Making money out of trading financial packages worth fuck all, for silly amounts. All well and good as long as the merry go round doesn't stop. But stop it did, and who instigated that? Harlequin. Their clients made huge profits foreseeing the crash, and not letting on. In effect Harlequin screwed the world and walked away unbelievably rich."

"And you think it's all run from this Hotel Zanzibar?"

"I do. Everything points to it. All the back doors, through all the shell companies led me to one place. Hotel Zanzibar."

"So what do you propose we do about it?"

"I want to go there myself. Book in as one of their guests, and have a root round. See if I can ferret out this Làngfèi shíjiān, and possibly that rogue agent that took it, Paul Rivers."

"Do you really think he's still alive? He'd be, what?" Coverdale leaned forward, put his reading glasses back on and flipped through the folder, "a hundred and twenty three."

"If Làngfèi shíjiān can do what it's clearly capable of, then that wouldn't surprise me in the least. He probably just sits in his own little time bubble, and nips back and forth in time to do whatever he wants."

"Well, if that's the case, how will you find him? He may not be in the same time thingy.. zone, dimension, whatever, as you."

"There's got to be something there. Everything points to Hotel Zanzibar. He's got to be there, or able to be got at from there."

Coverdale drummed his fingers thoughtfully on the folder in front of him, staring at it at the same time. He seemed to come to some sort of decision. "This is what we'll do. I'm convinced you're right, and this Hotel Zanzibar is it's centre of operations. Let me have a word with our friends across the river." By that he meant MI6, whose remit lay mostly outside the UK. "See if we can put an operation together. A small team from the SBS landed by submarine. They could be in, and take out whatever's necessary in no time."

"No," said Mark, quite firmly. "That will never work. They'll be constantly on the watch for something like that, and don't forget, they can also keep a watch through time, looking back for just such an eventuality to make themselves scarce when the attack happens."

"Yes, of course." But then Coverdale brightened. "Mind you, it would take out their centre of operations. They'd need to start all over again, and we can keep watch for it."

"It would have no effect. With the foreknowledge Làngfèi shíjiān gives them, they can have a whole new set up ready to roll at a second's notice. It would be a complete waste of time."

"I see. Of course you're right. So what do we know of the actual hotel? How do we get in there, and more importantly for our budget, how expensive is it? I can't see somewhere that exclusive and secluded is going to be in the Premier Inn, expense account level."

"It's not on Expedia, TripAdvisor, or any of those websites. It has it's own dedicated website, and that's the only way you can book, and yes, it's very expensive."

"Go on, how much?"

"You're looking in the region of £12,000 per night. But that includes transfer from Tortola, in the British Virgin Islands. It boasts a cordon bleu restaurant, and exclusive beaches. Mind you, it's the only hotel on there. Research seems to indicate that people on BVI use the term Hotel Zanzibar to refer to the island, as well. The only other thing there is a small harbour for the ferry to dock. A couple of local fishing boats use it. A small town, little more than a village, that provides most of the hotel's workforce, and the ruins of a villa up in the jungle that covers a hill on the East side of the island. Oh, and there's also a beach bar in the small cove next to the hotel's beach."

"So much, and only £12K a night. How on earth does it pay for itself? I can't see many people paying that sort of money to stay there, no matter how exclusive."

"That's the beauty of it. It doesn't have to pay for itself. It just needs a few guests to tick over. The eccentric rich, that want sun and privacy, and to be waited on hand and foot."

"Of course, and if it was seen to be thriving, but empty, questions would be asked. It would certainly arouse unwanted curiosity. I see what you mean, Mark.

"Leave this with me. I need to speak to a couple of people."

"You're not taking it to the Director, are you?" Mark sounded a little alarmed.

"Christ no. That political buffoon leaks more than a sieve. No, I need to speak to D. Ops, and my opposite number across the river. I'll be in touch tomorrow morning."

11am the following morning found Mark Hill and Derek Coverdale once again ensconced in SCR2. "You've got the green light," said Coverdale. "We can send you for a week. If no results by then you get out and come back home. We assume the guests are watched, so your every move will be monitored once you start nosing around. If things get too risky you get out."

"How, exactly?" interrupted Mark.

"There's two Royal Navy submarines undertaking exercises in the Atlantic, just East of the British Virgin Islands. You will be provided with a miniature emergency beacon. Get to the Eastern side of the island, set it off and they'll come and get you. Same procedure if you get what you're going for."

"How long have they been out there? Two of our subs being sent into the region just before I get there could set alarm bells ringing. And why two?"

"Don't worry they're already out there, been there for about two weeks already, on a joint exercise with the US Navy. Once you're en route we'll send a coded message to them to take it in turns moving close into the British Virgin Islands and listen out for you.

"All you've got to do now, is book the hotel and return flights. Which legend will you be using?"

"I've been thinking about that," said Mark. "I think I'll go under my own name. It's possible they know I've been looking into them, and they know I'm with MI5. I'm hoping it might provoke a reaction, and give me a lead."

"That sounds incredibly dangerous. Are you sure about that?"

"I know it's risky, but it's a risk I'm prepared to take. We..., I've, come all this way and I don't intend to come away empty handed."

"You'll need a gun. We'll get one of the new compact Glock 9 millimetre with a polymer frame, out to you en route. Just let us know your flights, and we'll let you know the arrangements."

"Thanks," said Mark, standing up, "I was going to ask. I'll do all the booking from home, on my own laptop, so there'll be no trace back to here."

"How soon will you be going?" Coverdale also stood up.

"In the next couple of days, hopefully. As soon as I can get a booking at the hotel, and flights."

"Right." Coverdale offered his hand, and Mark took it. Coverdale gave a firm shake. "Good luck, Mark. Get me those flight details as soon as, and I'll let you know how and when we'll get the gun to you."

Dr Hill got his gun, and two spare magazines of 9mm ammunition at San Juan airport, in Puerto Rico. Just as he was clearing security, one of the security officers directed him into a side office. Inside was a man he'd met briefly, in Thames House, a year or two ago. "Dr Hill," he extended his hand. "David Ingleby, currently Two I.C. Puerto Rico station." They shook hands. "If I could just see your passport?"

"Certainly," said Dr Hill and passed it across.

"Thanks," said Ingleby. He flicked through the passport, checking the details. He then opened his briefcase, took out a rubber stamp and stamped the passport. "There you go." He handed it back. "You now have temporary diplomatic clearance. I can now give you this." Putting the stamp back in his briefcase, he then withdrew a heavy duty hard plastic case, locked with a diplomatic seal. He handed it to Dr Hill. "It's a loaded Glock 26 with two spare magazines of ammo, and quick release belt holster. Brand new weapon. Only range test firing. Used one before?" The question almost rhetorical.

"Only on the range." He picked up the case and shoved it in his shoulder bag. "Let's hope I don't need it."

"Of course. Getting it to you like this, though, must mean you're involved in something pretty heavy. So good luck." He picked up his briefcase, shook Dr Hill's hand once more, and left through a side door. Dr Hill went back out onto the concourse. There was no one outside the door, just the usual throng of passengers and staff you'd find milling round any airport terminal. Slinging his bag over his shoulder he went off in search of a coffee before he got on his plane to Tortola. The bag seemed heavier, not just with the weight of the case, containing the gun, but what it entailed. The full implication of what he was embarked on started to really come home to him. Of course he knew it was dangerous, and he was basically a desk jockey, no field agent. Certainly not a man of action. He also knew he had to do this, and he was the only man who could. The only man who knew the full story. Even the comprehensive file he'd given to Coverdale didn't paint the full picture. A lot of it was more summary than full detail. He was convinced he'd find the answers at Hotel Zanzibar. Now it was just a short hop by local 'plane, and a boat trip. Then he'd find out.

Chapter 42

The bow dropped into a trough, spray flying as it pushed into the next swell. Rising up again, Dr Hill caught his first glimpse of the island. A grey smudge on the horizon. He'd stayed at the forward rail of the promenade deck ever since they'd cleared Guana Island. The wind and spray clearing his head after the long journey from London.

"There it is." Captain Philips joined him at the rail. "About another twenty minutes or so."

Dr Hill nodded, acknowledging the information. Then, "Quite a swell out here."

Captain Philips smiled. "It will get a little calmer the nearer we get to the island and we come into its lee. The swell out here is rolling straight in off the Atlantic." He turned and went back to the wheelhouse.

Soon the grey smudge turned green, then the lush green of tropical forrest. The whole island seemed covered. At the back what appeared to be a mountain, again covered by green. As they drew closer he made out a secluded bay with a white sandy beach. Towards the back were some parasols. Right at the back was a large, white, five storey building. Edwardian in style, with a terrace, partially glazed, running the entire width of the building, extending round each end and with wide, central steps leading down to the beach. This, presumed Dr Hill, was the actual Hotel Zanzibar. The ferry altered course to port as they drew closer. Soon the hotel was obscured by the headland and the water became much calmer. They approached a natural harbour. A narrow bay, with steep headlands that culminated in cliffs Dr Hill estimated perhaps eighty to one hundred feet high, dropping straight into the sea. A concrete quay had been built along each side. At the back a short beach then a road on a level with the two quaysides.

Captain Philips edged his boat slowly and gently to the quayside on his port side. Shouts from crew and men on the quayside as lines were thrown across. The sudden rise of engine noise, as they were thrown into reverse. Then quiet. Mooring ropes tied off and the rattle of the gangplank being run up to the side. He'd arrived. Dr Hill stood at the top of the gangplank, suitcase in hand. A white Range Rover pulled up on the quayside. On its front door a gold monogram H.Z., the letters separated by a palm tree. He ran his eye over the car, the slightly larger pillars, the special tyres. This wasn't any ordinary Range Rover, this was a Range Rover Sentinel. The virtually bomb proof vehicle of choice for heads of state, senior politicians and crime lords. He wondered why on earth they would need one here. A man got out of the car and came up the gangplank to him. He was black, about six foot tall, slim, but muscular. He wore charcoal slacks, with a razor sharp crease, a short sleeved white shirt that almost dazzled against his black skin, and a blue tie, in the centre of which was a duplicate in miniature of the H.Z. monogram on the car's door. With a broad, friendly smile he reached out and took Dr Hill's suitcase in his left hand and offered him his right. "Dr Hill, welcome to Hotel Zanzibar. My name is Thomas and it is my pleasure to drive you to the hotel."

"Thank you, Thomas," said Dr Hill, shaking the proffered hand, "Lead on." They climbed aboard, Dr Hill in the passenger seat rather than the back. Thomas swung the car around and drove smoothly away down the quayside. At the end he turned right onto a road that ran across the back of the harbour, through a small picturesque town with brightly painted buildings. None of the buildings was higher than one storey, with the exception of the stone building facing the harbour across the road. A simple sign, white letters on navy blue background, that said Port Authority. Dr Hill noted that there was no mention of a name either of the port, or the island. There were quite a few people about. Into the town there was a square on the left. This was filled with market stalls selling mostly vegetables and what seemed locally caught fish.

"It's about fifteen minutes to the hotel." Thomas brought Dr Hill's attention back to their small journey. "When we leave the town the road takes us inland around the headland. The island is quite hilly, so the road winds a fair bit."

"So, if I wanted to come into town, I'd need to get a taxi then," queried Dr Hill.

"Oh there are no taxis on the island, Dr Hill," said Thomas, with his usual smile. "Everything you need you'll find at the hotel. If you did want to go in to town for some reason though, I or another member of staff will gladly drive you in."

Dr Hill merely nodded. Looking out the passenger side window he noticed a road leading off to the left. It was metalled, but obviously unused judging by the cracks in the surface and the size of the weeds sprouting from them and encroaching in on both sides. A few yards in, a pole barrier lay across the road. Originally red and white, now mostly just rust and flaking paint. Behind the barrier, the road rose with the hill, turned left and disappeared into the dense trees that now sprung up on each side of them, now they'd left the town. "Where does that go?" he enquired.

Thomas glanced across. "That leads to nowhere," he said with a slight chuckle. "At least nowhere useful. On the top of the mountain, well, our tallest hill, there's the ruins of a villa. It was quite something, a large villa with views out over the Atlantic. That was the main road up to it. Private, of course. There's another, unmade road, at the far end of this one we're on where it ends by the cove beyond the hotel."

"What happened to it?"

"Fire," replied Thomas. "Fire and hurricane."

"Really?" Dr Hill sounded somewhat incredulous.

"Yes. The fire started before the hurricane hit. Got quite a hold before anyone could get there to help. Then the rains started. Everyone thought that would help, but then the winds came. Destroyed what was left."

"Who lived there?"

"The owner of Hotel Zanzibar."

"So where does he live now, in the hotel?"

"No. Apparently he lives in seclusion in a big house on Tortola."

"When did all this happen?"

"Oh, years ago, before my time here. Back in the sixties I think."

A knot manifested itself in Dr Hills gut. Fuck. What if that's where this Làngfèi shíjiān is. He may be stuck out on this bloody island on a fool's errand, when the answers are all back on Tortola.

"Are you ok, Dr Hill?" asked Thomas, glancing across at him.

Dr Hill straightened himself up and cleared his throat. "Fine, yes, thank you Thomas. Just a bit tired from the journey. It's a long way from London."

Thomas' smile broadened. "It is indeed, Sir. Well, here we are." He swung the Range Rover off the road to the right and onto a semicircular drive that fronted an imposing Georgian style building five storeys high plus an attic, judging by the row of dormer windows. Driving in through the far entrance, he pulled up in front of the canopied hotel entrance so it was on the passenger side. A boy of about fifteen came up and opened Dr Hill's door. A slightly gangly youth about five feet six inches tall in an identical uniform to Thomas.

"Welcome to Hotel Zanzibar, Sir" said the boy. The sir came out as 'sah' in his pronounced West Indian accent.

"Thank you," said Dr Hill.

"Terry," called Thomas from the back of the car, "could you come and take Dr Hill's bags, please?"

He ran to get the bags, then followed Dr Hill into reception with them.

It appeared Thomas was also the Head Receptionist. As Dr Hill entered the hotel, Thomas marched smartly behind the reception desk to greet him. "If you'd just care to register, Dr Hill, and give me your passport for a few minutes."

"Certainly." Dr Hill handed over his passport and busied himself filling the registration form. This is it, he thought, I'm here, now, and in all probability Rivers, or whoever's behind all this knows I'm here, and why.

"Thank you, Dr Hill." Thomas broke into his thoughts. "We've put you on the third floor, overlooking the beach. Room 304. I'm sure you'll find it comfortable, but please don't hesitate to come to me if you have any problems, or if the room doesn't suit." He gave his big smile, then held the room keycard out to the bellboy. "Terry, take Dr Hill's things to room 304. Dr Hill, please feel free to have some refreshment before you go up. Terry can see to your things." He handed the passport back to Dr Hill, along with a second keycard.

"Thank you, Thomas, I think I might just do that." Terry leaned down to pick up the shoulder bag. "No, that's OK, I'll bring that up after." Dr Hill slung the bag onto his shoulder and was about to head into the bar when a tall man with a slim athletic build, yet broad shoulders, came up to him.

"Welcome to Hotel Zanzibar, Dr Hill," he said. He had close cropped silver hair, and almost Ethiopian features. Dr Hill put his age at about fifty. He was dressed in a similar fashion to Thomas, but his shirt was the palest silver grey, and unmistakably silk. "I'm Mr Patterson, the hotel's General Manager. I do hope you enjoy your stay," he shook Dr Hill's hand with a firm grip, while looking him straight in the eyes. Dr Hill felt a little unnerved, but returned an equally firm grip. "If there's anything you require, or have any problems whatsoever, please don't hesitate to contact me. I'm always here." His bright white smile didn't extend to his eyes, Dr Hill noticed.

"Thank you," acknowledged Dr Hill, then walked on into the bar.

The bar could only be described as splendid. One side was all French windows, currently open and letting a warm gentle breeze in. The bar was opposite. Long, copper topped and panelled with cherrywood. The glass shelves behind, mirror backed and smartly laden with many exotic bottles, plus some very expensive rare brandies and whiskies, were tastefully lit with concealed lighting. The tables and chairs were well spaced out. Round cherrywood tables, glass topped and smear free. Four comfortable studded leather chairs to a table, also cherrywood with dark red leather. The same style in the low backed barstools arranged equidistant along the bar. Behind the bar a tall slim grey haired black man in a white shirt and black bowtie, was trying to look busy polishing a glass. At Dr Hill's approach he put glass and cloth to one side and came over. "What can I get you, Sir?" he said with a smile.

"Just a beer, please," replied Dr Hill.

"Any particular preference?" He indicated a long row of beer taps, all sparkling chrome, with condensation covering the lower portions.

"Heineken?" asked Dr Hill.

"Heineken it is, Sir. Please take a seat, I'll bring it over."

"Thank you," said Dr Hill. He surveyed the room. Only one table was occupied. A woman in her late fifties, or early sixties, wearing a loose floral summer trouser suit, was sitting over by the French windows, what appeared to be a gin and tonic on the table in front of her. A couple of tables were occupied out on the terrace. The place seemed sparsely occupied. Dr Hill took a table near the centre of the room. As he went to the table, the woman raised her glass to him and drank. She didn't speak. Dr Hill smiled and nodded, then chose a chair that was at an angle to her table, so that he didn't have to look directly at her. As he put his bag on the chair beside him the barman arrived with his beer.

"Here you are, Sir." He placed a coaster. Not a beer mat, a coaster, on the table and the glass of beer on it. "My name's Edward, Sir. If you need anything just ask."

Dr Hill took a long draught from his beer, then sat back in his chair. "Travelled far?" It was the woman. An American accent, but well spoken.

Dr Hill glanced across and smiled briefly, "London," he said, then picked up his glass for a second mouthful.

"Then you have travelled far. No wonder you need that drink." Dr Hill smiled across at her. That's all I need, he thought, some nosey bloody woman latching on to me as soon as I get here. However, he was relieved as she drained her glass and stood up. "I will leave you in peace, " she said. "It's time for my swim. I have a strict schedule. Gin and Tonic, swim, gin and tonic, swim. It's surprising how many swims I have during the day." She walked out through the French windows. It brought a smile to Dr Hill's face as he finished his beer, then beckoned the bar tender for a second.

Room 304 was, to say the least, opulent. No fitted carpets in this climate, but highly polished and even floor boards, with expensive Persian rugs laid tastefully around in strategic places. Antique furniture in a mixture of styles, mostly colonial. Matching oxblood leather sofa and armchairs, and an old chest as a coffee table, in the lounge area. Sliding double doors led to the bedroom. The bed was a king size four poster, with gauze drapes. The ensuite was the size of Dr King's entire bedroom back home. Italian marble tiling on the walls, riven stone flooring. A large, free standing bath, twin circular carved stone sinks, in front of illuminated mirrors. A shower cubicle that was more of a wet room in its own right, with multi jet sprays and a steam room option.

Dr Hill's clothes barely filled one half of the antique French armoire, in the bedroom. Terry had done a good job of unpacking the suitcase, and putting Dr Hill's things away. He'd even left drawers slightly open, in steps, so that Dr Hill could see where he'd put what. His toiletries were arranged neatly in the bathroom, and the empty suitcase placed in a small cupboard just inside the room, presumably for that very purpose. Arranged on the chest coffee table were leaflets about the hotel and its facilities, including restaurant details. Apparently it opened at 6:30am for breakfast, then remained open until midnight. It detailed menu changes throughout the day, but all it really told Dr Hill was that if he wanted something really exotic for dinner, he'd best go after 7:30pm, or pre order it with the head waiter.

Dr Hill dropped the leaflet back onto the chest and walked out onto the balcony. It was only a metre or so wide, but enough for a couple of rattan chairs and glass topped table. It ran the full width of his room, with French windows in both lounge and bedroom. A gap of a metre, or so, separated his from the rooms on either side. The sun was almost to the horizon, the surrounding sky a salmon pink. He lent on the rail and took a deep breath, taking it all in. I'm not here to enjoy myself, he told himself, but by Christ I'm going to make the most of it. It'd been a long day. He looked at his watch and decided to take a nap before dinner, then an early night. He went through to the bedroom, kicked off his shoes, and just flopped onto the bed. He was asleep in seconds.

Chapter 43

When he awoke, the room was in darkness. Some light came in through the open French windows, casting shadows on the ceiling. He checked his watch, 9:47pm. He hadn't meant to sleep that long, and felt muggy and heavy with tiredness. Still he dragged himself off the bed, pulled his clothes off and stumbled through to the shower. After suffering unexpected jets of water from various directions, he finally got the hang of it and washed the travel dirt away.

Dressed in pale stone chinos, tan brogues and a pale blue open neck shirt, he made his way to the restaurant. Again he noticed the opulence. Louis XIV chairs and tables (he suspected they were genuine) spaced generously around the room. Along one side semicircular banquets, upholstered with the usual buttoned oxblood leather. Opposite, slide back full length windows opened out onto a terrace overlooking the beach and sea. He was greeted by a short, slightly tubby black man in immaculately pressed trousers, a broad ribbon down the side. He wore a Maitre D's short jacket over a crisp white shirt, with a black bow tie. "Good evening, Dr Hill." Word gets around fast. "I'm Patrick, the head waiter. Would you prefer to sit inside, or on the terrace, this evening?"

"Thank you," said Dr Hill. "Inside I think. Perhaps over there." He indicated one of the banquets, midway along.

"Of course, Dr Hill." He escorted him over, saw him seated, draped the napkin across his lap, and handed him the menu . "Can I get you anything to drink?" he asked.

"Just a scotch, please. Chivas Regal, if you have it." He got that in first.

"Certainly, Sir. I shall bring you the wine list directly." He turned, raising a finger to a waiter standing at the station at the end of the room. The waiter walked swiftly over and handed the wine list to Dr Hill with a smile and the slightest of bows. As he retreated, the Maitre D' reappeared with Dr Hill's scotch. Dr Hill thanked him and took a sip of Chivas, it's warm glow comforting him. He perused the menu and chose something light. Despite the shower and the Chivas Regal, he still felt travel weary and not very hungry. He chose the British Virgin Islands' national dish, fish and fungi. He paired it with a glass of crisp Sancerre, condensation dewing the outside of the glass. The fish came expertly cooked, as he expected, flaky and light, with a delicate, seasoned flavour. Not having paid a great deal of attention to the menu, he expected the 'fungi' part of the dish to be some sort of mushroom sauce. Instead it was a kind of porridge affair made, he discovered, with okra and yellow cornmeal. Still, the whole thing was delicious, although he couldn't eat it all. He apologised to the waiter, who collected his plate. "Not at all, Dr Hill, the end of a lengthy journey can often dampen the appetite," replied the waiter.

After his meal Dr Hill sauntered through to the bar. He was relieved to see that the American woman, sipping her G&T on his arrival, was nowhere to be seen. A couple were sat out on the terrace. Even at this late hour, the warmth of the day still lingered and the French windows were wide open. There was one other occupant, a man sat at the fair end of the bar with a glass of beer in front of him. At this time of the evening, the bar lights were turned down low. Even the lights on the shelves behind the bar were quite dim, so the man's features were fairly indistinct. He didn't pay him much attention. He assumed the barman knew his way around his bar so well he didn't need the lights to be particularly bright. He looked up as Dr Hill entered the bar, who was surprised to see that Edward was still on duty. "Dr Hill, what can I get you?" he asked pleasantly.

"Scotch, please," replied Dr Hill,."Chivas Regal."

"Certainly, Sir, I shall bring it right over." Dr Hill took a seat at a table near the French windows, with a view out to the beach, and the ocean beyond. At this time of night, the ocean was inky black, indistinguishable from the equally black sky. The horizon was marked by being a place where the stars stopped. There was no moon, but here, without the light pollution of big cities, or popular resorts, the sky was literally bejewelled with stars. Occasionally a wave would catch and reflect the starlight, like some flickering lamp. The terrace was lit by a string of subtle lights strung above the railings overlooking the beach. As in the bar, tea lights flickered in coloured glass holders on each table. Edward brought him his whisky and he sat back, nursing it in his hands before taking a sip. When he put the glass down on the table he turned his attention into the room. The man at the bar seemed to have left, and Edward was fiddling with something below the bar. Then the man from the bar walked out past Dr Hill's table.

"Good evening, Dr Hill," he said as he passed.

"Good evening," replied Dr Hill, paying attention to the man properly for the first time. As he passed he turned his head toward Dr Hill and smiled, dipping his head in acknowledgment to the reply. Dr Hill's returning smile died on his lips and his mouth hung open as the man walked on. A creeping coldness came over him, almost making him shiver in the evening's warmth. Paul Rivers had just walked past and bid him good evening. It was definitely Paul Rivers. He was slightly heavier than the old photographs, perhaps ten pounds or so, but it was him. The only difference was this man had greying hair at the temples. Dr Hill watched him walk through the French windows. It almost seemed that there was a swagger to his walk as he crossed the terrace, then disappear down the steps onto the beach. Once he'd got over the shock he quickly got up, nearly tripping over his chair. He rushed out on to the terrace, but couldn't see him anywhere. The beach was in total darkness and, although not particularly bright, the lights strung between the posts above the railings helped to obscure the view.

He walked over to the couple having their nightcap. "Excuse me, but did you see where he went?" They were probably in their late sixties, tanned and healthy. Neither of them seemed overweight, nor did they have the wiry skinniness that often comes with age. Their clothes, though casual, screamed big time money, underlined by the Patek Philippe watch on the gentleman's wrist.

"I'm sorry," said the woman, with an Italian accent. "We were not paying attention, were we Aldo?" She was a very beautiful woman, Dr Hill realised, for all her years. High cheek bones and a wide Sophia Loren like smile. Her unashamedly silver hair was cut short, in a boyish style that seemed to accent her large dark eyes.

"Indeed we weren't," replied Aldo. He was dashingly handsome, but with a certain cruelness about him. He gave a chuckle. "Maria and I leave the island, tomorrow. We're going home to see our first great grand child."

"It's a boy, they have called him Rudi," beamed Maria.

Aldo smiled, perfect white teeth. "Rudi, What kind of a name is that? Kids, eh?"

"Well, sorry to have disturbed you," said Dr Hill. "Have a safe journey, tomorrow, and congratulations." He smiled and turned back towards the bar. He'd used the brief conversation to calm himself down, and strolled casually back into the room. He collected the remains of his scotch and wandered over to the bar. Edward was restocking the wine cooler and looked up as Dr Hill settled onto a bar stool.

"Another Chivas Regal, Sir?" he enquired.

"Thank you, yes," said Dr Hill, emptying his glass and putting it down on the bar. When Edward returned with his fresh drink he asked, "Who was that man at the bar, earlier?"

"Man, Sir, What man?" A peculiar sense of unease crept over Dr Hill.

"The man who was sat at the end of the bar, there." He inclined his head to indicate which end of the bar he meant.

"Oh, that man," said Edward. "He comes into the bar from time to time. He is a very discreet and confidential man. He asks that his name is kept quiet." Edward immediately went back to his restocking.

"Well the world and his wife seem to know my name," he blurted it out louder, and more abruptly, than he intended. "Sorry." he realised the whisky and the wine, plus the travelling, was starting to have an adverse effect on him. He'd better get himself to bed. He'd make better sense of it in the morning, with a clear head.

"I'm sure, had you asked, they would have kept your identity quiet, just as well," replied Edward. A certain dismissive attitude to his voice.

"Goodnight, Edward." Dr Hill drained his glass and got up from his bar stool.

"Goodnight, Sir," said Edward.

Chapter 44

Dr Hill breakfasted late, on the terrace. The Italian couple from last night, Maria and Aldo, were just leaving the restaurant. They exchanged pleasantries, and he again wished them a safe journey. The American woman was sipping a coffee. She smiled and nodded a hello to Dr Hill from her table by the railing. It was already hot in the sun, which hung in a blue cloudless sky. There was hardly a breeze, the sea a flat calm, small waves lapped gently at the shoreline. Dr Hill also took a seat by the railings overlooking the beach, two tables away from the American woman. He placed a leather binder on the table, opened beside his place setting. There wasn't much of interest in it, and he made some desultory notes during breakfast. More a ruse to deter anyone from attempting to join him. He was thinking of the American woman in particular.

"You must be very dedicated." The American woman was standing next to his table.

Bugger! He thought as he smiled up at her. "Beg your pardon?" he enquired.

"To come to a paradise like this and carry on working." She took off her sunglasses and waved them in the direction of his binder, "and at breakfast, even."

Dr Hill closed his binder in as casual a manner as he could muster,."Oh, you know." He paused, then, "Just some notes for something I'm working on."

"It must be very interesting." Her words hung there.

"Modelling," said Dr Hill, after a slight pause. "I'm a traffic modeller. Trying to work out a new model for traffic flow." He hoped that sounded suitably boring, yet tried to inflect enough enthusiasm to ensure she got the message. Keep me company and I'll bore the pants off you with my theories of traffic flow. "I'm a consultant," he added, to preclude any questioning as to why a glorified town planner could afford The Hotel Zanzibar.

She put her sunglasses back on. "Well, I'll leave you to your modelling." She smiled and walked away.

Dr Hill finished his breakfast in grateful silence. Just the gentle susurration of breaking waves a hundred yards, or so, down the beach. He walked back into the hotel, to the foyer. His intention to go out the front of the hotel, and stroll round to the next bay. In the foyer Mr Patterson was on his own, behind the reception desk.

"Good morning Dr Hill," said Mr Patterson. "I trust you slept well."

"Yes indeed," replied Dr Hill. "Tell me, there was a gentleman in the bar last nigh, late on. About fiftyish, dark hair greying at the temples." As he spoke he noticed Mr Patterson's expression start, imperceptibly, to close up. The eyes hardened. "I feel I know him from somewhere, but I only realised after he left. I don't suppose…"

"I'm afraid some of our guests demand absolute confidentiality," interrupted Mr Patterson.

"Of course, I understand perfectly," responded Dr Hill. "Perhaps I'll catch him in the bar, this evening"

"Indeed, Dr Hill. Enjoy the rest of your day." Mr Patterson gave a cold smile and moved his attention to some paperwork behind the reception counter.

Dr Hill walked out in the fierce heat of the sun. It seemed doubly intense now, after the cool air-conditioned hotel foyer. Donning sunglasses he walked off in the direction of the next bay. A small cove he was told was just a short walk round the back of the headland.

As the cove came into view, Dr Hill thought twenty five minutes in this heat, a bit more than a short walk. He was pleased to notice the beach bar, at the back of the beach. An open structure with a thatched roof. The bar running round all four sides and all the bar paraphernalia on an island in the middle. A few bar stools and, most welcome of all, shade. He made straight for it. There was one other patron, a tanned portly man of about sixty. A straw Panama lay on the bar top, next to a glass of beer dripping condensation. The very sight made Dr Hill thirsty. He glanced at his watch. Coming up to midday. Near enough, he thought. The barman came around the bar at Dr Hill's approach. Dreadlocks and a straggly beard going grey. Bob Marley quietly sang "No woman, no cry" from the speaker fixed to one of the roof support posts.

" 'ey man, you look like you needing' a drink," he flashed Dr Hill a dazzling smile. One gold tooth glinting in the sun.

"A beer, please," said Dr Hill, settling on to a bar stool.

"How you likin' our little island?" he asked, taking the top off a bottle of beer, dewed with condensation.

"Very nice," said Dr Hill, then added. "I'm staying at Hotel Zanzibar."

"Of course you are," laughed the barman. "Everybody stays at Hotel Zanzibar. You can call me Dave."

"Well cheers, Dave," said Dr Hill and took a long swig from his bottle.

"And you can call me Eddy," said the portly man, raising his glass to Dr Hill. He was well spoken, but at the back of it Dr Hill could detect the remains of its East end origins.

"Mark," responded Dr Hill, raising his bottle in salutation.

"When did you arrive?" enquired Eddy, "Yesterday?"

"Indeed I did." said Mark. "All the way from London."

Eddy nodded. "Bit of a schlep. Done it myself a few times. My business is based there, although I'm semi retired, now. Spend most of my time here. Have a small financial investment advisory company. We do alright for ourselves. Select group of clients. Select set of investments." The hairs on the back of Mark's neck felt as if they were electrified. Was this the conduit through which all these investments had been made? Was he Harlequin? He managed to maintain an outer calm, even smiled as his mind raced. Why was he telling him all this? Had he been rumbled already? Then another thought brought an element of calm. The patrons of Hotel Zanzibar were, in general, very wealthy. Perhaps this was the preemptor of a sales pitch. He wants me to invest. "So what do you do, Mark? What's your line that enables a few days in the sun at chez Zanzibar?"

Mark trundled out his story about modelling traffic flow statistics. "Not very exciting, I know," said Mark. "but pays the bills." He added with a smile, raising his beer bottle.

"So it would seem," laughed Eddy. "Well, time for my daily constitutional." He drained his glass, put the Panama on his head and strode off along the beach. Mark noticed, as he walked from the bar, he was wearing light khaki shorts and flip flops, and for a chubby chap, had very muscular legs. He didn't so much walk, as march over the sand to the road at the back of the beach. On reaching the road he turned right, away from the hotel. Intrigued Mark turned to the barman, Dave.

"Dave, where does that road lead?" he asked.

Dave straightened up from heaving a crate of beer in front of a fridge, ready to stock it up. He looked in the direction David was looking, "That road there? That don't lead nowhere, just up into the hills." He turned to Mark. "It used to lead to the old house many years ago."

"The old house?"

"Yeah, man. There was a big ol' house up there, in the hills. Burned down years ago. Jungle's takin' it back now. Roads no more than a track after the first couple hundred yards. Mr Ed likes to walk as far up it as he can. Says the exercise does him good. Sure makes him thirsty, know what I mean?" he laughed. "You wanting' a refill?" He nodded at Mark's empty bottle. Mark thought it a good idea in this heat. Dave opened him a fresh bottle and tossed the empty into the bottle box behind the bar with the ringing rattle of glass on glass. "Don't know how far he goes," continued Dave. "but sometimes he's gone up there for hours. Must go to the very top. If you go past the ruins of the old house you're only a few yards from the top. Then it drops almost vertical, into the sea. You get a great view out over the Atlantic Ocean." Mark thought that this must be the same place he was told about when he was being driven from the harbour to the hotel. Dave nodded to himself. "Nothin' between you and Africa."

Chapter 45

After a late lunch, Mark strolled down the beach and found a sun lounger in the shade of a parasol, away from the other few people sunning themselves. A quick look round, and no sign of the American woman. He lay back and closed his eyes, listening to the gentle susurration of the waves lapping the shore. He was soon asleep.

"Dr Hill?... Dr Hill." The voice stirred Dr Hill from his sleep. Edward, the barman, was standing beside the sun lounger tray in hand. On it was a glass, dewed with condensation, containing ice, slices of lime and lemon, and a cloudy liquid. "I thought you might care for something cooling. It's my own concoction, ginger pressé."

Mark squinted against the sun, sat up and put his sunglasses on. "Thank you, Edward. Nice timing." He took the proffered glass and took a long draught. "That's just the ticket." Edward smiled, did a little semi bow and walked back up the beach. Dr Hill finished his drink and looked around. Two people were in the sea swimming, another was just walking out. It was the American woman. In her swimsuit he could see that she was quite trim, with a tan that was just the right side of being too dark. It was clear she looked after herself, her legs and arms were well defined, but not excessively muscled. Mark was standing up to go back into the hotel.

"Dr Hill," she called out. "anybody would think you were trying to avoid me." She flashed him a bright white Hollywood smile and bent down to pick a towel off her sun lounger, only a few yards from him. Standing up she tossed her head, flinging her wet hair out of her face.

Bugger! thought Dr Hill. That's all I need. But another part of him thought Hmm she is rather attractive, though. "Not at all." He answered with a smile. "It's just that I wanted to check over some notes, in my room"

"Pity," she responded. "I was hoping you might join me for a gin and tonic."

Mark made a decision, straightened up and smiled back. Thinking this could be a mistake, but what the hell. "Actually that sounds a lot better than checking notes. A gin and tonic sounds just the job."

She came up to him and put her hand through his arm, guiding him towards the terrace. "That's more like it," she said. This close, he could smell the ocean on her. A combination of salt water and sun. At the steps to the terrace she used Mark to balance herself while she brushed sand off her feet and slid them into a pair of expensive looking leather flip flops that were at the side of the bottom step. They took a table on the terrace by the railings and ordered their drinks. Gin and tonic for her, a beer for him. "So, Dr Hill," she said, as Edward placed their drinks on the table. "Tell me all about yourself, and your fascinating life in traffic modelling." She said it with an impish smile, and a glint in her eye.

"Please call me Mark," he said.

"And I'm Susie, with an S." She offered her hand across the table and Mark shook it. They both smiled.

"I doubt you'd find traffic modelling fascinating," he continued.

"Try me," she said, leaning forward and resting her face in her hands, elbows propped on the table. A wide smile on her face.

"Well, I'm looking at modifications to the systems currently in place in Rio de Janeiro. It's quite a mess." Fortunately he'd brushed up on his legend before coming out to Hotel Zanzibar, even reading up on it during his flights out. He knew the rudimentaries of the traffic system in Rio, and its problems of too much traffic flowing into the same place at one time. The same with most big cities, so no surprises there. All the background was in place. Should anyone investigate, they would indeed find that the Rio de Janeiro authorities had indeed hired a consultant, Dr Mark Hill, to look at their traffic problem. Even if the Rio authorities didn't know it themselves. They would also find out, should they enquire further, that said Dr Mark Hill was currently on a well earned vacation somewhere in the Caribbean. Specific destination unknown. Which is just how Hotel Zanzibar would want it, and he assumed they'd checked as soon as he'd made a reservation. He just hoped they hadn't put two and two together, with Dr Mark Hill of Her Majesty's Government, quite yet. Though he realised it would probably only be a matter of time.

"So how do you plan to resolve their situation?" asked Susie.

"Oh, it's early stages at the moment." The stock answer. "I need to get a handle on the current system in place, then analyse it's breakdown. It can all hinge on something as simple as reversing the traffic flow in a couple of main arterial routes into the city, or it can mean totally redesigning the whole traffic system. New one way systems, coordinated traffic lights, the whole shooting match."

"And so far what do you think?" She's really going for this, thought Mark. This is more than the odd throw away question to start a conversation.

"I'm tending towards the latter," he replied.

"And what about you?" she followed up. "What brings you all the way out here on your own? No wife, or partner?"

An inward sigh of relief as the topic of traffic modelling was left behind. "I'm divorced," he replied. "What about you? What brings an attractive woman like you out here on her own? If you don't mind my asking."

She sat back and laughed. "No, I don't mind. I'm widowed. My husband died five years ago of pancreatic cancer. Seven weeks from diagnosis to death." The smile had left her face, and a distant look came into her eyes. "In a way it was mercifully quick, and the doctors made sure he wasn't in any pain when he passed. Anyway," she straightened up and the smile came back, "I have two grown up sons and my husband left me enough to ensure I can enjoy the life to which I'm accustomed."

"What do your boys do?"

"Oh, they're grown men now. The eldest is just turned forty. He's a political adviser. The other is thirty-eight, a concert violinist and gay." She'd sat back in her chair, more relaxed now she was talking about her boys. She was obviously proud of them both. "He came out in 2000."

"What did your husband say?"

"Well, we'd guessed as much for a couple of years. He just said "Tell me something I don't already know." Gave him a great big hug, then went back to watching the game on TV." She took a sip from her gin and tonic, "So, why did you divorce?"

"It all just seemed to have run its course. Jean, my wife, sorry - ex wife, couldn't have children. We tried IVF for two years to no avail. Then I was spending too much time away on various contracts around the world. There was no third party involved, although she's now living with some guy called Andrew, who owns a property development company. Met him once, seemed quite a nice chap, actually."

"And you?" She looked pointedly at him. "No significant, or even not significant other, to keep you company?"

"Not at the moment, no." They chatted for a little while longer.

Then, "Well, I guess I better go and get a shower," she said. "How about we meet in the bar, later. Have a drink and dine together? That's if you haven't got any notes to go over." She grinned at him.

"Oh I think I could give the notes a rest for the night," said Mark, "As for a drink, then dinner together, well I'd like that very much."

"Great, it's a date, then. Meet you in the bar at seven thirty." She got up and picked up her bag and towel off the back of the chair. Mark stood up with her. "See you later." She put her hand on his shoulder and kissed his cheek before walking off into the hotel. As she leaned in close, he smelled the sea on her again. Mark sat back down with, what he knew was, a silly grin on his face. Edward came over to collect the glasses and he ordered a Chivas Regal. He felt like treating himself. He sat back and gazed out from the terrace. Looking over the beach to the sea and the horizon he thought to himself I could get used to this. I may be on assignment, but no reason not to enjoy it while I can. He was fairly sure Eddy, the man at the beach bar was involved in some way. He even had a suspicion that Susie may have some links to this business, but he put that all on the back burner. He thought about a pleasant evening with an attractive woman. He also wondered what to do if Paul Rivers made an appearance.

Mark was sitting at the bar when a hand rested on his shoulder. "G and T, please, Edward," said Susie, climbing onto the adjacent bar stool. She was wearing a long black chiffon dress with gold trim around a plunging neckline, and a gold belt cinching in her waist. Her long black hair shone in the light from the bar, the few silver streaks shimmering. "Well good evening," she smiled at Mark.

"Well, good evening to you too." He grinned back at her. "You look fantastic."

She leaned back on her stool and looked him up and down. "You don't look so bad yourself." He was wearing a slim fitting mid blue silk suit, with an open neck white shirt. A handkerchief in his top pocket adding a splash of colour. "I'm glad you were already here. I'm not fond of guys that keep a girl waiting."

"Oh, I'd never do that. Besides, Dutch Courage." He held up his glass of whiskey.

"You? Dutch Courage? I think you're kidding me." She picked up the gin and tonic Edward had just put down in front of her. "Anyway, here's to a lovely evening. Cheers." They clinked glasses.

The small talk continued and they went in to dine. They both had fish, and Mark again went for the Sancerre, ordering them a bottle. Susie was easy company and Mark felt relaxed. More so than when he first arrived. After they'd dined they went out onto the terrace and sat at a table by the rail. The warm, balmy air was totally still. Just a gentle swell visible on the sea. A white line where the small waves gently broke on the sand. A gibbous moon, low over the headland, reflected in the water. Edward appeared and placed their drinks on the table. A gin and tonic for her, a Chivas Regal for him. Mark sat back in his chair, "So, is this it for you?" he asked, smiling. Indicating the beach and their surroundings with his glass, before taking a sip.

"You mean Hotel Zanzibar?" She turned in her chair and folded her arms along the top of the railing. She looked out over the beach toward the sea, a surprisingly young posture that Mark found quite alluring. "Well, I do spend a lot of time here."

"Don't you get bored?"

She looked round at Mark, with a broad smile. "Not now." She turned back and looked out at the beach before turning back to the table. "I do travel some," she added. "I have an apartment in New York, and one in London. Tite Street, Chelsea, do you know it?"

"I know Chelsea," said Mark. "Nice area."

"It's handy for business," she said. "My broker is based in London."

"I thought you said your husband left you well off," said Mark, then, "Sorry that was rude of me."

"Not at all," said Susie with a laugh. "He did. A lot of it was in stocks and shares, although there was a substantial amount of capital, but the shares bring in a very good income, even in these straitened times."

"You must give me your broker's name," said Mark. "I could do with some good investment advice." He smiled back at her, but the alarm bells were ringing.

"Well, you can meet him, he's staying here now. You may have seen him. Chubby fellow, walks a lot. He often goes up into the hills walking. Don't know where he is tonight, though." She looked around. "I don't see him anywhere, and he wasn't in the restaurant."

"His name wouldn't be Eddy, by any chance?" asked Mark.

"Why yes. How could you possibly know that?"

"I met him this morning, at the beach bar in the next cove. He went off for his walk. Up into the hills, as you said. Apparently there are some ruins up there. An old mansion that burned down?"

"That's right. Went up there once, myself. This is a couple of years ago, at least. Quite a slog, I can tell you, and not much to see once you get up there. Apart from the view that is. The ruin's just what you'd expect. Hardly a wall standing, just a load of rubble and some timbers, all overgrown. But the view! The sea's about a hundred feet below you and you can see right to the horizon. Nothing at all between you and, well, Africa, I suppose."

"Someone else told me that recently," mused Mark. "So he handles your investments. How did you find him?"

"Oh, I didn't. Dick, my late husband, had been dealing with him for years, even when he was still at Maguire Landers."

"Maguire Landers?" queried Mark. "Didn't they go bust in the fall out from 2008?"

"They sure did," said Susie with a smile. "Just a few short weeks after Dick retired. It's almost as if he knew something was going to happen. He moved all his money, plus his pension fund, out of Maguire Landers, and put it in Weston Deer. One of the very few banks in the USA, perhaps the world, to not be hit by the sub prime fallout.

"Anyway, you were asking about Eddy. Dick was dealing with Dunbar, Eddy's company, before all that happened."

"Do you think he tipped your husband off?"

"I sometimes wonder that, myself." A wistful look came over her, and she looked out over the railings toward the sea. Then she turned back to Mark. "Well, it's been a lovely evening, but it's time for my beauty sleep." Susie stood up and Mark stood up with her.

"Let me walk you to your room," said Mark.

"You're very gallant," said Susie,."but I'm fine. Thank you for a lovely evening. I guess I'll see you tomorrow." She came round the table to him, put both her hands on his shoulders and kissed him. This time full on the lips. There was still that faint scent of the sea on her, underneath a light perfume. She stepped back and smiled up at him. "Goodnight, Mark." She turned and walked back into the hotel. He watched her go, unsure of his feelings. He realised he was very attracted to her. He had half hoped she might invite him back to her room, but no that was just fanciful. He'd only just met her, for God's sake. He also had those alarm bells going off. He was now certain she had something to do with all this, Harlequin and it's clients. What if he got mixed up with someone, emotionally involved even, with one of the players. He sat slowly back down and picked up his glass. He'd hardly touched his Chivas Regal. He took a sip, and stared off into the middle distance.

Chapter 46

The following morning Mark ordered breakfast in his room, and stayed there till almost noon. He was supposed to be doing some work on Rio de Janeiro's traffic system. It would look strange if he spent too much time out and about, much as he really fancied the idea of spending more time with Susie. He'd wander down to the beach and explain he had been working.

He walked down the terrace steps onto the sand and looked around for Susie, or some sign of which sun bed was hers. He soon spotted it. A colourful towel spread over it and her beach bag he recognised from yesterday, but no Susie. He looked out to sea to see if he could spot her in the water, but no. In fact no-one was in the water. With a start he looked around. He'd been so intent on looking for Susie, he hadn't noticed that there was nobody on the beach, either. All the accoutrements were there. The towels, bags, bathing costumes draped over the backs of sun beds, but the beach was completely devoid of people.

He became aware of a figure beside him, the soft sand masking any sound of his approach. He turned quickly. Paul Rivers stood there, a smile on his face. "Dr Hill, I wonder if you could spare a moment or two." He half turned, and indicated the terrace steps with his outstretched arm.

Mark realised his mouth was open with surprise. He abruptly closed it, his mind racing. Then, "Why, what appears to be the problem?"

Paul Rivers retained his smile, even gave a little chuckle. "Come now Dr Hill, I know who and what you are, and you know full well who I am. Shall we?" He moved off toward the terrace. He turned at Mark's reticence. "I assure you no harm will come to you, you are in no danger. Well, not from me, anyway. I dare say

Susie Keelan may have something to say when she finds out you're not the traffic flow consultant you claimed to be." He moved off. "Do you mind if I call you Mark? Please call me Paul." He trudged up towards the terrace steps, his off white linen trousers flapping slightly in the light breeze. Mark noticed he was barefoot, his tanned skin contrasting with the trousers and the white T shirt he was wearing. Mark followed him, his flip flops dragging in the sand. Paul led him across the hotel foyer and to a door opposite the reception desk marked "Private". He opened it and ushered Mark through. "I thought it best we have our little tête-à-tête in private."

"Where is everybody else?" enquired Mark.

"They're having a meeting," replied Paul. "deciding what to do next."

"About what?"

"Why, you of course." He replied with a laugh.

"All of them?"

"Oh yes. Every guest here is part of the group, so to speak."

"So why advertise, and why let me come?"

"That's easy." They'd come to what looked like a service lift. Instead of a call button there was a key switch. Paul produced a key, inserted it into the switch and turned. The lift doors rattled open to reveal a very utilitarian lift interior, just a metal tread plate floor and scuffed metal walls and ceiling. It was illuminated by a bulkhead light on one of the side walls. Below it was a panel with another key switch. No other buttons, lights or switches were apparent. Again, Paul inserted his key into the switch and turned. The doors rattled shut and the lift jerked and started to slowly ascend. "I was expecting you to come eventually. So of course, when you sent a request for a reservation I was ready to accommodate you. As for advertising, it's very low key. No social media, whatsoever, very discreet. Our prices mean we get very few requests, and we vet them thoroughly. If we think they are likely to be recruited to our little group, then they get a reservation. If not, then we are fully booked for the foreseeable future. Here we are." The doors rattled open to reveal a short corridor. It looked scruffy and unused. The carpet was worn through to the backing in several places. A side table, against the left hand wall, was thick with dust. It was all lit by a grey light that managed to push its way past the grime on the window. It suddenly felt cold, causing Mark to shiver and rub his arms. He was only wearing his khaki shorts and navy polo shirt. Paul chuckled. "Yes, it is a bit strange. You'll get used to it." The corridor contained two doors, one on each side. Paul made for the one on the left, past the dusty table. As he was unlocking it, Mark took the opportunity to look through the window. Though the dirt he could make out what looked like a garden. Overgrown and gone to seed, brambles crawling through the undergrowth. To either side tall trees, rocking in a strong wind which buffeted the window, making it rattle. Beyond the garden, nothing, just a distant view of a grey windswept ocean, spray being whipped off the wave crests. Mark assumed the garden ended at the cliff edge, many feet above sea level. "Shall we?". Paul's voice brought him back with a start. Mark followed him into the room, and Paul closed the door behind him. It was a complete contrast to the shabby, neglected corridor outside. The room was spacious, but still cosy. Honey coloured wood paneling to the walls, warmly lit from several table and standard lamps. Within a stone fireplace and mantle, a small log fire burned, taking the chill off the air. A small chesterfield sofa and matching armchair faced each other across a carved cherrywood antique low table. All placed in front of the fire. Across the room was a large mahogany desk flanked by two tall windows that gave out on to the same bleak scene Mark had witnessed from the window in the corridor. Mark's eye was drawn to what was on the desk. At one end was an ornate bronze and gold, highly decorated hexagonal cylinder. At the other a weird looking contraption, all glowing glass valves, wiring and fine copper tubing mounted on a wooden base. It looked, for all the world, like the insides of an old fashioned wireless combined with an experimental teasmaid. Between these two, looking totally incongruous, sat a MacBook laptop computer. Snaking from a USB port, on the side of the MacBook, a lead ran to the curious valved object.

Mark pointed to the ornate cylinder, and turned to Paul. "Is that what I think it is?"

"The smart answer would be for me to ask you what do you think it is, but I think we can forgo the charade. Yes, it is. It's why you're here. Why we've come this far, and why all my guests are currently in heated debate about what to do next." He looked around the room, then back at Mark. "Before we go any further, I think it might be a good idea to get changed out of these beach clothes into something more appropriate." He opened the door opposite the entrance and went into what appeared to be an apartment, furnished in the same comfortable style as the first room.

"More appropriate for what?" demanded Mark, "and more to the point, where the hell are we?"

"All in good time," answered Paul. "I promise I will explain everything. What that artefact is, what it does and more importantly, the consequences.

"Now, I suggest we get changed, then make ourselves comfortable back in the study. We've a lot to go through, and a lot to do."

Chapter 47

Dressed in a simple dark blue suit, open necked shirt and brown brogues, Mark took his seat in the armchair by the fire. Paul sat opposite, on the sofa. He was wearing a dark grey, almost black suit, black shirt and black Chelsea boots. At his throat he wore a yellow paisley cravat and in his breast pocket a matching handkerchief. On the table between them was a tray, sat upon which was a French press full of coffee, two coffee cups, a milk jug and sugar. Paul leaned forward and slowly pushed the plunger down in the French press, then poured out two cups of coffee. "Help yourself to milk and sugar," he said. "So, where to begin? How much do you already know?"

Mark took a sip of his coffee. Black, no sugar. "Well, I know you robbed a bank and fucked off with a couple of million quid of other people's money, and a very special piece of equipment, the property of HMG." He nodded in the direction of the desk.

"Yes, well. Not strictly true," said Paul, cradling his coffee cup with his fingertips. "For a kick off Làngfèi shíjiān never was the property of HMG. Why do you think they got us to break into the vault of Swifts Bank, on Pall Mall, and nick it?"

"You were serving officer of the Crown. The moment you personally took possession, it became the property of the Crown."

" A moot point. You would have done exactly the same, had you been in my shoes."

"How can you say that? You don't know me. You may think you do, but you don't."

"Mark, listen to me. It's not about knowing you, it's about having the knowledge that Làngfèi shíjiān imparts. It's far too powerful and important to be given to a government, any government. It would make them think they could rule the world. It would be utterly catastrophic. Why do you think it was kept hidden in a Taoist monastery for over two thousand years. The man Zhao Goa was it's keeper. He thought it safe in London, he didn't want the Chinese to get hold of it. If I hadn't opened it, he would have come looking for it and killed anybody that got in his way."

"So why, what happened when you opened it?"

"It's a bizarre, otherworldly artefact. Literally it's not of this world. When I opened the cylinder and picked up the thing inside it immediately attached itself to me. I was its keeper. I instantly knew it, I instantly knew what it was and how it worked, and a million other things beside.

"For instance, you've not remarked on how youthful I look for a man one hundred and twenty-three years old."

"I was going to come to that. I assume it's down to Làngfèi shíjiān?"

"Yes. Once you take hold of it, you become its keeper. It prevents you ageing. Unfortunately it also immediately removes its protection to the previous keeper. When I took hold of it, I became its new keeper. Zhao Gao had been its keeper for over two thousand years. Can you imagine that? Being alive for over two thousand years. He was born in two hundred and fifty nine B.C. Nearly three hundred years old already, when Christ was born. He was Chief Eunuch to the first emperor of China, Qin She Huang. Name ring a bell?"

"You mean the emperor buried with the Terracotta Army?"

"That's the fella. Zhao Gao worked for him. Well, actually there was only one person Zhao Gao worked for, and that was Zhao Gao. He masterminded all sorts of Machiavellian plots when Qin She Huang died. Principally to get his younger, and fairly useless son on the throne, with himself as Prime Minister and virtually running things. However, it all went tits up, as these things usually do, and collapsed in just fifteen years. History says Zhao Gao was killed, but he wasn't. He, and a few buddies disappeared to a Taoist Monastery, where Zhao Gao remained.

"He'd used Làngfèi shíjiān to further his position all through Qin She Huang's reign, and thought he could use it to take over. However, it doesn't quite work like that, as he found out. He realised how dangerous it was, and that he must remain its keeper. Keeping it hidden from the world. That all changed when the Japanese invaded Manchuria, and he sent it to London for safe keeping."

"So, if you're the keeper, now, what's happened to Zhao Gao?" puzzled Mark.

"He died. The instant I took hold of Làngfèi shíjiān he ceased to be its keeper, and all its power and protection was transferred me. He would have died almost instantly."

"So if I jumped up and grabbed it, I would take over it's power and you would die?"

Paul grinned and held up his right hand. On the middle finger was a broad bronze and gold ring, with an intricate pattern inlaid. "Not while I have this. It's my remote control, if you like. While I have this, you can grab hold of Làngfèi shíjiān, run off to London with it. You won't be able to do a damn thing with it. It'll just be a big paper weight."

"Well that begs the question why Zhao Gao wasn't wearing it. Why send it all the way to London without the ring?"

"A good question. He'd just got tired of it, I suppose. He could see the way the world was going and felt burying it in a bank vault was as sure a way he could think of to put it out of harms way, so to speak. He was behind the murder of Lau Huang, after it was deposited. He pulled a few strings to manipulate the diplomatic immunity thing for the murderers, but the Chinese government really knew nothing about it. Just some minor officials making a mess of things, and when they got back they put them in front of a firing squad. His visit to London was more a check up that it was as safe as could possibly be. He now knew the bank wouldn't let anyone into the vault without proper authority, and that was highly unlikely. His interview with MI5 made him think they would't have much luck either, else why speak to him. So that's why he disappeared back to China.

"I'm sure when I grabbed hold of Làngfèi shíjiān, and he lost his contact, the only thing he felt was relief."

"That's all well and good, but what about all the money you stole? Some people lost fortunes."

"They did, and some of them deserved to. However, many of those who, shall we say, had more legitimate losses, got their money back and then some."

"How so?"

"I got them involved in the early stages of using Làngfèi shíjiān to play the markets. I set up some stock brokers, and got them to invest on what I knew would be a sure fire thing. Which neatly brings me back to Làngfèi shíjiān and what it actually does. It transports you instantly through dimensions. So, for instance, I could instantly be in London, or New York or where ever. It can also transport you in time. But only back in time. You can't go into the future, only back then return to the time you started from. I could go back and watch MI5 pick up Zhao Gao, in the 1930's, but I could only get back to this point in time, the here and now."

"So how did you get it to work for you?"

"I waited. I waited and I watched. I waited for some absolute dead duck, in the market, drop to rock bottom, practically giving the stock away, then suddenly spring back up. A mine that seemed worked out, about to go bankrupt, when suddenly they discover a new, rich seem and the stock rockets. I'd go back and buy up a load of rock bottom stock. Through several companies, of course, so as not to set any alarm bells ringing. Then come back and enjoy my, now, high priced stock. It worked for everything. Like I said, mines, shipping, manufacturing. You'd be surprised how many companies almost go bust, then pick up again. And all the guess-work's taken out."

"And the sub-prime market?" asked Mark, raising his eyebrows.

Paul grimaced and tightened his lips. "Ah, the sub-prime market. I thought you might ask that. Some of the group got a little greedy. Thought they could set the ball rolling themselves, then reap the benefits. Unfortunately they didn't fully understand Làngfèi shíjiān. Most of them don't even know of it. They think I just weave some kind of magic with algorithms and complicated, predictive mathematics. Stupid sods started the ball rolling too close to the now. I wasn't far enough into the future to be able to see it's effect. Just had to let it roll. Then when someone pulled the plug, there was nothing to bet on. Nothing about to bounce back. A few of the group lost everything. One threatened to blow the whole thing about what we do here. He had to be dealt with. No great loss. Selfish little shit, the main instigator behind S.P. You could say it was his idea. He'd floated it to the group. I said no, but he went ahead anyway. The others we helped out. Some seed cash to build up their stock again, that sort of thing.

"These days I just dole out advice to Dunbar. All at one remove, via Harlequin. Have you met Edward Chiles-Martin?"

"Do you mean Eddy, stocky chap likes to walk in the hills?"

"I do indeed. Eddy runs Dunbar, mostly at a distance from here. He's got staff in the office that do all the work. Contacting clients, passing on the information. All very discreet, and all in the name of Harlequin. Makes Dunbar a sort of cut-out. There's only a few staff, and all highly paid. Helps to keep them on side." Paul stood up and went over to the desk. "I think it's time you met Harlequin." Mark got up and joined him. Paul indicated the contraption on the desk linked to the MacBook. "This is it. It has a rather more mundane name. It's actually a multi dimensional communicator, or MDC. Làngfèi shíjiān keeps me well up to date on the world of modern technology, even a little ahead in this case. It allows me to connect to the internet at a time in the past."

"How do you mean?" Mark asked, with furrowed brows.

"Basically I can send an email to arrive yesterday, or last week, whenever. It's how I communicate with Dunbar. I see something worthwhile in our interest. We recently had a failing ferry company, about to go to the wall, several thousand jobs in jeopardy, stock worth next to nothing. Next thing you know, government steps in with a rescue package. Business picks up, stock shows a healthy improvement. So I email Dunbar. I send the email to get there just a couple of days before the government commits. It's in the wind, so a few sudden purchases don't raise any eyebrows, just some speculators betting on the government stepping in. They're not to know that I already know they have. It's that simple." Paul smiled and held his hands out palms upwards.

"What about big influences, though. What would happen if you went back and made some big changes?"

"What sort of changes?"

"You know, physical changes to the world, at large. Stopped someone being killed, that was. I don't know. Killing Hitler, for example. What happens then?"

"Nothing," said Paul. A darkness came over him. "It's funny you should mention killing Hitler. I did."

"What!"

"I killed Hitler. Used Làngfèi shíjiān to transport into the Olympic stadium, in 1936, and blew his brains out. Then hot footed it back to my current time. Nothing. Nothing had changed. Hitler still survived till 1945. The Holocaust still happened. It's as if causing historical change like that sends another world off parallel to ours, with the alternative consequences happening there. While our world carries on as if nothing happened.

"Small things, like following the markets have no effect. I don't cause the market changes, I just benefit from prior knowledge. I don't actually manipulate the past."

"So why worry about it falling into the wrong hands? If they can't manipulate the past. There's not a lot they can do, surely."

"They can see how things are turning out and put things in place that don't alter the past. They manipulate the future. Place-men, if you like. Someone in a position of power, given the information about what's going to happen in order to take certain actions at a later point. Depending on its outcome, they then feed back other information. It's a matter of short steps. Not too far in the past, so the outcomes can be observed. Then a short jump back to fine tune, so to speak. With manipulation like that, you could rule the world. You don't need bombs or wars, it's far more subtle. Just a nudge here and there. Enough to cause a reward, or a disaster."

Mark felt totally out of his depth. The horror of the capabilities of Làngfèi shíjiān was chilling. He was beginning to see why Paul Rivers had done a runner with it. It's one thing making a few million off the information, but if any of those clowns, currently in power got their hands on it. Utter disaster. "So what do you intend to do now?" asked Mark. "If you knew I was coming. I don't see."

"I need to show you something," said Paul. He went into the second room and came back carrying two dark coats. He handed one to Mark and put the other one on himself. He then went over to the cylinder and opened it.

Chapter 48

The room was suffused in a blue light from within the cylinder. Mark looked on, fascinated, as Paul lifted out Làngfèi shíjiān. Round, but slightly thicker each end, like a fat dumbbell, gold rods running its length connecting the ends. The blue glow was like an aura around it. Ornate symbols and inlays covered its surface. Small windows had shapes and symbols moving behind them in a sort of amorphous display, with thumb wheels beside each one. Paul pressed one end and a short wide cylinder emerged. It glided slowly out till Paul took it and lifted it. "Just pop this on your wrist," he said to Mark, who could now see it was a bracelet. "Hold your hand out." Mark did as he asked, and Paul slid the bracelet over Mark's wrist. When he let go the bracelet seemed to shrink and fit itself snuggly to Mark's wrist.

"What's this?" A note of alarm crept into Mark's voice.

"Nothing to be worried about," said Paul, calmly. "It just links you to Làngfèi shíjiān and me." He held up the hand with the ring on it. Then he closed the case and placed Làngfèi shíjiān on top of it. "Shall we?" he said. He turned the ring, so the ornate top was on the inside, then touched it with his thumb.

The world changed. Mark had the sensation of both falling and ascending quickly at the same time. His senses became completely confused. The sound was everything, all sounds, terrifying and lyrical, soothing, musical and angrily discordant. Although Paul remained roughly in focus, everything else was a blur. Shapes and colours both recognisable and alien, shapes and colours he couldn't begin to describe. As suddenly as it started, it stopped. It was all in an instant.

Mark found himself sitting with Paul on a bench in a seaside shelter. In front of them a grey, choppy, uninviting English Channel. Mark looked to his left at the dilapidated ruins of Brighton's West Pier. Shut down in the mid 70's, now showing the marks of years of neglect. "Doesn't burn down for a good few years, yet," said Paul, interrupting Mark's thoughts. "Come on." He stood up and walked round to the right. Mark followed him, he knew exactly where they were headed. They walked the couple of hundred yards along the front, then over to the pavement. Across the road was the building containing Andrew Henly's apartment. Instinctively Mark looked up at the top floor windows, to see if anyone was there. "Here we go," said Paul. A taxi drew up at the entrance to the building. Mark's heart was beating a tattoo in his chest, he could hardly breathe. He watched his 25 year old self come out of the building, get into the taxi and drive off. He looked back up to the windows. Andrew Henly appeared at one of them, glass in hand. Mark wasn't sure whether Andrew was raising his glass to them, or the world in general. "Time to go," said Paul, and walked back the way they came. "So you see, Mark when I said I've known about you for some time, I really mean it".

"But what, I mean how, I mean, I don't know what I mean. How did that just happen?"

"This," said Paul, raising his hands and indicating the world around them, "is 1986. Like I told you, it transports us back to a time and place I specify. When we go forward, it will return us back to the exact moment we left."

"What would have happened if I'd gone across the road and spoken to my earlier self?"

"Honestly? I've no idea. I've been back and seen myself on a few occasions, but I don't ever recall any interaction."

"What do you mean you don't recall?"

"Exactly that." By now they had reached the seaside shelter and Paul sat back down on the bench. "I don't recall any interaction. If I did, it's been completely wiped from my memory, and history."

"I'm still trying to get my head round this. Right now we're sat on the front in Brighton, in 1986."

"We are indeed. If you were to go across the road and find a newsagents, you could buy a paper with this very date, and all the headlines from today. It's not some simulation. You're not observing from outside. We are actually, right now sitting on the front, in Brighton, in the year of our Lord nineteen hundred and eighty six."

Mark sat looking out to sea. A tatty coaster made its way toward Shoreham harbour, a few miles along the coast. They'd just travelled across the world and thirty three years, yet to everyone else in the world it didn't even register. He realised, in that moment, how fantastic and terribly dangerous Làngfèi shíjiān was. He turned to Paul, "Can we go back now?"

"Of course." Paul glanced around, checking they weren't observed. He touched his thumb to the ring. Again, the sensations and colours. The sounds and the light. Then he felt the floor beneath him and the room they'd left snap back into being. They were standing by the desk. Mark put his hand out to steady himself and felt the bracelet go loose on his wrist. "I admit, it takes some getting used to. May I?" He held his hand out towards Mark's wrist. Mark held it up and Paul easily slid it off. He offered it up to the end of Làngfèi shíjiān and it slid smoothly back in, unaided. It became part of the whole, indistinguishable from the rest of this remarkable artefact. Paul took their coats back into the other room. When he returned, Mark was still standing by the desk, a stunned look on his face. He ushered Mark to the armchair, then took his seat on the sofa. "I've no doubt you have questions." He smiled and raised his hands, "Fire away."

"I don't know where to start. I came out here to track down your Làngfèi shíjiān. I didn't expect this "

"You called it My Làngfèi shíjiān, not just Làngfèi shíjiān."

"Well it is yours. You control it and there's some sort of bizarre link between you and it." Paul inclined his head in acknowledgement. "But this," he indicated the room, "How? I mean we got in a lift in the hotel, yet this isn't the hotel, is it?"

"Well, no." said Paul. "This is the house at the top of the hill, or rather, a displaced version of it. The actual building burned down, as I'm sure you've already been told, but Làngfèi shíjiān maintains this version of it. There are a couple of entrances to it. The lift, that we use. Làngfèi shíjiān senses it's me, and brings it here. Anybody else, even if they had the key, would just end up on the top floor of the hotel, opposite two permanently locked rooms. There's nothing in them, just keeps the customers happy to think that's where I live. The other entrance is up the jungle path. You pull some creepers away and there's an arch with a dilapidated looking burnt wooden door. It's anything but dilapidated. To anyone rummaging around they'd go round the arch, to the other side, and see the equally burnt other side of the door. However, if you're known to Làngfèi shíjiān, authorised so to speak, the door would open into the corridor outside." He waved toward the door to the office from the corridor.

"I'm beginning to think nothing's going to surprise me any more," said Mark. "but all you've done with this is make money. Stupid amounts of money to live your fancy life style, and your coconspirators likewise." He started to sound indignant. Damn it, he was indignant. All this, just to line his pockets. "Is that all you can do."

He almost spat the words out. "This fantastic article, Làngfèi shíjiān, and you just line your, and a few friends' pockets."

"Oh don't you get all indignant on me, Dr Mark Hill. You don't know the half of it. You, and MI5, have been so busy looking for it, and find out what happened to me. Digging into where the information comes from and who uses it. You've not even thought to look in the other direction."

"What do you mean, the other direction?"

"After they've made their money. Where it goes."

"We know where it goes, into their fucking pockets to lead the high life, courtesy of their offshore tax havens."

"And that, Mark, is where you are so wrong. Sure they're wealthy, and live a good life, but they channel far more through charities, trusts and charitable foundations. We put the money to work where it's needed. In the past few years we've spread out more donations than Bill and Melinda Gates. We can't cure the world, and if we did do it like the Gates', people would sit up and take notice, too much notice. We cannot afford prying eyes.

"That's why I've allowed you up here. I need to convince you that there's nothing here. To go back and tell them it's all been smoke and mirrors. I died years ago, but left behind a set of algorithms I used to predict the markets. Then a few select, and secretive people kept it going."

"I couldn't possibly do that," said Mark, indignantly.

"What's the alternative?" asked Paul. "We can't bump you off. MI5 know where you are, and why. If you suddenly disappeared it wouldn't be long before we had the SBS, or SAS tramping up the beach in the wee, small hours. Then again, you can't possibly let it fall into the hands of that bunch of self serving, useless idiots in charge of it all. And I don't just mean the current lot.

Any of them. None of them would be able to resist using it for their own ends. It would be a world wide disaster."

Mark remained silent for a while. He could see where Paul was coming from, but he couldn't figure a way out. "So I go back, and say what? It would need to be convincing, and I don't think your 'smoke and mirrors', algorithm theory would stand up to close scrutiny."

"Possibly. There are other possibilities. You could stay here, for instance. We could send back some email correspondence saying a distant relative has died, left you pots of money and you've decided to retire, and spend some time traveling. That would keep them off your back."

"Nice idea, but wouldn't work. My ex-wife wouldn't believe it, for a start. She'd start pestering the office and causing a scene."

Chapter 49

They were interrupted by a knock at the door. Paul seemed almost as startled as Mark, then recovered his composure. "That's probably Eddy," he said, and got the door.

Eddy Chiles-Martin came into the room looking somewhat out of breath. His long khaki cargo pants were rumpled, and grass stained around the bottoms. His floral shirt was unbuttoned half way and there were sweat patches under the arms. He went over to the fire. "Christ, that's some schlep up here," he moaned, "and why is it always so fucking cold in here?"

"What way did you come?" demanded Paul.

"Up the hill track, in through that arch under the creepers and through the door. Fucking gives me the creeps. That weird sensation when I come in through that door."

"Did you come alone?"

"Of course I fucking came alone. We've made a decision." He tipped his head towards Mark.

Paul heaved a sigh of annoyance. "I told you. I'm dealing with it. I also told you I would come down to you, when I'd finished."

"Yeah, well, some of us didn't want to wait."

"What you mean is you didn't want to wait."

"Well it's a good job I didn't. You seem to be getting pretty friendly with matey, here." Again he indicated Mark.

"I am here, and I've got a name," said Mark, angrily.

"You can shut the fuck up," said Eddy belligerently, stepping towards Mark. Mark stood to face him square on.

"For fuck's sake. Pack it in!" shouted Paul, now on his feet "I'll decide what's what in this house. My house, my rules. So, Eddy, you shut the fuck up and sit down, or get out."

Reluctantly Eddy sat on the sofa, perched on the edge. "Beginning to think you might be losing your edge. We didn't just discus Dr Mark fucking Hill. We discussed you. Your info's been a bit slim, lately".

"That, My Dear Eddy, is because not much has been happening worth our investment. You follow the markets. Have you seen anything going belly up, recently, that's had a sudden miraculous turn around?"

"That's because you didn't give us the nod. If we'd got in they would have probably turned," said a sullen Eddy.

"You're wrong, Eddy." Paul had remained standing, with his back to the desk so he could face both Eddy and the now reseated Mark. "I give the nod to invest because I know they're going to turn around. It's not a question of if!"

"How can you possibly know?" responded Eddy. The whole idea sounded incredulous. Mark maintained his silence. He realised that, although Eddy was allowed into this inner sanctum, he really didn't know the half of it. "I admit your laptop contraption," he waved towards the MDC, "comes up with some pretty amazing results, but come on. It can't predict the future".

"Oh, but Eddy," said Paul, giving Mark a quick glance, "it does precisely that. I have to work damn hard on it to maintain a discreet distance in time, so we have the edge. Why do you think I spend so much time up here?"

"Is that why you keep it so cold up here?" answered Eddy. "I've heard these super computers need to be kept cold. I know that's a laptop, but that thing it's connected to, that has do be kept cold, yes?"

"In a way, yes." said Paul. "That's also why you can't see this place from the outside."

"Come again?"

"You can't see it from the outside, because it doesn't exist in your normal time. It's how it knows the future." Again he glanced at Mark. Mark understood he needed him to go along with him.

"He's right," said Mark. "Paul was just explaining it to me when you came in. It seems hard to believe, yet here we are."

Eddy looked across at Mark, then back to Paul. "We decided he's a threat, and needs to be got rid of." He pointed across at Mark, "He knows too much. No thanks to you. Seems he now knows more than me."

"I told you," said Paul going round his desk and taking a seat in the leather and mahogany captain's chair, "I'm sorting it out." He rummaged around in a drawer, "Ah, here we are," he said, and raised a gun from behind the desk. A Glock, not unlike the one in Marks luggage, but not quite so brand new. He stood up, as did Mark, a look of surprise and confusion.

"What the fuck!" cried Mark.

"Now you're seeing sense," said Eddy. "You've got to do what you've got to do." Then Paul shot him. He turned slightly, extended his arm, and shot Eddy through the right eye. The sound of the gunshot made Mark's ears ring in the confined space, An expression of horror as he looked across at Eddy's ruined face, his body slumped to one side on the sofa. A spray of red all over the back of the sofa, even sprayed on the wall behind and on the carpet, along with bits of tissue and skull fragments.

"What the fuck?" shouted Mark for the second time.

"That's twice you've said that," said Paul, putting the gun away. "It was inevitable, and it wasn't just because you're here. I'd seen this coming for while. He'd been getting too inquisitive. Not happy just getting the information to pass on and reap the rewards. No, he was getting ideas above his station. Felt he could do a better job if he was in charge. He'd also made noises about the philanthropic side of things. Wasn't fond of giving any of his money away." He picked up a phone that Mark hadn't noticed. A landline partially hidden behind the curtain on the window sill to the right of the desk. He dialled just one digit. After a second's pause it was answered. "Ah, Mr Patterson. Mr Chiles-Martin has checked out. If you'd be so kind as to clear his room, and then attend to matters up here? Thank you, Mr Patterson."

"So what happens now?" Mark was still standing, looking around. The bloody mess, Eddy's slumped body. Totally confused as to what was going on.

"Shall we go through," said Paul, opening the door into the other room, and ushering Paul through, "Let Mr Patterson tidy things up." This room was as sumptuous as the previous. Again, a fire crackled in the grate. "Please sit. I think we could both do with a stiff drink after that." He went over to a tray of drinks on a sideboard, and poured two large brandies. "Armagnac OK?" He brought the drinks over and handed one to Mark, who took a grateful sip. "As I said earlier, we can't bump you off for the afore mentioned reasons, which I think is what Eddy had in mind. Don't worry, he's not the first. However, he may be the last." He sat down at the other end of the oxblood red chesterfield that accommodated Mark. There was a slight noise from the other room. "Just Mr Patterson," said Paul. He took a sip of his brandy, then sat back, nursing the glass in his lap and gazing at the fire.

"So what happens now?" asked Mark, "I've just witnessed a murder. I'm on government business, supposedly tracking you and that Làngfèi shíjiān thing, in there. What do you propose, I'm mean, what the fuck!"

"Let me think," said Paul, in response. "I have an idea that may suit all of us, but I really need to think it through. So, If you'll let me sit here quietly and work it out. Feel free to help yourself to another drink. I'm fine," he added when Mark reached across for Paul's brandy glass.

So the pair of them sat quietly, gazing into the fire. Mark sipping his recharged brandy, Paul deep in thought.

Chapter 50

They'd sat quietly for about a quarter of an hour when Paul seemed to come to a decision, and stood up. "I'm just going next door" he said and left the room. Mark had almost fallen asleep. A combination of two large brandies, the warmth from the fire and the reaction to the shock of Eddy Chiles-Martin's murder. Paul's abrupt announcement and departure brought him to with a jolt. After a few minutes he hauled himself off the sofa, placed the brandy glass on the side and followed Paul back into the other room, the study. His mind was a swirl of confusion. The travel to 1986 and back, the explanation, the things Eddy was saying and his sudden shooting. He dragged a hand over his face as he went through the door. The room was spotless, not a sign anything untoward had happened, let alone someone having their head blown off. Paul was at the desk, the MacBook laptop open in front of him, busy typing away. "Be with you in just a few minutes," he said without looking up.

"What are you doing?" asked Mark, as he took a seat on the edge of the sofa. He didn't particularly want sit where Eddy met his death, but if he sat in the armchair he would be facing it.

"Just some emails and documentation," he carried on typing, "trying up loose ends. Telling Dunbar that poor Eddy met his death in a boating accident. Impressing on them the need for discretion. They can carry on as normal for a while yet. He'd become more of a figurehead than an active partner, of late."

"Won't there be questions? What about the body?"

"Taken care of. The body was quite damaged by the boat's propeller, and besides the coroner on Tortola is, shall we say, friendly? Poor Eddy will go back home in the finest coffin you can buy, along with all the proper paperwork."

"You seem very flippant about all this," said Mark, with a hard edge to his voice. He didn't like the way things were going. Involved in a murder and its cover up, while on a mission for Her Majesty's Government, in the guise of MI5, which, he suddenly remembered, wasn't supposed to undertake operations abroad. There really should have been more MI6 involvement than just slipping him a gun at the airport, in Puerto Rico.

"At a hundred and twenty-four you get used to all sorts of things." He glanced up and smiled at Mark, "You also get tired, very tired. Do you have any idea what it's like not to age?"

"Oh spare me." Said Mark, in exasperation. "You wanting sympathy?"

"Of course not, but there are considerable drawbacks. There's the boredom, there's only so many things you can do before you're doing them all again." Mark gave a snort of derision. "But it's not that. There's falling in love, and watching your loved one grow old while you stay young. Can you imagine the resentment, then the jealousy. You explain things to them, try to get them to understand. But the jealousy just gets worse as they know you're going on as your young self when they die. Probably taking a new lover a fraction of their age. Puts a strain on the relationship."

"I'm sure you got over it." Said Mark, coldly.

Paul closed the laptop and looked across at Mark, "Just letting you know. Forewarned is forearmed, as they say."

"How do you mean?" A note of consternation crept into Mark's question .

"I've made a decision. It's the only possible answer to the situation we find ourselves in." He took a long hard look at Mark, pausing to take a deep breath that he then let it out slowly. "You have to take over."

Mark gasped and reeled back, as if punched in the midriff. "What?! You cannot, in all honesty, be serious, surely? You seem to forget I work for MI5. That has very serious implications. How, for a start, do you propose I do that without MI5, and in all probability MI6, coming looking. And it won't just be a case of the SAS tramping up the beach early one morning. There'd be a total shitstorm. This whole operation would collapse like a pack of cards. They'd take Làngfèi shíjiān back for the security services to investigate. Then, no doubt, have a grand old time seeing what they could do with it."

"I'd thought of that. And I doubt Làngfèi shíjiān would get back to Britain. Someone would get curious and have a look. Then they'd do exactly what I did, and disappear. The whole rigmarole would start over again.

"You have to take over. In fact I've preempted things, so to speak."

"Preempted?"

"Yes, you died earlier this week, on your way here. You fell overboard from the ferry. Emails and documentation has been sent. The initial emails were sent to the day you arrived, so they've been aware of your demise, so to speak, for a couple of days. Captain Philips has filed his report. You were the sole passenger, and it wasn't realised you were missing at first. They made a search of the area, but found nothing. The currents are very unpredictable and it's assumed your body washed out into the Atlantic. We're just waiting for them to tell us where to send your things."

Mark was speechless, Just staring at Paul with his mouth half open. A horrible sinking feeling in the pit of his stomach. He had figured a way do get rid of him without raising an alarm back home. When he spoke, the words were little more than a whisper, "Jesus fucking

Christ, what's happening to me." He looked around the room. How would he make his escape. Paul was still sat at the desk, there was a gun in the drawer and he could pull that out and fire before any chance of escape.

Paul smiled, then gave a resigned sigh, "Look, Mark, what's done is done. We can't change that."

"But that's just it, Paul." Shouting, now, "you fucking well can. That ability is what this is all about."

"No," said Paul as he got up from the desk. He came around and held out both hands to Mark. "See?" He wasn't wearing the ring. Mark looked up at him. Was he just looking tired after all the current events? Or were those lines on his face.

"What have you done?" said Mark, standing up in font of Paul. Paul picked the ring up off the desk, took Mark's right hand, and placed it in his palm.

"You'll know what to do, it will tell you," said Paul. Barely perceptibly he was ageing in front of Mark.

Mark felt a tingling from the hand that held the ring, then it spread throughout his body. Strange sensations, unlike any he'd felt before. He reeled back onto the sofa, a dull, relentless pain seemed to suffuse his body. Then a searing pain in his head. Images, impression, emotions , knowledge of things previously unknown flooded in. As the sensations receded he looked across at Paul, now sat in the chair opposite. He'd aged about ten years, maybe more. He was ageing before Marks eyes. "Paul?" There was genuine concern in his voice, "Paul, What's happening to you?"

"Don't you know? Làngfèi shíjiān. You are now it's keeper. I'm no longer under it's protection. I don't have long. It's all yours now, Mark. Use it wisely, as I have tried to.

"Now, I need a favour." He leaned forward in the chair, and struggled to his feet. He was a stooped old man, his clothes hanging from the emaciated frame.

"Help me outside." His voice had changed. It was still Paul, but a weaker huskier voice. "I would just like to sit and look at the ocean one more time. There's a bench in a small clearing just in front of the ruins. We can sit there for a while." He put his arm out to Mark, who took it and helped him to the door. He stuffed the ring into his trouser pocket in order to open the door. In the corridor Paul indicated the door opposite. Outside he bade Mark take him round the side. As they came to the clearing Mark had to almost carry Paul to the bench through the long, unkempt grass. Once seated, Mark steadied Paul and they both looked out to sea. "This is my favourite spot." Pauls voice now weak and reedy. "I know you'll do your best, Mark. It was time." He fell silent

They sat in silence, looking out to sea. There was a rustle from beside Mark. He turned and looked at Paul. He was dead, the flesh gone from his bones. Just a skeleton. Even the clothes were now falling apart. Mark stood up and as he did so Paul's remains collapsed off the bench, into the long grass. Mark stood for long minutes. Despite the heat of the day, it was just warm in this glade. The other side of the island to the hotel, and the sun. Shielded and shaded by the trees, the jungle keeping the fierce heat at bay. He turned from Paul's remains and looked out to sea. It was indeed a magnificent view. The sun glinted and sparkled off the ocean waves as far as the eye could see. The horizon many miles away at this height, several hundred feet above the crashing waves below.

Mark put his hand in his pocket and took out the ring. He looked at it, then slid it onto his right middle finger. It was an exact fit. He walked back to the office and picked up the keys from the green leather desk top. He locked the office door, then went to the lift and inserted they. The door rattled open and he stepped inside. Again inserting the key, the doors closed, and the lift started down. At the bottom the door creaked open, and Mark walked into the corridor of the hotel. As he approached the door, it opened, and Mr Patterson stood there. He held the door open for Mark.

"They're waiting for you in the bar, Dr Hill," he said.

Mark stepped through, into the hotel foyer. "Thank you, Mr Patterson."

***

Author's Note

This is entirely a work of fiction. Any resemblance to real events, whilst highly unlikely, are purely coincidental.

However, certain characters mentioned did exist, but their actions and dialogue in this story is completely fictitious.

Captain Vernon Kell, later to become Major General Sir Vernon Kell was actually head of MI5 at the time in question, you can Google him and look him up on MI5's website. He was also referred to as 'K'. Though all the events described are totally fictitious.

Sir John Simon was Home Secretary from 1935 to 1937. Again all the events in which he appears in this story are entirely fictitious, and I've been a bit flexible with his time in office.

Zhao Gao, as mentioned in the text, was chief eunuch to Qin She Huang (247 - 221BC), the first emperor of China. He of Terracotta Army fame. Zhao Gao manipulated the succession of Qin She Huang's younger son, Hu Hai, to the throne on his death. Then virtually ruling through him as his Prime Minister. He was eventually killed.

It may appear that my locations for MI5 H.Q. seem a little erratic. This reflects the various locations it occupied around the capital, over the years. I've tried to be exact with the setting and the time in question. Any errors are mine alone.

Colin South
November 2020

Printed in Dunstable, United Kingdom